CHRISTMAS CAFÉ

AT SEASHELL COVE

ALSO BY KAREN CLARKE

SEASHELL COVE SERIES
The Café at Seashell Cove
The Bakery at Seashell Cove

BEACHSIDE SERIES
The Beachside Sweet Shop
The Beachside Flower Stall
The Beachside Christmas

Being Brooke Simmons
My Future Husband
Put a Spell on You

THE
CHRISTMAS
CAFÉ
AT SEASHELL COVE

Karen Clarke

bookouture

Published by Bookouture in 2018

An imprint of StoryFire Ltd.
Carmelite House
50 Victoria Embankment
London EC4Y 0DZ

www.bookouture.com

ISBN: 978-1-78681-588-0
eBook ISBN: 978-1-78681-587-3

For my sister, Julia, with lots of love.

Chapter One

'Is that big enough for you?'

'I've had bigger.' The woman's mouth curled down in disappointment. 'Especially from that young guy who used to work here.'

'How much bigger?'

'He knew I liked a generous portion.'

I hovered the knife over a quarter of the chocolate cake. 'Is that big enough for you?'

The customer considered it through spiky eyelashes, as if its dimensions were as crucial to her life as breathing. 'I suppose that'll do,' she conceded.

I brought the knife down and began sawing, but instead of producing a neat wedge, the cake collapsed in on itself, buttercream oozing out of the middle and white chocolate shards shooting off the top.

'You've got it upside down,' the customer pointed out, her voice dripping sarcasm.

'I'm not very good with knives.' I flashed the blue plaster around my thumb, where blood had started to seep through. 'You should see me with a spoon though!'

She gave me a revolted look – either squeamish, or hangry. Probably the latter. Being hungry was the only thing that made me angry.

'Let me try again.' I passed the back of my hand across my lightly perspiring brow, then turned the knife over and swiped the blade through the cake, but it didn't resemble so much a slice as a heap of crumbs and frosting. I tried to stuff the buttercream back inside, and pressed some shards of chocolate into the frosting.

'You're not expecting me to eat that?' The woman's eyes almost vanished under the force of her frown. 'I've been looking forward to my Monday morning cake all weekend.'

'It still tastes delicious.' I pushed my finger through a drift of squished-out buttercream then licked it off. 'It's yummy!'

'Tilly, what the bleedin' 'ell are you doin'?' Gwen, the café manager, shot over and tackled the knife off me before lobbing it at the sink – probably breaking one of the health and safety rules she'd drummed into me earlier. 'Ain't you got other work you should be gettin' on wiv?'

She waggled her head meaningfully in the direction of the café's new extension, which I'd been overseeing for the past couple of months and was in charge of styling. Unfortunately, there'd been a leak from a burst pipe, which meant the floor had to dry out completely before the new floorboards could be laid and the rest of the work completed – which was proving stressful with only a week until Christmas Eve, when the café was hosting a party.

'You know I can't do anything at the moment,' I said, watching her hack out a fat slice of cake and heft it onto a plate for the disgruntled customer, waving away her money. 'On the arse,' she said, casting me a dark look that suggested Maitland's Café was on the brink of bankruptcy, thanks to me.

'Gwen, you're a superstar.' The customer's face transformed into an affectionate smile, despite Gwen's stony demeanour, and she trotted happily to one of the empty tables and whipped out a paperback.

'You were supposed to be coverin' for me on me break, not scarin' the customers away.' Gwen's narrowed gaze cased the café, which was empty apart from the woman, and a middle-aged couple at a table by the door, cradling cups of hot chocolate like baby birds. Both had beaming Santas on their matching Christmas sweaters.

'There aren't any customers to frighten away,' I pointed out. There'd been a rush, which Gwen had managed single-handedly, but it had soon quietened down. Thankfully, since I was learning that being a waitress was not my forte.

Gwen clearly agreed. 'Come back Tamsin, all is forgiven,' she grumbled, clearing up the mess I'd made, scraping what was left of the cake into a Tupperware box. 'Even Dom could slice a sponge, and 'e looked like 'e didn't know 'is own name 'alf the bleedin' time.'

Tamsin and Dom, the waiting staff, had left to go travelling after falling in love at the café over the summer, and their replacement – a timid man called Jerry, so scared of Gwen he flinched every time she looked at him – had come down with a cold, leaving the place short-staffed. The owners were away on a cruise – with my parents, as it happened – so it had felt natural to offer to help while I waited for work to recommence on the café's new function room. Well… not natural, exactly. Working for a boss, being told what to do and keeping regular hours didn't come naturally at all, but I was doing my best.

Which clearly wasn't good enough for Gwen, who ran the café with an iron hand, and a glare that could curdle milk. 'I'd be better orf on me own,' she concluded. 'You should stick to what you do best.'

She was either referring to my flair for interior design – which didn't extend to a proper career (a word I was allergic to), or the guided walks I led along the coastal paths, but there weren't many visitors to Seashell Cove in December, so my services there were redundant.

'I'm trying,' I told her.

'Very tryin'.'

'Isn't Cassie coming in later?' Cassie was the owners' daughter, and one of my best friends. 'Unless Danny's whisked her off somewhere?' She'd mentioned her boyfriend was behaving oddly, as if he was up to something.

'She's still paintin' that woman, ain't she?'

'Ah yes, I'd forgotten.' Cassie, an artist, had been commissioned to paint a portrait of the Mayoress of Kingsbridge, who wanted to present it to her husband for Christmas. 'Apparently, the woman keeps changing her mind about how she wants to be portrayed,' I said. 'Sexy but serious is the latest brief.'

Gwen snorted. 'She should just paint a picture of an 'ippopotamus in a tutu,' she said. 'That would be close enough.'

'Gwen! That's not very… *sisterly.*' I glanced pointedly at the combat trousers and steel toe-capped boots she was wearing with her navy Maitland's fleece.

'That woman refused plannin' permission when me cousin wanted a stable in 'er back garden for 'er donkey…' Gwen paused, her pebbly-gaze shooting past me. 'Brace yourself.'

I turned to see four elderly women approaching the counter, tugging off assorted hats and scarves and unbuttoning their coats. Their faces lit up when they spotted Cake of the Day – a gooey, chocolate Yule log sprinkled with icing sugar to look like snow and decorated with a plump, sugar-paste robin.

'Seashell Cove's finest,' one of them said, pointing a wonky, arthritic finger. 'You won't find better cake anywhere in Devon.'

'Or sliced more badly,' Gwen muttered, giving me side-eye. 'Go on,' she added, probably sensing my panic – a feeling I'd rarely experienced before stepping behind the counter. 'I'll manage the Golden Girls.'

My shoulders relaxed. Gratefully leaving her to it, I smiled at the women as I slipped past, but they didn't notice, their attention focused on placing their orders with Gwen, seeming undaunted that her fists were bunched on the counter, as if she was about to vault over and wring their necks. Her unique customer service style was legendary, and part of the café's attraction.

After pausing to tweak a couple of starfish decorations on the Christmas tree I'd helped Cassie put up at the weekend – styled in seaside colours to match the interior – I stepped through the plastic-covered archway into the extension, pausing briefly to breathe in my favourite aroma. While some people raved about newly baked bread, cut grass or clean laundry, the smell that tickled my senses the most was freshly sawn wood.

It almost seemed a shame to have plastered over the timber-framed walls, but I liked the smell of fresh plaster too. In fact, if it were possible to bottle the smell of a new-build, I'd wear it as perfume.

I stood for a moment and looked through the windows that stretched the length of one wall. From this angle the cove itself was less visible – unless you were out on the terrace – but the view was just as striking, even in winter, when the colours were muted, and the wind was gusting clouds above the swell of water.

I glanced around; picturing the empty room furnished with tables and chairs and filled with people, and experienced a thrill of anticipation. Since helping makeover the café the previous year, business had boomed to the point where customers were being turned away, and Gwen's bright idea to build an extra space that would double as a function room for celebrations and parties had been greeted with enthusiasm.

It had made sense to do the work after the summer season, and there'd been a wait for planning permission, but now the race was on to finish the project in time for the party on Christmas Eve. The paint couldn't go on the walls until the floorboards were down, and there was some electrical work to finish. Everyone was on standby until Ted, my floor man, deemed the floor dry enough to go ahead.

I squatted to double-check the paint colour – Sea Mist – and realised I was several tins short. They'd been delivered the previous day while I was out, chasing down some light fittings, and I'd forgotten to check the order when I got back.

'Damn,' I murmured, pulling out my phone. I blamed my preoccupation on Rufus. I'd been trying to decide whether or not to accompany him to his brother's wedding at the weekend. We'd only been seeing each other for six weeks – my longest relationship to date – and it felt like it might be too soon. Did going to a wedding together scream *Us next!* or was it no different to attending a dinner party? I was more used to breaking up with men than going to social events with them, and I'd felt the conversation required a delicate touch. In the end, I'd invited Rufus to the café to talk about it over coffee, and maybe a slice of cake, and—

'TILLY! LOVER-BOY'S 'ERE!'

Blowing out a sigh, I stood up and slipped my phone back into my pocket.

The paint – and everything else – would have to wait a bit longer.

Chapter Two

'I'm just not sure I'm ready to go to a wedding.'

'It's not as if it's *ours*.' Rufus sounded slightly regretful. 'I know you're a free spirit, it's one of the things I lo— like about you, but you said yourself, you were ready to try a grown-up relationship, and that involves us going places together.' He stopped walking and looked at me, hands on his coat-clad hips. I didn't like it when he stood like that. It made him look like a teacher. Which he was, but I wasn't one of his pupils, to be given a hundred lines. *You* will *go to the wedding, whether you like it or not.*

'We do go places together,' I protested. 'We go out for meals and drinks.'

'I mean, around other people. Our families, for instance.' He glanced at the rumpled sea and fudgy sand before trailing his gaze up the grassy headland to the café. 'You couldn't even sit in there with me for long.'

I glanced at the sky, where weak sunlight was trying to break through a bank of cloud. 'I needed some fresh air, that's all.' The truth was I still hadn't worked out what it was I'd wanted to say, and once we'd covered the weather, and I'd updated Rufus on the lack of progress in the function room, and he'd told me he'd been working on his best man's speech for the wedding, I'd leapt up and asked Gwen if I could take an early lunch break.

'Be my guest. It's not like I'm 'ere on me own,' she'd said with heavy irony, but I knew she wouldn't have let me go if she'd thought she couldn't manage.

'You know I don't like being cooped up indoors for too long,' I said to Rufus.

'Is that what you think it'll be like at the wedding, because it won't be.' His fine-featured face was puckered with concern. 'There are lovely grounds outside the Abbey, we can have a nice walk after the ceremony, if you'd like to.'

'It's not that.' I jammed my hands in the pockets of my shearling jacket, wishing I'd worn gloves and a scarf. Possibly a woolly hat. After a mild spell, winter had arrived with a vengeance, and the weather forecasters were predicting a white Christmas.

'What's it really about then?' His voice became a bit punchy, and I could suddenly see him trying to control his sixth-formers – a difficult bunch by all accounts – at the college in Ivybridge where he taught biology, and where we both lived (separately). 'I mean, I thought we were getting on well.'

'We *are*,' I said. 'I'm just not used to this whole couples thing.' My laugh was meant to imply emotional dimwittery, and his head swooped back, as if he was seeing me properly for the first time. His eyes – the same winter-grey as the sea – looked watery.

'I know *that*.' He blinked into the wind. 'I've already told you how flattered I am that you chose me to be your first "proper" boyfriend,' he scratched little quote marks in the air, 'and I'm so happy that your father introduced us.' He swiped at his hair with his fingers. 'I really think we've made a connection, Tilda, and want to take our relationship to the next stage.'

'My name's Tilly.' He'd thought Tilda the more 'grown-up' version of my full name, Matilda, and had tried to make a thing of it, probably hoping I'd find it cute. 'I do like you, Rufus, I really do…' I stopped. He looked older than his thirty-eight years, and it struck me it was *my* fault. He was upset because I hadn't committed to the simple act of going to his brother's wedding. I reminded myself that my dad had recommended Rufus… no, not *recommended* him, he wasn't a brand of toothpaste, but he'd designed an eco-friendly house for Rufus's parents and got to know them well, and thought I might like to 'try dating someone different to your usual type'. He'd meant the type I didn't bother introducing to my family, knowing there was no point, and I blamed turning thirty for finally caving in. My birthday, three months earlier, had brought with it a sense that my life wasn't quite as satisfying as it had been – that maybe there was something missing. It didn't help that my two best friends had fallen in love within months of each other (not *with* each other), highlighting the fact that I'd never come close to saying those three little words. Not that I could visualise saying them to Rufus yet, despite the novelty of being wined and dined by a man with a job I found genuinely fascinating, and shared musical tastes with – anything from the nineties and Alanis Morissette – but it was very early days.

'Does it bother you that I'm shorter than you?' He puffed himself up to his full five feet nine, broadening his shoulders and pushing out his chest.

'Oh, Rufus, of course not.' I couldn't help smiling, even though my face was numb with cold. 'Most men are shorter than me, I'm used to it.'

'If you're worried about this…' he flattened a hand to the collar-length gingerish hair he combed creatively to disguise a thinning patch '… I was going to have it shaved for the wedding. My sister reckons I'd look like Jason Statham.'

I wondered whether his sister was partially sighted. 'It's got nothing to do with your hair,' I said truthfully. 'It's habit, I suppose. You know I've never made it past a month with anyone before.' I felt my way carefully, knowing he didn't approve of what he called my 'dalliances'. 'Going to a family wedding seems very… *grown-up.*'

'That's because it is.' Rufus's shoulders dropped. 'Come along, you'll love it,' he said persuasively. 'I've been looking forward to showing you off to Grant.' A half-smile rose to his lips – more confident now he'd sensed me weakening. 'When I showed him a photo of you, he asked if you were a model.'

'That's nice.' I was never sure how to respond to compliments about my appearance. I'd been approached once by a model scout, at the airport with my parents on our way to Canada – probably because I was tall and gangly, so stood out – but I'd known in some deep-rooted way that modelling wasn't for me. 'Where is the wedding again?'

'It's in Exmouth, so not far.' I had the impression that if we'd been talking on the phone, he'd be throwing a victory punch. 'Honestly, Tild— Tilly, we'll have a great time, you'll see.' His eyes shuttled to my lower half. 'I'm looking forward to dancing with you,' he said. 'They say if you're a good dancer, you're good in the bedroom department, though I don't think we've anything to worry about there.'

'Bedroom department?' It sounded like something Mum would say. *What's he like in the bedroom department, Tilly? You want a man who knows what he's doing!*

He reached for my hand. 'We make a good pair, Tilly, you and me.' His fingers were freezing. 'I'll never forget our first night together, when you said I had a good body.'

I glanced round, imagining my friends' reactions if they could hear this conversation, but there was only a disinterested seagull strutting about on the sand. 'Well, you do,' I agreed. Divested of his clothing – including the sort of billowing boxers favoured by my dad – his body was tanned and muscly (he'd confessed to starting a work-out regime after one of his sixth-formers said his granny could beat him in a fist fight) and, I admit, our encounters in his hotel-like bedroom had been pleasant so far – though I'd sensed him reading more into them than I had, saying he loved my 'laid-back vibe' and that I was the yin to his yang. 'It's very nice,' I added, as if complimenting him on a new tie.

'I don't mind you using me for my body.' Letting my hand go, he flapped his coat open and shut like a flasher in what I assumed was an attempt at appearing irresistibly sexy. 'But I'd like there to be more between us than the physical.'

The physical? 'Right,' I said, wishing we could fast-forward a week, so that the wedding was over and he could stop being weird. 'Well, I suppose there are worse ways to spend a day than watching someone get married.'

'Oh, great, that's great.' He rubbed his hands together. 'So, you'll definitely come?'

'My word is my bond,' I said, hoping he didn't want it in writing.

'You won't regret it, Tilda.'

'Tilly.' Out of the corner of my eye, I noticed a black streak of fur tearing across the beach. It was a sleek-haired dog, barking as it darted to the water's edge, and I remembered someone had recently bought the old cottage on the other side of the headland.

The dog was frisking about, barking at the waves, and I hoped he wasn't about to run into the sea. Often deceptively calm in the cove, the water possessed strong undercurrents and there were rocks further out where ships used to run aground.

'How about Mattie?' Rufus was saying.

'Sorry?' I dragged my gaze back to see him flick up the collar of his coat, his hair flapping sideways in the wind.

'Mattie's got a nice ring to it.'

'I prefer Tilly,' I said. 'It's my name.'

'You could call me Roo.'

I stared. 'I… don't think I can.'

His face coloured down to his neck. 'Don't you think it's nice when couples have pet names?'

'I think it's supposed to happen organically.' I bit the inside of my cheek to stop myself laughing, sensing he wouldn't like it. 'When they've got to know each other much better.'

'All the more reason to take our relationship to the next stage.' Before I could ask him to please stop saying *next stage*, his head shot forward and he pressed cold lips to mine before backing away, his round-toed boots sinking into the sand. 'I'm going to go now,' he said, as if I'd been trying to detain him. 'I'll give you a call later, make sure you haven't changed your mind.' He mimed putting a phone to his ear, and waved with his other hand.

I waved back, stamping my feet. I felt like a Popsicle and needed to move to warm up, and was aware of a sweeping relief as I watched him walk back up the winding path to the café. *It's only a wedding,* I told myself. Dad would be pleased I'd agreed to go. *Date a man who deserves you, Tilly.*

Stop messing about with beach boys. He'd meant surfer types and I had to admit, I'd had my fill of them. Maybe my sister would approve of my 'grown-up' relationship too, and stop treating me with her usual contempt. I just wished I hadn't boasted to her about a well-paying design job I'd had lined up – to prove that I was capable of working just as hard as she did – which had fallen through at the last minute. There was nothing else on the horizon. It wasn't that I needed the money, thanks to the savings I'd accrued from jobs I'd done over the years (unlike Bridget, I didn't covet expensive furniture, or have a mortgage to pay), but she'd been driving home how a satisfying career would give meaning to my 'empty life'.

Shivering, I started walking, pulling my chin into the fur at the neck of my jacket, deciding that once I'd filled my lungs with fresh air, I'd drive to the supplier and pick up the rest of the paint.

As I strode out, my gaze travelled the length of beach I knew so well and had missed a surprising amount when I'd moved to Canada with Mum and Dad, twelve years ago. A movement caught my eye and I paused. A boy had sprinted onto the sand from the same direction as the dog, a bright blue towel flaring from his shoulders like a cape. Like the dog, he was hurtling towards the sea, shouting, 'Digby!' in a high, panicked voice. 'Digby, come back!'

I shifted my gaze, heart stalling when I saw the dog's head bobbing about in the water. The weak sunshine had retreated, and the sea was a choppy mass of foaming grey that I knew was capable of sweeping a person (or animal) away in minutes.

'Wait!' I called, starting to run as the boy flung off his towel and ran through the waves in his pants, but he either didn't hear me, or was too intent on rescue to see the danger.

I picked up speed, adrenaline charging through my brain, the salty wind stinging my eyes as I threw off my jacket and peeled my sweatshirt and T-shirt over my head. I slowed to a stumble to kick off my boots, and when I looked up, the dog had made it back to the beach and was shaking off water in a spraying arc, but the boy was struggling in the sea, drifting close to the rocks.

I waded out, sucking in a breath as the icy water gripped me. 'Hang on!' I yelled, before ducking beneath the surface, swimming away from the beach with steady strokes as the current wrapped around me. The freezing water prickled my scalp and shot up my nose, making me splutter and gasp, while the undertow tried to pull me off course. I kicked harder and swam faster, as if I was back at school, my coach urging me on.

Come on, Tilly, you've got this! You're winning, come on, Tilly!

I raised my head, caught a flash of saucer-wide eyes and a slick of dark blond hair, and then I was beside him. 'Just go floppy,' I panted, grabbing him under the arms. Making sure his face was above the water, I struggled back to the shore in a one-armed crawl, my legs thrashing frantically against the undercurrent, distantly aware of someone shouting from the beach.

My lungs felt on fire, and my neck was burning from the effort of holding the boy, and then he was being lifted from me by whoever had been shouting. Suddenly weightless, I half-crawled onto the soft wet sand and collapsed, gasping and choking for air. After coughing up a mouthful of salty water, I rolled onto my back, sounds rushing in as I blinked at the oyster-pale sky: boyish protests; a deep male voice, sharp-edged with panicky relief, and a series of staccato barks that came closer and a long pink tongue unfurled to lick my face.

Chapter Three

'Are you OK?'

Twisting away from my canine face wash, I spotted a pair of sand-gritted feet by my head. 'I'm fine,' I tried to say, but my teeth were chattering like wind-up novelty gnashers and the words didn't quite make it out.

'Christ, you must be freezing.' As soon as he said it, I became shiveringly aware of my half-naked state, having stripped to my bra and jeans, both of which were clinging like a second skin.

'The boy…' I pushed myself upright and scanned the frothing sea, as if he might still be out there.

'It's OK, he's fine.' Behind me, the man's voice had a touch of urgency. 'Here, put this on.'

Before I could process what was happening, the view disappeared in a shroud of navy, musk-scented wool, and I began to struggle as though I was being taken hostage. 'It's my sweater,' the man said, and the view reappeared as my head popped through the neck-hole, my dripping hair clinging to my cheeks. I shoved my arms in the sleeves and hugged my waist, shudders rippling through me. 'Where is he?'

'Over there.'

Twisting round, I saw the boy chasing the dog back up the beach, a man-sized jacket dwarfing his frame, as if he hadn't been on the verge of drowning minutes earlier. I'd half-expected a crowd to have gathered, or paramedics to be rushing over with foil blankets, but apart from a distant dog walker the beach was still deserted, and it was doubtful we'd have been seen from the café, unless someone had been on the terrace.

The whole episode already felt dreamlike.

'Thank god he's all right,' I said, pushing awkwardly to my feet. A wave of dizziness overtook me and I stumbled against the man.

'Take it easy, you're probably in shock.'

For a moment, I leaned against a solid wall of chest while a pair of strong hands rubbed my arms, as if trying to get my circulation going. I couldn't remember the last time I'd placed my head on a man's chest, apart from my dad's when I was little, which meant he was taller than me. His skin felt warm through his T-shirt, and I could hear his heart, thumping as hard as mine was.

'You saved my son's life.' His voice rumbled through me, and I recognised a soft, Home Counties accent – Hampshire, perhaps. Not *Made in Chelsea* posh, but well educated. 'If you hadn't been here, and I hadn't just happened to look out of the window…' A convulsion ran through him. 'I don't think he even realises—'

'Why was he running about on the beach on his own?' A shot of anger propelled me backwards, and I looked at him properly for the first time, noting that I had to tilt my head. *Wow.* OK, so he was attractive: rumpled dark-blond hair, a matching, close-cut beard and eyes the colour of swimming pools. He was in his late-thirties, maybe older; it was hard to tell when his face was creased with anguish. 'Your son could have died!'

'Don't you think I know that?' A frown cut between his eyebrows. 'It was because of the dog. He must have got out somehow.' He was wearing black jeans, fitted around strong thighs. 'I must have left the back door open.' I dragged my gaze up to his face. 'Jack would never have come out, otherwise. I thought he was still in the bath.' At least that explained the towel – now pooled around his feet – and why the boy had only been wearing pants.

'Do you know how many people die trying to save their dogs from drowning?'

'I—'

'It was a rhetorical question,' I snapped. 'Nine times out of ten the dog survives and the owner dies.'

He ran both hands through his hair. 'Please don't keep saying those words.'

'What words?'

'Drowning. Dying.'

I stared in disbelief. 'Well, I'm sorry for pointing out that rushing into the sea in December, after your badly-behaved dog, is a recipe for death.'

'Please, stop.' His voice had lowered and I saw the boy – Jack – approaching, his hair almost dry already and curling around his neck. He was probably six or seven, skinny-limbed, ribs showing beneath the too-big leather jacket. 'I don't want you to scare him.'

'He *should* be scared.' I wished my teeth would stop chattering as I turned to look at the boy. 'You know you could have drowned out there?'

'No, I wouldn't.' Despite his big, scared eyes – a shade darker than his dad's – his tone was resolute. 'I could have easily got back on my own.' I could see he desperately wanted to believe it, but keen to drive my point home I pulled my head back and jabbed a finger to where a couple of rocks were sticking up out of the water. 'You were being carried out to sea. You could have been knocked unconscious.' I made a slapstick performance of bashing my head and sinking underwater, my eyelids fluttering shut.

The boy giggled. 'You're funny.'

My eyes snapped open. His response was so unexpected, I couldn't think of a single response before he'd turned his attention back to the prancing dog. 'C'mon, Digby.' They ran off once more, the dog tail-waggingly unaware of the drama he'd caused.

'I'm sorry about that.' The man bent to scoop up the soggy towel. 'Get your things and come back to the house to dry off. The least I can do is fix you a hot drink.' Straightening, he extended a hand. 'Seth Donovan.'

'Tilly Campbell,' I said automatically, ignoring his hand. 'He needs to take this seriously.' I gestured at the sea. 'You both do.'

Seth's arm dropped back to his side. 'Believe me, I do,' he said with a grimace. 'We both do, and I'll make sure nothing like this ever happens again. It's… Jack's…' He shook his head, as if the right words wouldn't come. 'It's complicated.' His tightly muscled arms were pimpled with gooseflesh and his jaw looked clenched, as if he was trying to stop his own teeth from chattering. Divested of his jacket and jumper, his T-shirt was no match for the wind, which seemed to have gathered strength, and his jeans were soaked to the knees where he'd run into the sea. 'Please, come back with me,' he urged. 'We're just up there.' He pointed to the path worn into the rocky hillside, the grey-stone cottage at the top stamped against the rise of another hill. 'You can't go home in that state.'

I glanced down at my sea-sodden jeans, then at my boots discarded on the sand, my sweatshirt, T-shirt and jacket nearby. I could easily grab them and leg it up to the café car park, drive home and leap under a hot shower; fix myself some drinking chocolate and hunker down on the sofa with my duvet for the rest of the day.

But home – our solid house, designed by Dad, with its elegantly proportioned rooms and sturdy walls – wasn't the same now Bridget was back with her two-year-old daughter, and right now, I felt… *what*? Looking at the heaving sea, pushing closer as the tide crept in – nothing like the flat expanse of silky, turquoise water I'd floated around in during the summer – I remembered striking out towards the boy. It had been ages since I'd swum like that, and although it had been frantic and frightening, it had also been… *exhilarating*. The whole thing had been over in a matter of minutes, but I felt different; and not just because I couldn't feel my legs any more.

'OK,' I said, my anger deflating as I retrieved my clothes and boots, hugging them to my chest, desperate now to get my sopping jeans off. 'I could definitely do with a hot drink.' My few hours at the café, and my chat with Rufus seemed ages ago. I wondered if he was home now, practising his best man's speech for his brother's wedding.

'Me too,' said Seth – I'd never met a Seth before – just as it began to rain. Not the soft light rain that south-west Devon was known for, but rain like needles of ice that made me squint unglamorously as we began a lumbering run towards the path. Jack and the dog had already vanished, presumably into the cottage, and the part of my brain that hadn't gone frigid with cold was curious to look inside. There'd been some gossip about the new owner, but I'd been too sidetracked by my sister's recent return home to take it in. Hopefully, Seth wasn't a suspected serial killer, posing as a loving dad. I wasn't getting that vibe from him, but a psychopath could appear charming and charismatic on the surface. Not that I thought Seth was either on first appearance, but the circumstances had been exceptional.

He turned back suddenly, tenting the towel over his head, then held out a hand as if to help me, but I had my arms full and quickly scrambled past him. I was used to rough terrain – admittedly not in wet socks – and didn't need the hand of a man who hadn't realised his son wasn't in the house, until it was nearly too late. What had he been doing that was more important than keeping an eye on him?

We finally reached the top of the hill, feet squelching through puddled mud, and then we were on the stony stretch of path outside the cottage. I fleetingly registered that the powder-blue paint was peeling off the front door, before Seth led me inside a low-ceilinged hallway criss-crossed with old oak beams. It was only when he'd reached past me to close the door that I realised how noisy it had been outside, with the rain and wind, the crashing waves, and the wailing cry of seagulls.

Inside, it was silent – almost too quiet – and I stood, dripping onto a carpet so densely patterned with tiny beige and green swirls it made me go cross-eyed.

'There's a lot needs doing,' Seth said. 'I mean, the building's structurally sound but the decor leaves a lot to be desired.' He sounded apologetic, anxious to explain why we appeared to have zipped back to the seventies.

'It does have a retro look,' I said, taking in the tobacco-coloured wallpaper, and a single swaying pendant light we'd have to duck to avoid. On my right was a steep wooden staircase, where pale light filtered down from a window on the landing, emphasising bare patches on the walls where pictures used to hang.

In spite of everything, I slid into design-mode, mentally planning the improvements I'd make if the place was mine: a mirror at the bottom of the stairs to bounce the light around; neutral walls to give the impression of space; a wooden floor (more hard-wearing than carpet) and touches of colour with a rug, some artwork, flowers – maybe a console table with drawers to store clutter, and a lamp on top for warmth.

'Come through to the kitchen.' Seth's voice ruptured my thoughts. 'It's nicer in there.'

'What about Jack?' I couldn't believe he didn't seem interested in where his son was, or what he was doing. He'd almost drowned ten minutes ago – even if Jack had been in denial.

'He'll be in his bedroom. He won't want me there.' Seth had turned away so I couldn't see his expression, but there was something in his voice – a sort of grim acceptance – that hinted at a troubled relationship.

'Even so, he must be shaken up,' I persisted, remembering the boy's wide-eyed shock as I'd approached him in the water. 'You should check he's OK.'

'I did and he is.' Seth's voice was curt. 'He'd hardly have run all the way back here, otherwise.'

I supposed he had a point. Through the gloom, I noticed a set of smallish damp footprints on the bottom two stairs, and the tinny howl of an animal floated down – presumably (hopefully) from a computer game.

Slightly unsettled, I dropped my boots by the door and trailed Seth down the passageway, noticing a couple of wood-panelled doors on my left. One was open, and I glimpsed a room with a hardwood floor, empty apart from a mole-coloured sofa, and a wide-screen television hanging on the wall. It was obvious Seth and Jack hadn't lived here long. There was no real sense of the occupants; not like at home, where every room reflected my parents' tastes, and mingled scents of ironing, coffee and Mum's favourite flowers wafted through the air. At least, they had before Bridget returned, and the smell of frustration and bad cooking had taken over.

There weren't even any Christmas decorations that I could see, unlike our living room at home, which was like a (tasteful) Santa's grotto – ostensibly for my niece's benefit, but really because we loved Christmas.

The cottage was warm, but dusty, and I swallowed a sneeze as Seth pushed through a half-open door at the end of the hall and beckoned me inside.

The kitchen *was* nicer – old-fashioned but cosy, with a grey flagstone floor and a dark red Aga slumped against the far wall. An inglenook fireplace drew my eye, furnished with hooks for pans, conjuring images of toasting forks and marshmallows. Digby, curled on a stripy mat in front, completed the picture-book image and thumped his tail in greeting.

'He must be shattered after his adventure,' Seth said, bending to fuss him, before moving to the sink to fill a squat, copper kettle. After the dimness of the hallway, the kitchen felt interrogation-bright, light flooding through a sash window above the butler sink. 'You should take your clothes off.'

'Pardon?'

Seth turned, and I saw that his eyes were topped by a strong set of eyebrows, and put him in his late-thirties. 'You'll catch your death, as my gran used to say.'

'Oh, right.' I dropped my jacket, sweatshirt and T-shirt onto a polished oak table, next to a bowl of rosy-skinned apples. 'I wouldn't mind getting out of these wet jeans.'

His brows lifted a fraction. 'Go upstairs and have a shower, while I make a drink,' he said, grabbing a tea towel and rubbing his hair until it stood in peaks. 'There's plenty of hot water, and clean towels,' he added. 'I'll find you something dry to wear, and then you can tell me how I can repay you for saving my son's life.'

Chapter Four

Following Seth's directions, I ran up to a narrow landing and through the second door on the right. Behind it was an airy but old-fashioned bathroom, with turquoise wall tiles, orange-pine fittings, and mushroom-coloured vinyl on the floor. I slipped inside and turned the key in the lock, Seth's words ringing in my ears. What did he mean, *repay* me? I'd been in the right place at the right time and happened to be a strong swimmer, that was all. Anyone would have done the same.

Still charged up, I yanked Seth's sweater over my head and wrenched off my jeans and bra, noting that the shower was attached to the wall above the bath. There were several inches of water inside, and a faint ring of scum clinging to the surface. Jack clearly hadn't emptied it when he stepped out, and he'd left his *Star Wars* pyjamas on the floor. There was an unopened bottle of shower gel on the side, suggesting he hadn't washed himself either, and I pictured an irate Seth, trying to persuade his son to bathe – perhaps even bribing him, the way Dad had once bribed me, promising I could have riding lessons if I kept my room tidy for a month. (I'd gone off wanting a pony by then, so it didn't really work.)

Keen to get warm – still shivery, in spite of the heat coming from an old-school radiator on the wall – I tugged out the plug and watched the water gurgle away before climbing into the bath. I switched on the shower and adjusted the temperature, dragging across a thick plastic curtain to stop water spraying the floor, indulging a brief fantasy in which I created a brand-new, country-style bathroom, with weathered-oak wall panelling and flooring, and a roll-topped bath with bronze taps positioned beneath the frosted glass window.

At least there was nothing wrong with the plumbing; as Seth had promised, the water was hot and plentiful, but the shower gel smelt overwhelmingly male – *a pungent aroma of Italian limes and pink peppercorns*, according to the blurb on the back; an expensive brand I'd seen advertised by a famous footballer. I wondered whether Seth had bought it to appeal to Jack – part of the bribe to get him in the bath. Maybe the boy was into football. Maybe Seth was. In fact, now I thought about it, hadn't the gossip I'd heard had something to do with his career? Or rather, his *ex*-career. Something sporty he'd retired from, but what?

I couldn't see any shampoo so used a squirt of shower gel, and once I was done, squeezed water from my hair and pulled back the curtain to reach blindly for a towel. The air was fuggy with steam, but it had cleared enough for me to meet Seth's startled gaze.

'What the…?' I grabbed a hand towel, which barely reached my thighs, while Seth froze in a half-crouch, a pile of neatly folded clothes in his arms.

'I'm sorry, I wasn't expecting you to have finished yet.' He discreetly lowered his gaze and placed the clothes on the toilet lid. 'I'll leave these here for you.'

'You could have left them outside the door.' I wondered whether he'd been spying on me. Unlikely, given that the shower curtain could have hidden a bevy of naked women, and he'd already seen me soaking wet in my bra. 'How did you get in?'

'I'm afraid the lock doesn't work.' His voice was apologetic and ultra-polite – hardly the tone of a pervert. He turned to leave, still carefully averting his gaze. 'I didn't want you to come out with nothing to wear.'

'Well… thanks.' I was equally polite.

'I'll pop your jeans in the dryer.'

'You don't have to.' My knickers were balled inside, along with my soggy socks.

'It's no problem.' He scooped everything off the floor, including Jack's pyjamas.

'I'll be down in a moment.'

'No rush,' he said, as though we were discussing the state of the economy at the sort of dinner party I wouldn't be seen dead at. 'There's a hairdryer in my room, if you'd like to use it.'

'No need,' I lied. My hair was growing out and needed more attention these days, or it ended up a hybrid of flat and wavy. 'You blow-dry yours, do you?'

As soon as I'd said it, I realised he probably had a girlfriend – or wife – and the hairdryer was hers. Not that there was anything wrong with men blow-drying their hair, but I preferred a wash-and-go attitude.

'Isn't it obvious?' He tossed his head and patted the back of his hair with his free hand. 'It needs a lot of help to look like this.' With a rather camp swivel he stalked out, closing the door behind him, and I realised I was smiling.

Dropping the skimpy towel, I stepped out of the bath and after drying myself, pulled on the jogging bottoms, rolling up the cuffs, before tugging on a pair of wool socks that were almost a perfect fit, and the sweater that had dried on the radiator. There was no underwear, and the clothes were obviously Seth's, so maybe there wasn't a wife or girlfriend. Thinking about it, the place lacked a

female influence. No feminine toiletries, either. I peeped inside
the pinewood cabinet above the sink, but there was only a pack of
toothbrushes, some toothpaste, and a bottle of cough medicine on
the shelf. I guiltily shut the door and studied my reflection in the
misty, mirrored front, surprised for a second that I looked more or
less the same as I had when I'd left home – apart from the slicked
back hair. And maybe my face – losing its summer tan – was a little
flushed, deepening the green of my eyes, but that would be the hot
water. Turning away, I opened the window, cold air tightening the
skin on my cheeks. The rain had stopped, and rays of weak sunshine
washed across the cove, turning the waves to a silver-tipped shimmer
as they broke onto the sand.

Aware Seth was waiting, probably wondering what I was doing,
I left the bathroom and was about to head downstairs, resisting the
urge to check the view from the landing window, when I heard what
sounded like a stifled sob from one of the other rooms.

Jack.

I hesitated, one hand on the wooden post at the top of the stairs.
It seemed wrong to ignore the sound but, equally, I didn't feel it was
my place to rush in and comfort the boy – if indeed he was crying,
and the noise wasn't coming from his computer game. My experience
with children, prior to Bridget coming home with her daughter, was
zero. By choice. The thought of being responsible for a small human
being was terrifying to me.

But when the sound came again – *definitely crying* – I found myself
padding towards a scuffed door at the end of the landing and pressing my
ear to the paintwork. I knocked, but there was no reply, so I turned the
knob and pushed. 'It's only me, the lady from the beach.' *Nice one, Tilly.
Not at all creepy.* 'Hello?' A muffled snort emerged from a cabin-style bed

pressed against the far wall, and I could just make out a hump beneath a moon-and-stars patterned duvet cover. 'Are you OK?' *Stupid question.*

I crept further into the room, which was filled with light from two long windows, one with the same outlook across the cove. It was neat and tidy inside, for a boy's room. The last one I'd encountered belonged to Cassie's brother Rob, and had looked like it should be cordoned off and declared a crime scene. Apart from Jack's bed, which had a desk area underneath, there was a white wardrobe and matching chest, and a shelf that ran the length of one wall, neatly lined with books, toys, and stuffed animals. The floorboards looked freshly sanded, covered with a patchwork rug in rainbow colours, and a floor lamp shaped like a rocket stood by the window. It was clear an effort had been made to make it look nice and welcoming.

'Is it all right if I come in?' I ventured, even though I already had. The duvet lifted as Jack turned onto his side, and I had a glimpse of his knobbly spine before it fell again. 'Should I take that as a no?' I'd defaulted to a jokey tone as I moved closer, noticing a discarded iPad thrown to the bottom of the bed. 'What game were you playing?'

The answer seemed unlikely to inspire conversation, as I knew next to nothing about computer games. I picked up the iPad, but the screen was blank and smudged with fingerprints, and didn't respond to my attempt at switching it on. Laying it down, I spotted a small gallery of framed photos on the wall by the bed, of Jack with various family members – mostly grandparents, judging by the ages (none with Seth, I noticed) and one in particular caught my eye. A much younger Jack, with neatly-parted hair, his wide-eyed smile injected with mischief, was in the arms of a woman about my age, with red-gold hair cascading over her shoulder and a smiling, cat-like face. Clearly his mum, despite their different colouring.

'Go'way.' Jack's voice was muffled by the pillow, but there was no mistaking his meaning, or the anxiety crackling through the duvet.

I hovered a hand above the cover. 'It's probably delayed shock,' I said, not sure why I was persisting, but there was something about his tidy room, the photos, and the sad little heap in the bed that was making my throat itch. 'That's why you're upset.'

'I'm NOT upset.'

It was practically a roar, and I jumped so dramatically it nearly made me laugh. 'I heard you crying just now.'

'I wasn't crying because of *that*.'

My hand stilled. 'Oh?'

He sniffed, but didn't say anything else.

'I nearly drowned once.' I said it in a conversational, hopefully non-threatening way, and immediately had a flashback to the classy Greek resort we'd holidayed at when I was six, with its interlocking pools and lagoons, where I'd spent practically the whole holiday. I was a keen swimmer, even then, and hadn't wanted to come out. Bridget, ten years older and fed up of 'keeping an eye' on me, had been swotting up on her maths homework (she'd been the brainy one) and didn't see me bang my head on the side of the pool and slip under the water. Luckily, the lifeguard had, but I'd never forgotten that feeling of looking up at the surface and not being able to reach it. 'I was sick afterwards,' I said to the shape of Jack. 'Not straight away, but that evening, after dinner. My dad said it was shock.' He'd felt guilty for asking Bridget to watch me while he and Mum 'had a rest' in their room, and they didn't let me out of their sight for the rest of the week, while Bridget coped with her guilt by ignoring me more than usual.

'Jack?' The duvet rose and fell in time with his breathing, and although I thought it unlikely he'd gone to sleep, I guessed he was pretending in the hope that I'd leave him alone. 'I like your dog,' I said, a final, lame attempt to get a response. 'I always wanted a dog, but my sister was allergic so we couldn't have one.' When that didn't produce so much as a twitch, I sighed and backed towards the door, one eye on the duvet, and started when Jack said, 'His name's Digby.'

Even though I knew, I said, 'That's the best name for a dog. If I'd had one, I'd have called it something silly like… Fleabag, or Winnie the Poodle.' *Was that a muffled giggle?* 'Sherlock Bones?' Deciding to quit while I was ahead, I left the room and gently closed the door.

'Did you really nearly drown?'

Spinning round, I met Seth's gaze once again. 'Bloody hell, you're everywhere.' I clutched my chest, wondering how many shocks my heart could take in one day. And I'd thought slicing cake was stressful.

'You were gone a while.' In the shadowy light of the landing, his eyes looked darker than before. 'I wondered what you were doing.'

'I was seeing if Jack was OK.' I swallowed. 'I thought I heard him crying.'

A host of emotions tramped over Seth's face. 'Did he tell you to go away?'

'He did.'

Seth rubbed a hand around his jaw. 'I'll send Digby up to keep him company. He loves that dog more than anything.'

I trotted downstairs after Seth, my heartbeat not quite returned to normal. Everything seemed heightened, as though I'd been slipped a drug that had sharpened my senses, and I couldn't stop staring at the hair on the nape of Seth's neck. 'He prefers the dog to me.'

'I'm sure that's not true.' I jumped again when he turned to look at me at the foot of the stairs, and I heard myself say, 'You're not from around here then?'

'No, I'm not,' he said. 'I was born and bred in Surrey, but I came here on holiday decades ago with a friend. His parents had a holiday cottage down the coast, and I remember having a brilliant time.' His smile transformed his face, wiping at least five years off. 'When I was looking for somewhere to settle with Jack, it popped into my head, and this cottage had been on the market a while so...' He tilted his head. 'I'm guessing you're local, though your accent isn't very strong.'

'Ivybridge,' I said. 'I'm working up at the café.' I pointed behind me, as though it was on the landing. 'Not in the café as such, I've been overseeing an extension—' I cut myself off. 'Anyway, I'd better go.' Jumping to the foot of the stairs, I pushed my feet into my boots, not bothering to lace them up, and reached a hand to the door.

'You can't go yet.' He seemed put out, as if I was an absconding house guest. 'What about your clothes?'

'I'll get them another time. We can do an exchange.' I gestured to his sweater. 'I've got to go and pick up some paint.' I also needed to return to some semblance of normality.

Seth's brow furrowed. 'But I've made some coffee.' He sounded almost flatteringly dismayed. 'And we haven't talked about how I can repay you.'

'You don't have to.'

'I do,' he said, pushing a hand through his hair. 'It's important.'

'It really isn't.' I pulled open the door, a gust of wind forcing my damp hair into my eyes. 'Just watch him more closely in future.'

'Tilly, wait...' He started towards me, but I was already outside.

'I'll see you around,' I called, and jogged away without glancing back, certain I could feel his eyes on me all the way back to the café.

Chapter Five

The first sound I heard as I entered the house, an hour later, tins of paint stashed in the boot of my car, was my niece banging a spoon on a pan lid (her favourite pastime). The second was Bridget, clapping and cheering as though her daughter had just composed her first symphony. I scoped the hallway for an invisible route to the stairs, hoping I wouldn't be spotted, which was pretty much how I'd felt since the night my sister returned a month ago, cradling two-year-old Romy like a priceless vase.

'Hi,' she'd said, into the stupefied silence that had followed. Bridget rarely travelled up from London, and never alone, and we'd been innocently watching *Say Yes to the Dress* (even Dad had been reduced to a puddle of tears when one of the fathers saw his daughter's meringue-like creation), and we couldn't quite comprehend that she was there, looking less like the Bridget we thought we knew.

'I need some bonding time with my daughter,' she'd announced, pressing a squirming Romy against her shoulder. 'I've taken a few months' unpaid leave from work, rented out the house, and I'm moving home for a while.' She'd audibly swallowed before continuing, as if on the verge of sobbing – except Bridget considered crying to be a weakness. 'My daughter's so precious and perfect…' another pause, while she scattered kisses on Romy's soft swirl of hair, 'and I won't have her messed up by that… by becoming the product of a broken family.'

Her gaze had briefly hardened into defiance before she'd added, 'She needs to get to know her grandparents,' as though Romy didn't have an auntie present too, and as if our parents hadn't tried to get their hands on their first and only grandchild since coming back from Canada. 'She's missing her father, and the house feels too big without him, and I…' more swallowing, while we'd continued to gawp '… I need a break from London.' Our jaws had finally dropped. Bridget Campbell, finance manager at one of Britain's leading airlines, and self-confessed control freak, was admitting to *needing* a break. 'Also, I can't find an au pair capable of meeting Romy's needs.' She made Romy sound like an invalid, instead of an apparently robust toddler. 'As her mother, I'm the only one who can do that,' she'd continued, seeming unaware that Romy was tugging her mother's hair out of its toppling bun, while intermittently shouting 'HUNGRY!' at the top of her lungs.

Once Mum had recovered the power of speech and suggested that Romy might need something to eat, Bridget had dug a banana out of her bag, peeled it, and fed her daughter a tiny piece, insisting any more would upset the eating routine she'd implemented, before spiriting Romy to the spare bedroom and tucking the wailing child into the neatly made-up bed.

At first, there'd been some novelty value in this new, Perfect Mum version of Bridget, but her general disdain (mostly of me) meant it had quickly worn thin. She didn't appreciate Mum and Dad's input, implying they were doing everything wrong, despite their very best efforts. Having missed the first year of their granddaughter's life they'd been keen to make amends once we were home, pleading to be allowed to take care of Romy while Bridget and her partner Chad

had a little break, but Bridget didn't do little breaks, and was reluctant to relinquish control. Secretly, we'd been amazed she'd found time to have a child in the first place, and even more so that she hadn't immediately returned to work. Bridget had been even more fiercely anti-motherhood than I was, and completely focused on her career – until she'd met Chad Drummond.

Until that point, despite running her life with military precision, my sister had shown appalling taste in men. There'd been a short-lived marriage in her twenties to a Frenchman who'd smoked cigars and drank little cups of espresso all day, followed by a fling with a minor politician who'd turned out to be gay, and a two-year affair with a Turkish man called Alvin, who'd worked in a call centre but wanted to be an actor. All had been dispensed with, once she'd realised she couldn't mould them, and then she'd met Charming Chad, who'd worked at the café where she allowed herself brunch on Sunday mornings. He'd turned out to be the love of her life, despite the job being part-time, and his work ethic underdeveloped. A self-styled inventor, he'd held a deep-seated conviction he was on the verge of producing something the world couldn't live without; like a plastic handle that attached to a can of drink, so it could be held like a mug.

'Why not just tip the drink into a mug?' Dad had queried – not unreasonably – when Chad pitched up one night and tried to persuade Dad to invest in his scheme so he could 'surprise' Bridget by becoming worthy of her affection.

'It was worth a try,' he said, in his charming way (I'd liked him) when Dad had declined the 'opportunity of a lifetime'. 'I'll have to do it another way.'

'Another way' had been to book a flight to New York a week later, and to promise Bridget that when he'd found his fortune and could make her and his daughter proud, he'd be back for good – news she'd conveyed briskly to Mum during their weekly phone catch-up, giving every impression it was nothing more than a blip in her neatly ordered life.

Clearly it had been more than that for her to want to return home and share a roof with her family for the first time in over twenty years – even if she'd made it plain she wanted things done her own way.

'I still can't believe you sent Mum and Dad on a cruise.' Her voice halted my tiptoeing progress across the polished-wood floor, and I turned to see her watching me from the living room doorway, arms folded across her thickly cardiganed chest. The old Bridget – whose LinkedIn profile described her as managing a portfolio of accounts and driving more than £14 million a year in revenue – wouldn't have been seen dead in a cardigan. She'd mostly worn satiny blouses, tucked into tapered trousers, and maybe a fitted jacket over the top, depending on the weather. The old Bridget had been sleek and streamlined, her autumn-red curls fiercely straightened, her face subtly made-up to hide her peppering of freckles, her diet strictly controlled and mostly green. *This* Bridget – though still undeniably stunning – had plumped up on a diet of carbs, her curls were held off her forehead with a bulldog clip, and her freckles stood out like crayon dots. I'd always envied them.

'I didn't *send* them on a cruise.' I tried to keep my body language relaxed, as Romy's pan-symphony ramped up a level, accompanied by intermittent shrieks. 'The cruise was already booked, they'd been looking forward to it, and I didn't think they should cancel.'

'And what you say goes around here.' She seemed to think I'd deliberately encouraged the cruise to punish her for coming back and stealing my limelight, which was utter rubbish. I'd given her the 'Dad's worked hard all his life and always put family first, and now he's finally retired it's time for him and Mum to have some fun', speech, but she'd taken that as a personal criticism. They'd wanted more children after Bridget was born, and had been nearly forty by the time I came along, and were now approaching seventy – too old for the level of childminding that Romy seemed to require, even if Bridget was reluctant to give them full rein (or any rein at all). It was clear Romy missed her dad – who'd apparently been as hands-on as Bridget would allow – and would often wake crying in the night. I'd seen how it was taking its toll on Mum; dark circles under her eyes from getting up when Romy refused Bridget's attempts at consolation. Even Dad – already at a bit of a loss without work to define his days – had started to stay out of the house for hours on end, after Bridget had criticised his attempts at engaging with his granddaughter.

'Don't do that, you might drop her,' she'd cry, surging forward to grab Romy as he swung her in the air, petting the child as though Dad had planned to throw her out of the window. 'Yes, I know you've raised two children,' she'd answer his protests. 'But things were different then.'

I wasn't even allowed near my niece. Bridget apparently had no faith in my ability to be a good auntie, so consequently neither did I. The one time I'd picked up Romy as a baby, drawn by her cherubic smile and chubby, flailing arms, Bridget had yelled so loudly at me to put her down, she'd almost slipped from my grasp.

'You don't pick her up when she's calm or she'll come to rely on it,' she'd said, wrestling her daughter back into her sling where she'd promptly burst into tears. It wasn't long after Romy's birth, and Bridget had flown out to Canada for our grandfather's funeral. I couldn't deny a swell of relief when she'd returned to London the next day – or the flare of sadness that followed, that we didn't have the sort of sibling closeness I'd witnessed among friends who had sisters.

'They haven't even been in touch,' said Bridget, snapping me back to the moment. 'It's not like there isn't a signal on the boat. You'd think with Skype and so on, they'd be on the phone all the time.'

I didn't mention I'd suggested they didn't call, in order to have a proper break, and it was a measure of how fraught things had become that they'd readily agreed.

'How's the regime going?' I said, unwilling to provoke an argument. It happened all too often in Bridget's company, to my endless dismay. She'd resented my presence since I ended her reign as the only child, thirty years ago, and nothing much had changed in the decades since. 'Are you still following the book?'

'It's not a *regime*,' she said. 'I'm hardly Kim Jong-un. And, yes, I'm trying.'

The book was a child-rearing tome Bridget had brought with her, written by a Danish woman with too much hair and a whimsical smile, who'd had her own TV show called *Hygge Parenting*. Its philosophies of play, authenticity, reframing (to help kids cope with setbacks and look on the bright side), empathy, togetherness, and No Ultimatums were fine in theory, but ignored the importance of Boundaries – even I could see that's what Romy needed during this transitional period in her young life – and clashed completely with Bridget's controlling nature.

'She's due some lunch.' Bridget glanced at the watch she'd taken to wearing, that used to belong to Dad. 'I just let her get this…' she made a circling motion with her hand at the room behind her '… out of her system first, so that she feels cleansed.'

I wondered how she could bear the noise, but knew better than to say anything. I wasn't a mother so I had no idea, as Bridget had pointed out before I left for the café, when I'd queried why she'd let Romy switch on the television downstairs at 7 a.m. and turn the volume to maximum. If we'd had neighbours either side, we'd have been reported for disturbing the peace. 'Frida says I mustn't acknowledge negative behaviour,' she'd said, as if she had a hotline to the author. 'You wouldn't understand, not being a parent.' I'd left her to it, reassured that at least Romy had been smiling, even if Bridget wasn't as she stirred a pan of something smoking on the stove.

'Shall I go say hello?' I tried to peer past Bridget, but she shunted sideways to block my view.

'Please, leave her alone.'

Jeez. 'I just think, you know, you should maybe tell her you want her to stop. It can't be much fun listening to—'

'*Fun?*' She pulled her head in so far, a double chin appeared. 'That's your favourite word, isn't it, Tilly? *Fun.*' She might as well have said *murder.* 'As long as you're having *fun*, life's a peach.' *Do not respond. Do not respond.* 'Is that what you've been doing?' Her wide-set ocean-coloured eyes – a perfect blend of our parents' – scanned my peculiar outfit and thinned to slits. 'Rolled out of your boyfriend's bed and couldn't find your own clothes?' Before I could respond, she held up a finger. 'Wait, what's his name again? Robbie... Ricky?'

'Rufus, actually.'

'Rufus?' Her expression smoothed out; became interested. 'You're still seeing him then? The guy dad recommended.' Now he sounded like a brand of floor cleaner. 'Good for you.' She nodded slowly. 'This must be the longest you've ever dated anyone.'

'True.' I swelled a little. Bridget sounded impressed, which hardly ever happened – scrap that; she was never impressed by me – and I liked it. 'We're going to his brother's wedding on Saturday.'

'Really?' Her eyebrows rose. 'A wedding? It must be getting serious.'

'M-hmm.' *Was she smiling?* She definitely wasn't frowning.

'He seemed really nice when he came to pick you up last week,' she said, though to my knowledge, she'd barely noticed him. I'd shot out of the front door the second he rang the bell, unwilling to indulge Dad's *Why don't we get both families together for a meal, now you two are an item?* fantasy. 'Good for you, Tilly. It's about time you had a grown-up relationship.'

Why did those three words put my back up so much? What *was* a grown-up relationship, anyway? One where you discussed Brexit without arguing, and remembered each other's birthdays? It wasn't as if Bridget had any room to talk, but I bit the inside of my cheek to stop myself saying so. I'd heard her crying in her room when she thought no one was around. I knew, in spite of herself, she desperately missed Charming Chad. Plus, I still had a long-buried hope that, one day, my sister and I would have a conversation as equals. Friends, even.

'What with all the work you've got coming in you're almost a fully-fledged adult these days.' She leaned against the door frame, seemingly enjoying herself now. 'Where is this design job you mentioned you had lined up?'

My brain scrabbled for a response she'd find acceptable, and couldn't find one. 'Actually, it's fallen through.'

She rolled her eyes. 'Isn't it about time you set yourself up as a proper business?' she said. 'I thought you were getting a website, doing it properly.'

'I was… I am.' At least, that had been the plan, after listening to her go on about it one evening over dinner – how having an amazing career would be defining, and that I should try it sometime, which had fired some ridiculous notion of trying to make her proud.

'Actually, I do have another job since this morning.'

'Oh?'

'I've been asked to redesign a cottage for someone in Seashell Cove.' Behind her, Romy had given up with the pan and spoon and was yodelling.

'You're never away from that place,' said Bridget. 'Who is this client?' She said client ironically, as if doubting their existence. *As well she might.*

'He's called Seth Donovan. He's moved to an old cottage overlooking the sea with his son.'

'Seth Donovan?' Bridget jerked as though someone had poked her. 'The Formula One driver?' Excitement sharpened her voice. 'I heard he'd moved to Devon.'

Formula One driver. That's what he'd been. Quite famous, apparently. He must be, if Bridget had heard of him. 'That's him.'

Her cheeks were tinged pink. 'He's always been my dream date,' she said, eyes shining. 'You know, the one you'd get a free pass with.' Her glow dimmed a little. 'Chad's was Ellen DeGeneres.'

I let that settle for a moment. 'He seems nice. Seth Donovan, I mean.'

Bridget shrugged aside whatever memory had risen. 'How on earth did you wangle the job?'

I haven't. I lifted a shoulder, indicating it had been easy with my powers of persuasion. I could see she was willing to be convinced, but decided not to tell her how I'd actually met Seth. It sounded too much like boasting to mention I'd saved Jack's life. 'It's a nice cottage,' I said instead. 'At least, it will be.'

'A cottage by the sea. How romantic.' She made a swoony face that nearly made me smile. Bridget wasn't the swoony type.

'I can get you a date with him.' The words shot out before I could stop them, but I remembered his insistence on somehow paying me back for saving Jack. Surely taking my sister out couldn't hurt, and it might bring back her smile again. Permanently. I knew he'd like her. Most men did; she had that indefinable something that drew them in. Plus, they both had a child, so they instantly had something in common, and it was about time Bridget moved on now Chad had been gone for months, doing goodness knows what in America. As far as I knew, they didn't speak any more as she'd decided it would be too confusing for Romy.

'You could get me a *date*?' Bridget's face had knotted into a shape I didn't recognise. 'With Seth *Donovan*?'

'He's single, isn't he?' *Wasn't he?*

'Well, yes… according to the *Daily Mail*.' Her shoulders rose. 'I looked him up when I heard he was moving here.'

'Well, there you go.' I sounded a lot like Mum. 'I'll have a word with him, if you like.'

Her expression was a mixture of hope and disbelief. 'That would be amazing,' she said. 'Listen, I'm sorry if I've been a bit… you know.' Her knees suddenly buckled, and Romy poked her curly blonde head through Bridget's legs and shouted, 'BISCUITS!'

'No problem,' I said. 'I'll ask him when I next see him.' I backed towards the stairs. 'I'd better just…'

'Go and change.' She flapped her hand while trying to unwedge Romy's head. 'I'll put the kettle on.'

Bridget wasn't the 'putting the kettle on' type. At least, she hadn't been. Not for me, anyway. For the first time in my life, it seemed I might be able to do something to make my sister happy. Now all I had to do was talk to Seth.

Chapter Six

'Why did you say you were redecorating his cottage, Tilly?' Cassie scanned my face with forensic interest. 'It's not like you to make things up.'

'Or to try and impress anyone.' Meg put down the tray she'd been carrying. 'Since when do you care what people think about you?'

My mouth watered at the sight of the snowman-topped cupcakes she'd brought over. 'She's my sister,' I said, reaching for a plate. 'Don't ask me why after all this time, but I apparently do care what my sister thinks.'

Silence fell and I watched as Meg settled next to Cassie and poured the tea, as though she'd forgotten she no longer worked at the café. Her forget-me-not blue jumper exactly matched her eyes, and complemented her wavy, pale-blonde hair. It struck me that if we were seasons, Meg was summer and Cassie was autumn, with her silver-grey eyes and chestnut mane, while my winter-pale skin and black-as-night hair suited the winter months.

'I know you've told us before that you don't get on with your sister,' Meg said. 'But I'm sure, deep down, she loves you as you are.'

'If she does, it's buried very deep.' I smiled. 'You've never really met my sister, have you?'

'We almost did, once.' Cassie broke off a chunk of cupcake and lifted it to her lips. 'Remember, she'd met that French guy in London and brought him home to meet your parents? We were up in your room, getting ready for the school-leaver's party.'

'I'd forgotten about that.' Meg stirred milk into her tea and added a spoonful of sugar. 'We were dying to meet her, but you said we should leave them to it and hustled us out of the back door.'

'Yes, because the Frenchman had made a pass at me in the kitchen before you two arrived and I couldn't face her,' I said. 'I was so tempted to tell her what a creep he was, but she wouldn't have believed me. Or, she'd have blamed me for "leading him on".'

'It sounds like she's still got issues,' said Cassie, after swallowing her mouthful of cake. 'No wonder you don't want to be at home so much these days.'

'Not while Mum and Dad are away.' That flash of sadness again. 'I just seem to wind her up.'

'It's such a shame.' Meg looped a tendril of hair behind her ear, her face wreathed with worry. 'Family's *so* important,' she said.

I looked at my two oldest friends, wondering how I'd survived without them for so long. I'd been seventeen when I'd moved to Canada with Mum and Dad, and after finishing college Cassie had fled to London where she'd lived and worked for years. Only Meg had stayed in Devon, pursuing her cake-making dreams, and the day after my return, I'd found her working at the Old Bakery and engaged to her childhood sweetheart. We'd picked up our friendship as if we'd never been apart, and Cassie's return six months later had sealed our little circle. Now, we saw each other whenever we could, which wasn't as often as I'd like as Meg was in love with someone new, as well as being in charge of the bakery, and Cassie – also madly in love – had more commissions than ever for her artwork.

Increasingly, I felt as if I was stuck in the past, while they'd reframed their lives – not in a bad way (and they never judged me like Bridget did), but by inhabiting a world I knew little about, with their satisfying jobs and healthy relationships. It was a world I'd been happy *not* to inhabit, but seeing how content they were had fuelled the notion that I was the one somehow missing out.

'Family's only important to Bridget now she wants it to be,' I said, taking a bite of my cupcake and pausing a moment to savour the sweetness on my taste buds. *It's enough to make your ears smile* was something Dad said whenever he ate something delicious, and Meg's cakes had that effect. 'She couldn't wait to leave home the minute she turned eighteen.'

'I don't know why, when your mum and dad are amazing.' Cassie licked her fingers. 'It's not like she had a terrible childhood, or anything.'

'I think she sees it very differently,' I said. 'Not that it was terrible, but that I had it easier than her, being ten years younger, and because they'd tried for so long to have me and spoilt me rotten.'

'There's nothing rotten about you, Tilly.' Meg's smile was wide and warm, and I couldn't help noticing her rosy glow, which was partly due to meeting Nathan and dumping her fiancé, who'd taken her for granted for years, spending most of his free time cycling in different time zones.

'You should have told her about saving that little boy,' said Cassie, wiping her lips on a paper napkin. 'Surely that would have impressed her more than anything.'

'It would have sounded like showing off and she hates that.' A memory of Jack's terrified face came flooding back. I hoped his experience wouldn't have lasting effects – except to remind him not to rush into the sea after his dog. 'I only told you two because I needed to get it off my chest. It was starting to feel unreal.' In fact, once I'd left Bridget to tend to Romy and put the kettle on, I'd fallen into a deep sleep on top of my bed, only stirring to shuffle under my duvet, and when I'd woken that morning, I'd wondered whether I'd dreamt the previous day.

'You do know his mother's dead, don't you?' Meg picked up her tea and blew on it.

'Seth's?'

'His son's.' She puffed out a little sigh. 'Seth Donovan is a tragic widower.'

'That's awful.' I remembered Jack huddled in his bed, and the photos I'd seen on the wall – the one with the woman I'd assumed must be his mum. 'Was it recent?'

'A few years ago, he was only three, I think. Probably too young to properly remember her.' Meg looked at Cassie, who was twisting her shiny hair back into a ponytail. 'Isn't that what your mum said?' As the owners of Maitland's Café, Cassie's parents got to hear the local gossip first-hand.

'It was a car crash,' said Cassie, dusting crumbs off the front of her chunky red sweater. 'Danny mentioned it. He's a motor-racing fan, and was gutted when he heard Seth Donovan had retired.'

'He was world champion for four years in a row, but lost to Lewis Hamilton a couple of times and decided to pack it in.' Meg gave a delicate shrug. 'What?' she said, when Cassie and I exchanged smiles. 'He came in the bakery once, in disguise, but one of the customers guessed who he was.'

'How?'

'Something to do with his tan, and his spectacles looked like they didn't have real glass in them, and he was wearing a hat even though it was sunny.'

'Inspector Poirot, eat your heart out,' I said.

'Apparently, he sold his amazing house in Italy last year and moved back to Britain. His parents had been raising his son, but Seth's got him back, at least for now. There's an issue around custody.'

'You gave him a good grilling then?'

'Of course not.' Meg clattered her cup down. 'The customer didn't say anything until Seth had left the shop with a couple of loaves and a lemon drizzle cake,' she said. 'We googled him after he'd gone.'

'What would we do without the internet?' My curiosity was not so much piqued as flaring in bright pink neon. 'What else did it say about him?'

'That he's an only child, his parents live in Surrey, his father's an art historian, his mother does something with horses, and it was his uncle who got him interested in motor-racing after taking him to Silverstone when he was eleven.'

'Is that all?'

Meg crinkled her nose, thinking. 'He married quite young, his wife was a model, and before he came back to Britain he was seeing an Italian woman—'

'I was joking,' I said, smiling as I tried to insert a feisty brunette into the cottage with Seth and Jack. 'I'm impressed by your powers of recollection, though.'

Meg grinned. 'Big Steve at the bakery got a bit carried away,' she said. 'I think he's got a little crush on him.'

Cassie toyed with her half-eaten cupcake. 'Are you really going to redesign his cottage?'

'Big Steve's?'

She tutted. 'You know who I mean.'

'Never mind a bleedin' cottage, what about this place?' Gwen materialised, a cloth in one hand and a bottle of squirty cleaner in the other. Only she could make both items look like weapons. 'You do know them floorboards ain't gonna lay themselves?'

'I do.' I gave her a winning smile. 'And you know I have to wait until the floor is properly dry.'

'It's dry enough,' she said, eyes pinched. 'I checked this mornin' when I got in. Crawled over it on me 'ands and knees, I told you.'

I'd checked my phone whilst stuffing my face with toast at home as Bridget attempted to foist burnt porridge on me, and had noticed some missed calls from the café. Gwen had even fired off a text: *The floor's dry, where the bleedin' 'ell are you?* spelt exactly like that, so I'd heard her cockney accent as plainly as if she was standing next to me. 'You know I trust your judgement, Gwen, but in this case, you have to trust mine, and – more importantly – Ted the floor man's judgement.'

'Nuffink to do wiv judgement,' she said, frowning so deeply she developed a monobrow. 'It's a fact.' She seemed more bullish than usual and I almost recoiled when she thrust her face close to mine and said, 'That room *will* be finished in time for the Christmas party, won't it?'

'I told you it would, and it will,' I said, surprised by her vehemence. 'I always keep my word.'

'Yeah, but fings 'ave already gorn wrong wiv the leak, and now you're behind schedule.' Gwen sprayed cleaner at the next table without looking. 'You've a deadline, in case you've forgotten.'

'I met my deadline when I fixed up the café last year.'

'That's true, she did,' said Meg, sticking her hand up like I remembered her doing in high school. 'I was here, and she did a fabulous job.'

'She did,' agreed Cassie, with a grin. 'I couldn't believe my eyes when I came back and saw what she'd done.'

'Why, thank you.' I modestly bowed my head. 'It was my pleasure.'

In all honesty, it had been the first time since completing my degree at Vancouver Island University that I'd felt a strong creative pull, having mostly dabbled while living over there. When Meg had mentioned that the Maitlands were thinking of updating their café, I'd leapt at the chance to flex my design muscles.

'Come with me.' Gwen beckoned me with a jerk of her head.

'What?' I glanced at the counter. Surely she didn't need my help. Jerry was back, looking self-conscious in a 'Santa's Little Helper' hat, firing terrified glances in Gwen's direction every few seconds, and Cassie had given herself the day off from painting the mayoress so she could help out if the café got busy.

'Floor,' Gwen barked, rubbing the table next to ours as if trying to remove its surface. 'Come and see.'

'Blimey, OK.' Exchanging looks with Meg and Cassie, I stood up, feeling an ache across my shoulders from where I'd held onto Jack the previous day. 'Get some more tea in,' I said to Meg – almost forgetting she didn't work at the café any more. 'I'll be back.'

The function room was chilly without any heating and I gave a little shiver. Feeling Gwen's presence behind me, I swung round. 'You really don't need to worry,' I told her, my voice echoing around the empty space. She'd tucked her cloth in her trouser pocket, and the spray cleaner dangled from her belt hook like a gun from a holster. 'Ted will be popping over again later, and once the floorboards are down, the painters will come and do the walls, and when the lighting's sorted it's just a case of making the room look Christmassy for the party.'

'That's a lot of whens and ifs and buts.'

'There weren't any ifs or buts.'

'I'm plannin' summink,' she burst out, looking around as if to check no one was listening. 'At the party.' Her biceps bulged as she belted her arms across her ample chest. 'That's why I want to know it's definitely goin' to 'appen.'

'Planning what?' It didn't sound good whatever it was, but that was just Gwen's demeanour. If she announced she'd won the lottery, her delivery would make it seem sinister.

''Is nibs.' This time, her head jolted in the direction of the café.

'Sorry?'

'Jezza.'

'Who?'

Rolling her eyes, she said, 'Jer-e-my,' exaggerating the syllables.

'Jeremy?' I could only think of the Labour leader, Jeremy Corbyn, but had no idea why Gwen would be talking about him. 'Jeremy who?'

Her glare could have crushed glass. '*Jerry*,' she ground out through gritted teeth.

Understanding dawned. 'Jerry behind the counter?'

Her eyeballs rotated. 'No, Jerry the bleedin' mouse, who do you fink?'

An image of her chasing him, cartoon-style, around the café, brought a giggle to my throat. 'What about him?' I managed, guessing Gwen wouldn't like me laughing at her. For all her machismo, she was a surprisingly sensitive soul. As if on cue, Dickens appeared, swaying around her calves while purring violently. She picked up the black and white cat and pushed him against her cheek. 'Look at 'is smilin' face,' she cooed, the corners of her mouth twitching upwards. I had to admit he did look smiley, despite only having one eye. 'I'm plannin' to snog 'im under the mistletoe.'

I glanced from her to Dickens. His whiskers were vibrating against Gwen's face and her eyes were screwed shut, as if in unbearable ecstasy. '*Snog* him?' Had she lost the plot?

Her eyes flipped open. 'Jerry,' she growled. ''Ave you listened to a bleedin' word I've said?' Dickens shot out of her grasp and disappeared – probably back to his velvet cushion in the office where he lounged most of the day, like a Saudi prince. 'Who do you fink I was talkin' abart?'

'But, why do you want to snog Jerry?' Maybe *I* was losing the plot. I simply couldn't imagine Gwen snogging *anyone*. Her mouth didn't seem designed for kissing.

'Why do you reckon?' Gwen strode across to the windows and looked out. The view was obscured by a veil of rain, and there was nothing much to see.

'It's supposed to snow this week,' I said. 'Did you know, the winters are so harsh in Montreal they built an underground city? I went there once, it was weird. We didn't get much snow in Vancouver, apart from one year, when—'

'Ain't it obvious why I want to snog Jerry?' She glowered at me over her shoulder, clearly not interested in the weather here, or in Canada. 'I fancy the pants orf 'im.'

I considered myself unshockable – even Bridget's return hadn't rendered me completely speechless – but found myself lost for words.

'You've gotta admit, 'e's pretty 'ot.' To my astonishment, her cheeks had turned a mottled shade of scarlet

'Well… I…' The truth was, I'd barely registered Jerry as anything more than a panicked face above a Maitland's shirt, and although he seemed perfectly natural and at ease with the customers, 'hot' was not a word I'd have chosen to describe him.

'You won't tell anyone, will you?' Gwen's tone was urgent now. 'I wanna make sure 'e's on board before we go public, like, though I know 'e wants me, I recognise the signs.'

I wondered what signs they were, when he seemed to go out of his way to avoid even looking at her, and tried and failed again to picture Gwen's lips attached to a man's. I knew she'd been through an unpleasant divorce in the past, and up until now had given every impression of being a man-hater. 'Snogging him at the Christmas party will be pretty public,' I pointed out.

Her eyes stretched. 'I'm not a *tart*,' she said, as if I'd accused her of plotting to have wild sex with him, in front of a thousand people. 'The party will create the right atmosphere, that's all.' She sniffed. 'When the moment's right, I'll get 'im in a corner and Bob's your randy uncle.' She tracked the room's dimensions, as if imagining how she'd tackle poor unsuspecting Jerry into submission.

'Right,' I said quickly. 'Do you, er, does he, um… are you sure you're not misjudging the situation, Gwen?'

She gave a terrifying chuckle. ''E wants me.' She passed a hand across her close-cropped hair. ''E just don't know it yet.'

She left me standing there, mouth half open, imagination spinning, and after I'd gathered my wits and checked the floor myself – it was definitely dry to the touch – I made my way back to where Cassie and Meg were chattering as if they hadn't seen each other for weeks. I was about to break my promise and relay what Gwen had said – knowing it wouldn't go any further – when I heard someone say my name.

'She's over there wiv 'er mates,' said Gwen, and I turned to see Seth Donovan walking towards me.

Chapter Seven

'You're not very good at disguises, if you don't mind me saying so.'

Seth waggled his tortoiseshell frames. 'What, these aren't convincing?'

'They don't even have proper lenses.'

'Is it that obvious?' Smiling sheepishly, he whipped them off and stuffed them under the dashboard. We were sitting in his car – an elderly, midnight-blue Renault – parked on the narrow road that led to his cottage.

'Is this part of your disguise too?' I touched the worn fabric of the seat. 'So people won't recognise there's a former racing driver in their midst?'

He put a hand over his eyes and let out a groan. 'I take it everyone knows.'

'Well, I didn't yesterday, but I do now.' Why was I attempting to coax out a smile when twenty-four hours ago I'd lashed out at him for not taking care of his son? Maybe it was because I needed to ask him if he'd take my sister out to dinner. Or because Meg's sad-eyed description of him as a tragic widower had got under my skin. As he'd approached me in the café, I'd noticed things I hadn't before; tension around his shoulders, a rigid set to his jaw, and a wariness in his eyes. It was as if he'd been thrust a thousand miles out of his comfort zone, and was only just holding himself together.

Even so, surrounded by ordinary people in the café drinking coffee, reading the papers and working on laptops, he'd stood out. Not just because he was attractive – though he was, even in fake glasses – but there was a sheen to him; an aura that marked him as different. Although he was wearing an ordinary black Puffa jacket over a V-neck sweater, with a faded T-shirt underneath, it was obvious he was used to a warmer climate, and the sort of service that probably came with silver platters and deferential nods – not a raucous, 'Ain't you gonna buy anyfink, you tightwad?' from Gwen, and a nervous titter from Jerry that made me think he was either desperate to please her, or petrified of being fired.

I looked at Seth now, gripping the steering wheel while the engine ticked over, blowing warm air through the vents. 'And your hat looks too new.'

He snatched off the green woollen beanie and bunched it in his hands, leaving his hair sticking up on one side. 'Don't you think you only recognised me because we met yesterday?'

I grinned. 'Everyone recognised you,' I said. 'You stand out like a…' I tried to think of something wittier than 'sore thumb'.

'Like a stranger in a small seaside café?' A glint of humour brightened his gaze.

'I was going to say like a Goth at a rave, and the café's not that small,' I said. 'At least, it won't be soon. And everyone in there was far too British to mention they knew who you really were.'

I'd been hyper-aware of several sets of awestruck eyes on us, and Cassie and Meg trading knowing smiles when he asked if he could talk to me in private, before leading me out to his car.

'Why were you looking for me anyway?' I said. 'Especially if coming out is such an effort.'

'Because you ran away from me before I had a chance to thank you properly for what you did.'

'You did thank me,' I reminded him. 'I accepted your thanks. End of story.'

'But I want to do something for you in return.'

The wind buffeted the car, making it rock, and rain pattered on the roof. The radio was on low, playing a Sam Smith song, making the car seem smaller and less full of air.

'Where's Jack?' I swivelled to look in the back of the car, as though he might be crouching there, but saw only a matted tennis ball on the back seat that I guessed belonged to Digby. 'You haven't left him on his own, have you?'

'Of course not.' Seth's eyes flashed. 'I'm not a complete idiot,' he said. 'My mother's come to stay for a couple of days.'

'Oh.' I deflated. 'Well, that's good.'

'Not really.' His voice grew heavy. 'You don't know my mother.'

It was practically an echo of what I'd said about Bridget to Cassie and Meg at the café and I nodded in understanding. 'Like that, is it?'

He shot me a look, as if my response had caught him off guard. 'She's not happy that we've moved here,' he said candidly. 'My parents want custody of Jack, and if they get it, they plan to send him to boarding school.'

I searched his face. 'You're joking?'

'Nope.'

'But that's so… *Victorian.*'

'That's my mother for you.'

'God.' I shook my head. 'I'm sorry.' I remembered Meg mentioning there were custody issues. 'It sounds serious.'

'She says it's in Jack's best interests and… I don't know.' He looked at his hat, twisting it in his hands. 'Maybe she's got a point, after what happened yesterday.' He lifted his head and directed his gaze through the windscreen. A speckled seagull had landed on the road, head cocked as if weighing us up. 'Maybe I'm not a fit parent.'

'That's rubbish,' I said, despite having nothing concrete to base my opinion on. After all, his son had run all the way from the cottage and into the sea in his pants without Seth noticing. But I'd seen how shaken Seth had been; heard the gruff love in his voice when he'd remonstrated with Jack, and the underlying terror at how close he'd come to losing him. 'He's your son.'

Turning his head, he gave me a look that went on so long, every inch of my face heated up. Even my nostrils felt hot. 'You don't know the whole story,' he said gravely. 'After Jack's mum died, my parents looked after him while I was away, competing all over the world. They gave him a stable home, albeit one with rigid rules. They practically have more rights to him than I do.'

I worked that around my head for a moment. 'Doesn't Jack have a say?'

Seth shook his head. 'He's only six,' he said. 'If it goes to court, they'll decide what's best for him.'

'It could go to court?'

'I'm afraid so.'

'Can't you share custody?'

'I want my son with me,' he said firmly. 'I'm not having him packed off to boarding school, like I was.' He shot me a look. 'I was fine, I came home at weekends, but I really don't want that for Jack.'

'But look what you've given up,' I said. 'You've retired from racing, sold your home in Italy, probably given up an amazing lifestyle, all to take care of Jack and give him a normal life. And that's on top of losing your wife.' I paused. 'That's got to count for something.'

Seth's face was a hybrid of faint amusement and horror. 'Wow,' he said, eyebrows raised. 'You've really done your research.'

The warmth in my face intensified. 'Actually, my friend told me most of it.' I sat on my hands to stop them waving about, and gave a wincing smile. 'Sorry,' I said. 'That must have sounded really rude.'

'The wonders of Google, I suppose.' He flicked a glance at the rear-view mirror and flattened his sticky-up hair. 'Hard to keep anything secret these days.'

'True though?'

'Some of it,' he acknowledged. 'Though I was ready to give up the *amazing lifestyle*, as you put it, anyway. It was pretty empty without…'

'Your wife?' I risked, trying to imagine how it must feel to lose someone you loved in what sounded like tragic circumstances. The thought of Dad without Mum – or vice versa – was unthinkable. Flip sides of the same coin, their lives entwined for nearly half a century, bound by all that history… to lose your 'other half' must be devastating at any time, but surely worse too young and in tragic circumstances.

Watching sadness settle over Seth's face, I was glad I hadn't experienced the kind of pain he must be going through. One of the benefits of not having had a serious relationship.

'Actually,' he said. 'I was going to say without Jack.'

'Sorry?'

'Didn't Google tell your friend that my wife and I were divorced by the time she died, and she'd been refusing me access to my son?'

'No,' I said, thrown. So, there'd been no love lost between Seth and his wife. But that didn't make it any less tragic for Jack, even if he was too young to remember much about his mother. 'I'm sorry to hear that.'

Ruffling his hair up again, Seth eased out a sigh. 'It's a long story,' he said. 'I don't come out of it that well.'

Normally, in male company, I shied away from exchanging too much personal information – even with Rufus – but my head was crammed with questions. Before I'd mustered the necessary nerve to ask any of them, he said, 'I'm actually looking to settle down now.'

'You are?' That was unexpected.

'Not just to find a mother for Jack, though I know he'd like one, and it would be good for him.' He grimaced. 'My mother's style of parenting is quite regimented.'

'It must be a bit confusing for him, being with you now.'

'He was becoming too quiet there, too introverted. It wasn't healthy,' said Seth. 'I know there's going to be a period of readjustment, but we're getting there. Moving here was a good decision, and getting the dog has helped.'

'So, now you're ready to start dating.'

He made a face. 'That's such an old-fashioned word, but yeah, I suppose I am.' He tipped his head. 'Are you volunteering?'

Now my whole body felt on fire. 'Definitely not.'

He recoiled a little from my tone. 'Sorry,' he said. 'Are you married?'

It was such an amusing concept, I couldn't help smiling. 'No, but I'm seeing someone,' I said. 'His name's Rufus.' Unexpectedly, I felt a wave of affection as I recalled my conversation with him on the beach – his eagerness to make things work – and it strengthened my resolve to try harder. 'I was actually thinking of my sister.'

Seth was frowning slightly, rubbing his fingers over his short beard. 'You have a sister?'

'I do.' I pulled my phone out of my jacket pocket, aware of him tracking my every move.

'I've got your clothes, by the way,' he said. 'They're in the back.'

'Oh. Thanks.' I flashed him a grin. 'I haven't washed yours yet.'

It was a weirdly intimate exchange. I couldn't remember ever discussing washing with a man. 'Here she is.' I angled a recent photo of Bridget and Romy towards him, their faces pressed together in a rare show of unity. I enjoyed snapping pictures, but there was something about my sister that discouraged me from pointing a camera in her direction. Mum had taken this one and forwarded it to me. Bridget's skin and eyes looked luminous – no sign of sleepless nights – and Romy, who took after Chad with her white-blonde curls and crystal-blue eyes, looked especially appealing. 'She's forty, but doesn't look it,' I said. 'Bridget, I mean. That's her name.'

'She's beautiful.' He spoke with obvious sincerity. 'You don't look at all alike.'

'Thanks a lot.'

'Oh god, I didn't mean—'

'It's fine,' I said. 'She got Mum's beauty and Dad's brains. I was the gawky, boyish bookworm growing up.' He was giving me such an odd look, I had to turn away. 'She lives in London, but she's home for a few months. We don't really get on, which is why I'm not there much at the moment…' *Why had I said that?* 'Anyway, it's a good opportunity for you to get to know her, and she's honestly really nice. It's just me she doesn't like very much.'

Seth looked like there were several things he wanted to say, and finally settled on, 'I don't think I've ever been out with a single mum.' He gave the picture another cursory glance, and I wondered whether looks weren't important to him. Or maybe he wasn't a fan of redheads and was just being polite. I remembered Meg's reference to an Italian girlfriend.

'She's lovely,' I said, laying it on a bit thick. Though, Bridget *was* lovely – around men. She'd left a trail of broken hearts before meeting Chad. 'Maybe it's time to ring the changes.'

'Maybe it is,' he said. 'But, I'm not sure—'

'You did say, if there was anything you could do in return…' I trailed off. It sounded tacky, after saying he didn't need to repay me.

'I did, and I meant it,' he said. His eyebrows drew together. 'This is repayment?' he said. 'You'd like me to date your sister?'

'At least take her out to dinner.' Now I sounded like a pimp. 'You'll get on,' I promised. 'You've got loads in common, and it would honestly make her year.'

'Well, when you put it like that.' He lightly bashed the steering wheel with his fist. 'You're on.'

'There's a restaurant called The Mill in Kingsbridge,' I said. 'It's really good, you should take her there. You could book in under a fake name, if you're worried about being recognised.'

'Such as?'

'I don't know… Don Sethovan?'

His eyes narrowed. 'Don Sethovan?'

'Well, you come up with something better.'

'Um… Van Donaseth?'

'We're terrible at fake names.'

He was the sort of person who smiled with his eyes before his mouth joined in, and the sight was surprisingly hard to look away from. 'I'll use my own name,' he said. 'Anything else I can do?'

A short burst of laughter escaped. 'Like what?'

'Oh, I don't know.' He looked thoughtful. 'I could pay for a nice holiday for you and your friends.'

I laughed again. 'I don't need a nice holiday, thank you. I spent ten years living abroad, and have only been back in Devon just over a year.'

'Make a donation to your favourite charity?'

'I already give money to charity.'

'There must be something else.'

'Honestly, there isn't.'

His smile drained away. 'I just want you to know that what you did was massive,' he said. 'My life could have been a whole lot different today, like a trillion times worse.'

'Maybe you should stop thinking like that.' He was sounding like a glass-half-empty person, instead of focusing on the positives. 'Maybe it was fate, or whatever, that I happened to be there, but Jack's fine,' I said. 'You're grateful, I get it. You don't have to keep on about it.'

That look again, slow and steady. 'I appreciate that you didn't immediately go to the press with it, or post about it online,' he said. 'We could do without that kind of attention.'

'Ah, but I didn't know who you were then.'

He narrowed his gaze, then realised I was teasing. 'I'm not just thinking about myself.' I hadn't thought that he was. 'Jack doesn't need to read stuff about me online, and I don't want to give my mother any more ammunition.'

'Well, no one will be hearing anything from me.' My phone vibrated. It was Gwen. 'I'd better go, my floor man has turned up early,' I said, after she'd blasted the information into my eardrum.

'Floor man?'

'There's a new function room at the café. I'm in charge of getting it ready for a party on Christmas Eve and there's still a lot to do.'

'In charge?'

'I'm sort of an interior designer.' It was what I usually said, prior to explaining that it wasn't a career as such; more of a hobby I loved, and that I didn't have my own business, but instead took on projects that appealed to me. Instead, I qualified the statement with, 'I *am* an interior designer,' remembering I'd told Bridget I was giving Seth's cottage a makeover. Would it be too much to ask him to let me do it, so soon after persuading him to take Bridget out on a date?

'You don't fancy having a go at my place, do you?'

My head whipped round. Had he really just asked me that?

'Obviously, I'll pay you,' he said, turning the heating down a notch. The car windows had totally steamed up. 'Actually, I'll pay double what you'd normally earn, it's the least I can do.'

OK, so he was offering me the job above the going rate as 'payback' for saving Jack, but still… it would mean I wasn't lying to Bridget about the job, and I *had* imagined refitting the cottage while I was there.

'You'd be doing me a massive favour actually,' he was saying, warming to the subject. 'My mother doesn't think the cottage is fit for habitation.' He clapped a hand to his forehead. 'I can't believe it.' His face clenched. 'You saved my son's life, and now I'm asking *you* for another favour.'

'It's not a favour.' I hovered my hand near his then quickly withdrew it. 'I'd like the job, so you're doing *me* a favour.'

His smile returned, and something peculiar happened to my insides. For a split second, I wished I'd put on a bit of mascara, and maybe my best sneakers instead of the ones with the tatty laces. 'Now, where are my clean clothes?' I said.

Chapter Eight

'You actually asked him?' Cassie sounded awestruck. 'I didn't think you'd go through with it.'

'To be honest, he didn't seem overjoyed. I think it's because he's never been out with a single mother, but I know once he meets Bridget he won't regret it.'

'She'd better be a lot nicer to you after this.' Cassie stepped to one side while Ted the floor man unpacked the floorboards, having deemed the floor dry and ready for business – leading to lots of high-fiving and a swoop of relief in my stomach. Meg had gone back to the bakery, but Cassie had pounced as soon as I walked back in, determined to extract every detail of what had happened after I left the café.

'He's crazy rich,' she said. 'We looked him up on Meg's phone after you'd gone, and let's just say he'll never have to work another day in his life – if you can call driving a car work.'

'Racing's a skill,' I said, 'and money's never been an issue in our family, so it's not like Bridget would be interested in that.' Seeing Cassie's face, I realised how that sounded. I sometimes forgot I was one of the lucky ones; that I'd never wanted for anything growing up, because Dad's career as an architect (award-winning) had afforded us a better lifestyle than most of the people I'd gone to school with. Not that he'd been remotely flashy with the money, once it started rolling in. It was more that there'd been no worry around it, and our house hadn't been mortgaged, and bills had been paid without question. Holidays were plentiful, and Christmases and birthdays extravagant without being over the top, but we'd had to work for our pocket money like everyone else; or rather, Bridget had. I'd been perfectly happy to do without. 'I'm just saying, Bridget wouldn't be interested in his cash.'

Cassie nodded. 'Fair enough, but Seth probably doesn't know that. I bet he's used to women wanting him for more than his good looks.'

'I get the feeling that's the last thing on his mind at the moment.'

'Imagine if he ends up marrying into your family,' she said. 'Wouldn't that be weird?'

'It would a bit.' A showreel ran through my mind: of one dinner leading to another, a declaration of love, an introduction to each other's children and family, followed by wedding bells and the patter of more tiny feet.

'Just let me know when and where you'd like me to meet your sister,' he'd said, as I got out of the car with my bag of clothing. 'And come to the cottage whenever you can, and we'll talk about that makeover.'

'Tomorrow?' I'd pushed. That way, when he met Bridget there wouldn't be any awkwardness if she mentioned me working for him.

'Tomorrow's fine,' he said. 'Although, talking of makeovers…' He'd looked through the rain-speckled back window, towards the café. 'Will you have time, if you're already pushed with this project?'

'I'll make time.' I squashed an image of Gwen's furious face, confident I could manage both. 'Anyway, I'd better get back.'

I'd jogged back to the café in a surprisingly carefree mood, not caring that my hair wouldn't thank me for getting wet.

'I thought he liked the look of you, to be honest,' said Cassie, while I squeezed out my fringe. 'You're not tempted?'

'He was wearing rose-tinted goggles because of what happened yesterday, that's all,' I said. 'I'm definitely not his type and, anyway, I'm seeing Rufus, remember?'

Cassie's eyes widened. 'What's it been now?' she said. 'More than a month?'

'Six weeks,' I said. 'I think I'm going to his brother's wedding on Saturday.'

'Think?'

'OK, I'm definitely going.'

'Good for you,' she approved. 'We should all get together sometime.'

'Together?'

'Well, we've only seen you with him once, that night in the Smugglers Inn, when he tried to hide while we did our routine.' She was referring to our All Saints tribute karaoke act, which I hadn't invited Rufus to. He'd turned up anyway, keen to 'see where you hang out', but hadn't stayed long after my hasty introduction – probably put off by my shockingly off-key vocals, and the salvo of questions fired at him by Meg. 'He's definitely different to your usual type.'

'Well, they do say opposites attract.' I was imitating my Scottish grandmother, who'd had a 'wee saying' for every occasion. 'Not that I've ever believed that.'

'Oh, I don't know. It depends what the opposites are.' Cassie – like Meg – fancied herself as something of an expert since finding True Love. 'Danny and I had totally different approaches to life when we met, but we've rubbed off on each other.'

'I'm sure you have.'

'Don't be smutty.' She smiled through a blush.

'I suppose he "completes you".' I put on my best moony voice, recalling the line from *Jerry Maguire* – which I'd secretly loved despite pretending it was lame.

'Ugh.' Cassie rolled her eyes. 'I didn't need completing, thank you very much. I suppose we do complement each other, though.'

'You do,' I agreed. 'Like Meg and Nathan.'

'Exactly. And I bet when you get to know Rufus better, you'll find you've more in common with him than you think.' She glanced at her watch, before I could ask her what she meant. 'I'm meeting a new artist in a minute. She's going to display her work here.'

'Hopefully her paintings will go down better than the last lot,' I said, wondering why Ted was standing around scratching his head, instead of getting on with laying the floorboards.

'That wasn't my fault,' said Cassie. 'He'd promised me something poignant from his latest collection, which I thought would be more studies of the local coastline, then cried when I said they weren't right. I felt sorry for him.'

'I don't think Seashell Cove was ready for abstract pictures of old ladies' hands.'

'I don't think anyone is.'

'You got a mixed batch here,' Ted's voice broke in.

'Sorry?'

Cassie gave me a sympathetic smile and backed into the café mouthing 'Good luck.'

'What do you mean, a mixed batch?'

'Half of them are a different shade to the rest.' He pointed to where he'd laid some of the boards out in a row. 'It's not obvious at first, but when you look more closely you can tell.'

I tilted my head for a better look, then moved across the room and studied them from a different angle. With light from the windows flooding across the wood, there was no getting away from it. Half of the boards were a subtly darker shade, and while it might not be noticeable once the tables and chairs were in, I would know.

'They'll have to go back,' I said, heart sinking. This was the last thing I needed.

'So, you don't want me to put them down?' A look of annoyance crossed his moon-like face. 'I already had to switch jobs around because of the leak.'

I sensed it wasn't the right moment to point out that the leak hadn't been my fault. 'I know, and I'm sorry,' I said. 'I'll pay you for coming out.'

'Fine,' he said, slightly mollified. 'That'll be eighty quid, plus my petrol expenses.'

'Petrol expenses? You've only come from Kingsbridge.'

'I charge twenty pence per mile.'

I rummaged in my back pocket. 'Here, I've got four quid in change.'

'There's no need to be sarcastic.' He practically snatched the coins I was holding out. 'I've got a business to run, you know.'

'So have I,' I said to his departing back, even though it wasn't strictly true. And now I was eighty-four pounds down and didn't have change for a cup of coffee, never mind a slice of the rich, fruity Christmas cake I'd spotted on the counter. I'd left my wallet in my rucksack in the car, and couldn't be bothered to fetch it.

Sighing, I called the flooring company to explain, and after arranging for the boards to be returned and a fresh batch delivered, I stared around for a while, realising there was nothing more I could do.

Leaving, I heard Gwen regaling a customer with a tale about how, when she'd lived in London, she'd seen the Queen in disguise outside Marylebone Station. 'Carryin' a shoppin' bag, she was, wiv one of 'er Corgis inside.' Jerry was hanging on her every word, blinking more than was natural.

'Where are you going?' Cassie caught me at the door, glancing back at a woman with mink-grey hair smoothed back from her face, holding a crate of framed pictures.

'Are they any good?' I said.

'I don't know, I haven't looked yet.' She grabbed my arm and lowered her voice. 'Is there a problem?'

'Wrong floorboards, would you believe?' I said, trying to keep the alarm from my voice. 'I've ordered some new ones.' Cassie bit her lip, eyes darting over my face. Her cheeks were deeply flushed, but it was warm in the café, and her sweater was a bit on the chunky side. 'What is it?'

She looked from side to side, like a cartoon spy. 'I know Gwen's already asked you, but the room *will* be ready in time for the party, won't it?'

A smile twitched at my lips. 'Are you worried it won't be done before Mummy and Daddy get back, and they'll tell you off and send you to your room?'

Instead of grinning, and possibly punching me, she said, 'No, no, it's not that.' Another glance behind her. The arty woman had put down her crate and was pointedly looking over.

'What is it then?'

'It's just…' Cassie bit down on her bottom lip, as if to stop any more words bouncing out.

'What's going on?'

She took a deep breath. 'I want to make an announcement, that's all.'

'Now?'

'No, not *now*.' She slapped my hand. 'At the Christmas party.'

'Oh?' I zipped up my jacket and looked at her more closely. She was almost vibrating. 'What sort of announcement?'

I could see her fighting to hold back, but she was terrible at keeping secrets these days – a legacy of not being honest for years, about her life in London. She'd only recently confessed to her parents about how stressed she'd been in her job, because she hadn't wanted to upset them. 'It's…' She dipped her eyes, to where her hand was resting on her belly.

'*Ohhhh*,' I said, realisation dawning, even as she snatched her hand away. 'You're—'

'Don't say it,' she hissed, darting a look towards the counter, but Gwen was still in full flow, the words "*is nibs, the Prince of Wales, blew me a kiss, but I told 'im I was married,*' carrying over, followed by a blast of laughter. 'No one knows, but Danny and me,' Cassie whispered, eyes glowing like lamps. 'We wanted to wait until it had been twelve weeks, which it will be on Christmas Eve.'

'Oh, Cassie, I'm so happy for you.' I felt oddly choked as her words distilled in my mind. I wanted to hug or kiss her, or pick her up and spin her round – something to mark the occasion – but it would have been a giveaway. We already looked odd, huddled by the door, talking in hushed voices. 'To be honest, I can't believe you've kept it to yourself this long.'

'I really wanted to tell you and Meg, but thought it might be tempting fate,' she said, the words spilling out. 'I actually didn't know myself for ages, even though I've been feeling sick every evening. I thought it was Nan's cooking, now she's gone vegan and keeps sticking hemp in everything.'

'I didn't even know you *wanted* kids.' I felt an odd little pang again – the sense of being excluded from something good; something that only happened to other people.

'I didn't either, but being around my nephew… let's just say, we'd already decided we were happy to let nature take its course.'

'Ew.'

Cassie giggled. 'He *is* really cute. The baby, I mean. I've bought him a little elf outfit for Christmas and can't wait to see him in it.' She'd become an auntie two months ago, and was relishing her new role, which had been something of a revelation. At school, Meg had been the one hankering after marriage and babies, while Cassie couldn't wait to escape and fulfil her get-rich ambitions, yet Meg was the one now focused on work, and 'not ready' to start a family. 'Do you know when it's due?'

'Sometime next June,' said Cassie. 'Promise you won't say anything?'

'Cross my heart.' I had to make do with grabbing her hand and giving it a tight squeeze. Catching a raised eyebrow from the artist, I guessed she thought we were having a lovers' tryst. 'I suppose it's a good way to let everyone know at once.'

'And the perfect Christmas gift for Mum and Dad.' She groaned. 'I've no idea what to get them.'

'At least you've the option of producing a piece of original artwork,' I said. 'I've no clue what to buy mine.'

'I could do one of my cartoon sketches of them if you like.'

'Oh, Cassie, they'd love that,' I said, wondering why I hadn't thought to ask before.

'Excuse me, Miss Maitland.' The artist gave an imperious click of her fingers. 'I haven't got all day.'

'Oops, I'd better go.' Cassie grazed my cheek with her lips. 'Thanks, Tilly-willy.'

'Don't ever call me that again.'

Outside, I zipped up my jacket to ward off the cold as I walked to my car; a beetle-black Kia Picanto, which Dad had bought for my thirtieth birthday, even though I'd been perfectly happy borrowing Mum's car, especially as she rarely drove any more.

In the driver's seat, I sat for a moment, thinking about Cassie's bombshell, and how lit up she'd looked, and something I couldn't name started rising beneath my skin.

'Oh, get a grip,' I ordered myself, and without knowing I'd intended to go there, I started driving to the leisure centre in Kingsbridge, mentally checking I had my bag in the boot. There was only one way to shake off whatever it was I was feeling, and that was by going for a swim.

Chapter Nine

In the pool there was nothing to think about but getting from one end to the other, arms scything through the water, my breathing carefully controlled the way I'd been taught by my swimming coach, Mr Mellor, all those years ago. He'd prided himself on spotting early potential and had been convinced I was an Olympic medallist in the making. The trouble was, I lacked a competitive streak. That particular personality trait had been passed straight from Dad to Bridget, who'd had enough for us both, while I took after Dad's mum, a woman who'd firmly believed in putting off until tomorrow – or even next week – what you could do today.

'Such a waste,' Mr Mellor would say, shaking his grizzled head when I refused to enter some race or other, but I swam purely for pleasure, for the feeling of being truly myself, and I preferred swimming in the sea. In Vancouver, I'd ignored the pool at home during the long dry summers, and swum in the ocean nearly every day.

'Shame you don't apply that sort of dedication to getting a proper job,' Bridget had groused on her first visit. She'd been busily pursuing her career in London by then, and hadn't been remotely tempted to relocate to Canada with us. 'You could be running your own corporation by now.'

After twenty quick lengths, I paused for breath, rubbing water from my stinging eyes. I knew chlorine was necessary in public pools, but hated its effects on my skin. The pool wasn't busy, and I almost shot out of the water when a man's voice said, 'I'd have thought you'd had enough of swimming, after yesterday.'

My watery eyes travelled up a set of hairy shins and muscly thighs, over a pair of black swimming shorts, across a flat stomach, up a toned, tanned chest, and landed on Seth Donovan's grinning face. 'What are you doing here?'

'I could ask you the same thing.'

'Isn't it obvious?' I pushed back my dripping hair, glad my costume was the sensible, black one-piece with the racer-back that I kept in the car – until I remembered he'd already seen me naked. 'I was swimming.'

'So I gathered.' I wondered how long he'd been watching me. 'I didn't realise it was you at first, you were going so fast it was hard to see your face.'

Hoisting myself up, I rested my elbows on the side, goosebumps rippling up my arms. 'I like to push myself.'

'Impressive.' He dropped down, so he was sitting with his legs dangling in the water, hands gripping the sides, his thigh close to my elbow. 'To be honest, I'm not a strong swimmer, and Jack isn't either – as far as I know – so I thought I'd get him some refresher lessons as we're going to be living by the sea.'

'Better late than never,' I quipped, not meaning to sound judgemental.

Seth's mouth pursed. 'I know, I should have thought of it sooner.' His expression clouded. 'I just didn't think—'

'Hey, I was kidding.' I shot a hand out to his knee where it rested for a moment before I snatched it away. 'Is he OK about it? I mean, after yesterday, he might not be too keen on being in the water again.'

'I thought about that,' he said, a touch defensively. 'But I figured it was like getting back in the saddle when you've been thrown off the horse. If you don't do it right away, you could end up with a phobia. Plus, unlike horse riding, being a good swimmer's kind of essential for survival.'

He was giving me that meaningful look again, and keen to divert him from thanking me once more, I said, 'Not worried about being spotted?'

His lips hitched into a smile. 'I reckon I need to get over myself, and stop thinking I'm going to be mobbed.' He glanced around the pool, which was empty apart from a pair of middle-aged women in full make-up with bone-dry hair, doing a sedate breaststroke side by side while chatting. 'I shouldn't think anyone here gives much of a sh— monkeys who I am.'

I returned his smile, and realised with a little shock that I was pleased to see him, even though we'd parted just hours ago. 'Where *is* Jack?' I said.

Seth's face froze, as if he thought he suspected him of leaving Jack at the cottage. 'He told me to wait out here, while he got changed.' He looked over his shoulder towards the shower area. 'Ah, here he is!' He shot to his feet, rubbing his hands, his voice and smile pitched slightly too bright – like a children's entertainer unsure of his audience's mood.

'Hi, Jack!' I threw him a little wave as he approached. He looked vulnerable and undernourished in his drawstring swimming shorts, his skin so white it was almost translucent. 'You OK?'

'Say hi to Tilly,' said Seth, ruffling the boy's hair a bit too vigorously.

'Hi,' Jack said brightly, his gaze shyly ducking away from mine as he stepped to the edge of the pool, shivering slightly. He gazed at the water with a mix of anticipation and terror he was clearly trying to hide.

'It's shallow here, so you'll be fine,' said Seth, still in that unnaturally jolly voice. It struck me that he didn't know how to be around his own child. Jack had been taken care of by someone other than the parent he was now with, and instead of Seth being himself, he was trying to be some fictional version of a 'Dad' – hearty and encouraging – and it wasn't working. No doubt Jack sensed his dad was out of his depth, just as Romy, though younger, sensed Bridget trying too hard to be the perfect mum and played up to it.

Seth and my sister were going to get on like a house on fire, I realised. They already had tons in common.

As if making up his mind, Jack pinched his nostrils together, screwed his eyes shut and jumped, creating an almighty splash that made one of the women shriek and dive for the side, as if she'd spotted a shark.

Noting Seth lowering himself into the water, she nudged her friend, and the two of them began primping their hair and rearranging their cleavages. Meanwhile, Jack surfaced once, blew out water, then sank back down again.

'Jack!' Seth spun round, up to his waist in water, an expression of naked panic on his face. As he inhaled, preparing to dive down, I instinctively touched his shoulder.

'Wait,' I said.

'What?' He blinked at me in confusion.

'He'll come up in his own time.' I spoke with a conviction I couldn't explain. 'He's either trying to prove something, or provoke a reaction,' I said. I remembered a boy of around the same age in a pool on holiday once, doing something similar in an attempt to win the approval of his dad; a strutting macho type in budgie smugglers, who'd talked to anyone who would listen about how he used to dive to sunken ships for a living, until his wife made him give it up.

'Or, he could be lying at the bottom, about to be sucked into the drain, or have held his breath so long he's lost consciousness, or... or...' Seth was pawing the water, as if he could part it and see more clearly, when Jack burst upwards, gasping for air, shaking water from his hair as he treaded water.

'See?' I murmured, but my heart was pounding and I felt a little bit queasy. What if I'd been wrong? I shouldn't be stopping Seth from doing what came naturally.

'See?' Jack echoed, though he couldn't have heard me, lobbing the word in his dad's direction. 'I can hold my breath for ages underwater.' The defiance was unmistakable and somehow moving. 'I counted up to twenty.'

'Well done, Jack, I'm proud of you.' Seth looked pale beneath his tan as he walked towards Jack through the water, the muscles rippling in his back and shoulders. The two women were spellbound, as if watching an unexpectedly good movie – or an exceptionally good-looking, half-naked man they suspected might be famous. 'Do you want me to race you?' he said.

Jack's face brightened momentarily, then, 'Nah,' he said. 'You'll let me win on purpose.'

'No way.' Seth flicked water at him, and I could tell he was trying his best to sound relaxed and cool. Jack shook his head, water dripping off his chin as he slid a look at me and away again.

'I could show you how to do butterfly stroke, if you like,' I offered.

He wrinkled his nose. 'Isn't that for girls?'

'Not really.' I was starting to shiver. I disliked being in water if I wasn't moving – unless it was outside in the sunshine. 'Men swim the butterfly at the Olympics.'

'Maybe.' He flipped over like a duck, legs wavering out of the water as he did a handstand. When he came back up, rubbing his eyes, hair flattened, the women applauded and a smile flickered over his face.

'They're advertising for an instructor, you should apply,' Seth said to me, his eyes fixed on Jack. 'I saw it when we came in. You'd be great at it.'

'Hmm,' I said. 'It's not a proper job though, is it?'

'Who cares?' He gave me a baffled look and, flustered, I dipped my face in the water to cool it down.

'Look, Dad!'

When I raised my head, Jack was pointing at the winding blue flume that dropped into the leisure pool on the other side. 'Can I have a go?'

'We could go down together,' Seth suggested.

'I can go on my own.' Jack levered himself out of the water.

'Be careful!' Seth called as Jack skittered across to the steps and began climbing the metal stairs without looking back.

'What am I supposed to do with him?' Seth spoke with such quiet despair I instantly wanted to rest a hand on his shoulder, his cheek – somewhere – and tell him things would be fine. But, the truth was, I had no idea whether they would be.

'Just keep on being there,' I said, pulling myself onto the side. 'He probably needs to know you won't leave him, like you've done in the past.'

I wondered for a moment whether I'd gone too far, but Seth was watching me retrieve my towel. He probably thought my default look was slightly blue and shivering. 'Are you going?' he said. 'It would be nice to chat a bit longer.' I sensed his unwillingness to be left alone with a son who appeared to reject him. 'How did you learn to swim like that?'

I regarded him steadily. 'Go and be with Jack,' I said. 'Don't take no for an answer.' I sounded like the opposite of Bridget's Danish child-rearing guru, who'd probably advocate leaving Jack alone to explore his boundaries, or something. 'I'll see you tomorrow.'

Once more, I found myself walking away from Seth – even though part of me wanted to stay.

❋ ❋ ❋

'Why didn't you?' said Meg, that evening. I was phoning her from my room, while Bridget attempted to concoct something for dinner. She was a terrible cook, but it was part of her mission as a 'proper mother' to provide healthy nutritious meals for Romy, and if I was around I was expected to eat with them.

'Too messy,' I said. 'You know I don't do complicated.'

'But we're not talking about a relationship with the man—'

'I know, I'm seeing Rufus,' I said, wondering when he was going to call – and whether I should call him. What did people in 'grown-up' relationships do?

'—just be his friend,' Meg continued smoothly. 'It sounds like he needs one, from what you've told me. And you're a good friend, Tilly. Look how you've been there for Cassie and me this past year.'

'Friends are different,' I said. 'I like having friends.'

'Men can be friends, too.'

I thought about that for a moment. I'd had male friends in the past, but they'd ended up wanting more than friendship and that's when things had got tricky. Still, if Seth found Bridget beautiful it meant I wasn't his type, and I'd already told him I was seeing Rufus. His comment about me applying for the role of his girlfriend had been a throwaway one, and any subsequent interest was because I'd saved his son's life – not because he was attracted to me.

'Maybe,' I said, hearing a ripping sound on the landing. I opened my door and saw Romy tearing pages out of a book and scattering them around her. She looked totally absorbed, her tongue poking out, and actually quite happy. 'It'll be a bit weird though, if I'm going to be working for him, and he's seeing my sister.'

'He's agreed to go on a date, that's all.'

'Yes, but once he's met her, he'll want to take things further,' I said. 'I actually think they'll be good for each other.'

'Have you told her yet?'

'No.' I felt an odd little dip in my stomach. 'I'm saving it for when I can't eat her dinner, so she won't smash my plate over my head.'

'She wouldn't do that?' Meg sounded deliciously appalled.

'Like I said, you—'

'—don't know my sister,' we chorused.

Meg laughed, then said, 'Oh, Cassie texted earlier and said there's a new problem with the floor at the café.'

'Not this again.' I made a huffy sound. 'Does everyone in south Devon know there's a problem with the floor?' Meg's laugh sounded slightly forced, and I remembered Cassie's other news. 'Is that all she said?'

'What do you mean?'

'She didn't tell you anything else?'

'Like what?'

'I don't know.' So, Cassie really *was* keeping mum. *Keeping mum.* I almost chuckled at my private joke. 'Yes,' I said. 'The floorboards were wrong, but I've ordered some more.'

'And the room *will* be finished in time for the party on Christmas Eve?'

I frowned. 'Why do you ask?'

'Oh, Tilly, I've had an amazing idea.'

Feeling I might need to sit down, I dropped on my bed, catching sight of myself in the mirror on my dressing table. My hair looked flat and lifeless, and my face was raw from the chlorine-water at the pool. 'Go on.'

'You know my dad has asked my mum to marry him?'

An involuntary smile travelled over my face. Meg had grown up thinking her father was dead, not alive and well and living in Ireland, completely unaware he had a daughter – until Meg appeared on a television show in the summer and he tracked down her mother, Rose. It was a proper love story, and even I'd been enchanted. 'I do,' I said, and allowed myself a smug smile. 'Have they set a date?'

'No, because you know Mum's not good at going out, and the thought of even getting married in a register office brings her out in a panic.'

'Y-e-e-e-s,' I said. 'Get to the point, Meg, or I'll be grey by the time you've finished.'

'Well, Dad and I have managed to persuade her to come to the Christmas Eve party, and see the new function room, and because she feels comfortable at the café, because it's familiar, I thought… wouldn't it be brilliant if they got married there?'

'*What?*'

There was the sound of running feet across the landing, and Romy shouting, 'GHOST!'

'What do you mean, *married?*'

'I mean, a friend of Nathan's brother got ordained so he could officiate at his wedding, and he's said he'd *love* to marry them. Mum and Dad, I mean. And I know Cassie's parents applied for a license—'

'The council has to approve fire and safety provisions, first.'

'Which they will?'

'Well… yes, as long as it's finished in time. Plus, Dad knows everyone in the planning department, so it'll be fine.'

'And it will be finished in time?'

'Of… of course.' How could I say anything else?

'Dad's in on it, obviously,' Meg rushed on, and I heard in the warmth of her tone how much she loved saying Dad. 'He's organised the rings and everything, and invited his family over, so everyone they care about will be there.'

'Wow, that's quite a plan.' I wasn't sure whether to be impressed or worried. Hopefully, Rose wouldn't twig what was happening and run.

'So, it *will* be ready on time?'

I looked at myself in the mirror. 'It *will* be ready on time,' I said, with my most solemn expression. 'I promise.'

Chapter Ten

'How have you managed to break your arm?' I shot up from the kitchen table, sending my fork flying. 'You're supposed to be on standby, and the floor's finally dry.'

'I know, I'm sorry, Tilly, I didn't do it on purpose.' The electrician sounded genuinely wretched. 'I was showing my nephew a judo move and landed awkwardly,' he said. 'I was going to send my brother over, but he's booked solid until the New Year. I'm so sorry.'

'Shit.' Bridget turned from the dishwasher to flash me a warning look, even though Romy was watching children's television in the living room. I'd already had to explain that there wasn't a ghost in my bedroom, I'd been chatting to a friend on the phone. 'OK, well, thanks for letting me know,' I said, modifying my tone. 'You don't have any electrician mates you could recommend, do you?'

'I'll see what I can do, but no promises.'

'I need to know as soon as possible.'

'I'll call you.'

'Thanks.' When he'd rung off I stared at my phone. How could this have happened on the back of my promise to Meg?

'Trouble?' enquired Bridget. She'd finished haphazardly stacking the dishwasher, her face still flushed with pleasure that she'd unexpectedly produced an edible meal – albeit fish fingers with potato waffles and peas.

'The mung bean stir fry burnt,' she'd announced, when I entered the kitchen after talking to Meg, nose twitching at the smell of charred onions. 'I haven't got anything left, so we'll have to make do with processed food tonight.'

'YAY!' Romy had cheered, clapping her hands, and proceeded to clear her plate with the enthusiasm of a diner at a Michelin-starred restaurant, only pausing to burp, then cackle with delight at her mother's look of horror.

'Nothing I can't sort out,' I said, hoping I sounded more confident than I felt.

'You'll have to be more organised if you're serious about your business.' As she rinsed her hands, I noticed she was still wearing the cheap, gold band that Chad had apparently put on her finger as a 'statement of intent' after she fell pregnant with Romy. 'You should always have a back-up plan.'

'I've never needed one,' I bristled. 'I've never not got a job done on time before.' That didn't sound grammatically correct, but she didn't appear to notice.

'Probably more good luck than management.' She often seemed put out that things usually fell into place, as if it had more to do with serendipity than any hard work on my part. 'I suppose it's because you're working for friends. They'll forgive you if you mess up.'

'I won't mess up.' I was stung by the unfairness. 'You've no real idea what goes on in my life, Bee, so stop looking for something to criticise.'

It was the closest I'd come to starting an argument, and a measure of how rattled I was. People I cared about had big plans for the party on Christmas Eve, and the function room was still nowhere near finished with less than a week to go.

'Don't call me Bee.' Bridget slammed the dishwasher shut and switched it on. Her hair looked wilder than ever, standing around her flushed face, and her eyes sparked with annoyance. The detritus of her culinary efforts was scattered across the worktop – bits of burnt beansprout, crumpled wrappers, badly diced carrots she'd forgotten to add to the stir-fry, and a swathe of crumbs from the loaf of bread she'd been comfort eating while 'cooking'. Proof that, in spite of her accusations, she was human too.

'What did you even do, all those years in Vancouver?' She folded her arms and leaned against the worktop. 'Loll about, I suppose, while I was working sixteen hours a day.' She clearly couldn't wait for me to answer.

'It was your choice to stay behind.' I put down the cloth I'd picked up to wipe the table with. 'I wanted to spend time getting to know our grandparents, and help Mum and Dad look after them when they got ill.'

Bridget's shoulders slumped. I knew she'd loved Gran and Grandpa. Mum had told me that Bridget missed them terribly when they decided to move to Vancouver, where Grandpa had been born and raised. 'You got the best bits,' I said. 'I was too young to remember them before they left.'

'I suppose.' The fight flowed out of her. 'I was pissed off at them for ages.'

'They weren't in the best of health by the time we moved there,' I said, though in truth, it was only during the last year or so that things had gone downhill. I smiled, remembering Grandpa, with his hair as white as salt, who'd loved his tools but was rubbish at DIY, and Gran, who'd given the tightest hugs and smelt of lavender hand cream. 'Also, I was at university for a while,' I reminded her, keen to put her straight on the 'lolling about' issue. 'And I travelled a lot.'

'Oh, travelling, how lovely.' She made a sour face, so I decided not to detail the places we'd visited: Niagara Falls, where the air was crisp and cool, and I'd felt the spray on my cheeks as the water plunged with a deafening roar, like a thick, white curtain; the majesty of the Canadian Rockies and the vast, wild beauty of Jasper National Park. She knew anyway, because Mum and Dad had constantly sent her emails and pictures, determined not to lose contact with their eldest daughter, even if she gave every impression of not caring. 'With Mummy and Daddy,' she sniped, reverting to being a teenager.

'Nothing wrong with travelling with your parents, if you get on with them.' The truth was, I enjoyed my parents' company, whether it was idling in dressing gowns with coffee and the Sunday supplements, or whale watching in Vancouver.

'Is that a dig at me?'

'No, *Bridget*, it was just an observation.'

We eyeballed each other for a moment. Time to flip the switch. 'I got you a date,' I said lightly. 'With Seth Donovan.'

'You did?' Immediately her eyes lit up.

I nodded. 'He's going to take you out for a meal. At The Mill in Kingsbridge.' I hoped he'd remember.

'Really?' Her expression had changed from rage to eagerness, and she thudded into the chair opposite. 'Tell me exactly what he said.'

'Er, he said he'd like to take you out to dinner.' Seeing she expected more, I embellished a little. 'He thinks you're beautiful and he can't wait to meet you.'

'Oh. My. God.' Flumping back, she fanned herself with her hand in a very unBridget-like gesture. 'I'm actually going on a date with Seth Donovan?' Her voice rose at the end, turning it into a question. I nodded, pleased with the effect my news was having. 'Is he as hot in real life?'

I pretended to give it some thought – remembered the sight of his naked stomach and muscular thighs at the swimming pool – and nodded again. 'Hotter,' I said, feeling the word somehow did Seth an injustice. 'I mean, he's attractive, yes, but there's more to him than that.'

Bridget's forehead rolled into a frown. 'What do you mean?'

'He's… he seems like a really nice person.' I wasn't adequately conveying the essence of him. 'He's struggling a bit with his son, though.'

Now I felt disloyal, especially when Bridget looked meaningfully in the direction of the living room, and said, 'Well, perhaps I can introduce him to some of Frida's child-rearing methods.'

'Maybe.' Judging by the angry Cockney accents emerging from the television – reminding me of Gwen – Romy wasn't even watching *CBeebies*, she was watching *EastEnders*. Unless Phil Mitchell was voicing *Bedtime Stories*. 'Although Jack's a few years older than Romy.'

'Like a big brother,' said Bridget, clearly getting carried away. 'Frida says it's good to mix with children of different ages, as they can learn from each other.' She grabbed a handful of the half-eaten loaf on the table, then dropped it as though it had burnt her. 'Should I lose weight?'

It was so unlike her to ask for advice, I was momentarily lost for words. 'Of course not,' I said, when the silence had gone on too long. 'You actually look great at the moment.' She gave a disbelieving snort. 'I mean, you might want to tidy your hair, and wear something nice, but you don't need to try too hard.'

'Really?' She looked at the blouse she had on – one of Mum's, with a fussy pie-crust collar. For some reason, Mum was stuck in the eighties style-wise, her wardrobe filled with swishy, long-sleeved dresses, slouchy boots, jumpsuits and frilly blouses. 'None of my things fit me since I came home.'

'I'm afraid I can't help on that front.' My own style was casual, bordering on 'student', consisting mostly of jeans, T-shirts, hoodies and sneakers. On special occasions, I might whip out a checked shirt or a drop-shouldered top, and I once wore a maxi-dress, but made it more casual by wearing a biker jacket. Due to my height, and lack of hips and boobs, I couldn't carry off a girly look, or the sort of power dressing my sister had favoured, pre-motherhood. I didn't own anything designer, and lost my sense of gravity in high heels. 'We'll sort something out, don't worry.'

'Did you give him my number?' Her eyes had a sparkle I hadn't seen for… actually, I couldn't remember seeing them sparkle the way they were right now. 'Do you even know my mobile number?'

I didn't, as we weren't in the habit of calling each other. Anything of note in my life was relayed to her by Mum in their weekly phone call, and she'd report back to me about what Bridget was up to. 'I'm going to the cottage tomorrow so I can give it to him then, or, better still, tell me when you'd like to meet and I'll pass it on.'

'I think I'd like to speak to him myself.' She was already slipping into bossy-mode. 'You might get something wrong, or forget altogether.'

'I'd hardly forget something like that.' I wished she'd have a bit more faith in me. Already, her approval from the day before felt like a distant memory.

'Remember when Todd Fogarty rang the house and asked you to let me know he'd got the mumps and couldn't pick me up to take me to the cinema?'

'I was seven,' I pointed out. 'I only answered the phone because I thought it might be Father Christmas replying to my letter.'

Bridget rolled her eyes. 'I can't believe you still believed in Father Christmas when you were seven.'

'Shush.' I jerked my head at the living room. 'You don't want Romy to hear you say that.'

'I'm not sure I should be encouraging her to believe a strange man creeps into her bedroom every year. What if it gives her a false sense

Karen Clarke

of security and one day, when she's older, she's faced with a burglar or
worse in the middle of the night and thinks it's normal?'

I couldn't help laughing. 'Bridget, that's ridiculous, of *course* she
won't.' Seeing she wasn't convinced, I added, 'You could always leave
her presents downstairs under the tree, to be on the safe side.'

'He'll still have been in the *house*,' she protested, as though she too
believed in Santa.

'Well, what did you tell her last year?'

'We were in the Swiss Alps last year, and sort of glossed over
Christmas. She was too young to understand it all, anyway.'

'Oh, Bee, you're never too young to understand Christmas.' I
leaned forward and placed my chin in the V of my hands. 'Don't you
remember how lovely our Christmases were growing up? The lengths
Mum and Dad went to, to make sure it was special?'

She gave a one-shouldered shrug. 'Maybe for you,' she said.
'Remember, I'd long grown out of Christmas by the time you were
old enough to appreciate it.'

'It was still a lovely time, though.'

I knew there were photos in big fat albums on the bookcase in the
living room and was about to leap up and get them, keen to capitalise
on her good humour about Seth, when she said, 'I know Mum and Dad
really tried, but I suppose what sticks in my mind are the miscarriages
before you came along.'

My mind stilled. I knew there'd been lost babies in the ten years
before I was born, because Mum had explained when I'd asked her once,
why I didn't have brothers (convinced they'd be better than sisters, as
Bridget was so unsuitable). She'd skipped over her explanation, referring
to it as 'trying hard' and rounding off with 'It was all worth it when
you came along, sweet pea.'

'The miscarriages weren't my fault,' I said, surprised to hear a slight wobble in my voice. *Cassie's pregnant.* What must it be like to lose a baby? Not once, but four times? I'd never discussed it with Mum, and she never referred to it either. It wasn't something you brought up over the dinner table – especially as Mum was such a happy person, and had never given any signs of someone suffering. But then again, why would she, once I came along?

'You didn't see her then, but I had to live with it,' said Bridget, as though she'd read my mind. 'Two Christmases our parents were all excited about a new baby, and two Christmases were ruined because it didn't happen. Mum was all mopey, and even though she tried to be excited for me, I'd catch her crying in the kitchen, or her bedroom.'

I looked at Bridget – saw sadness etched in the fine lines round her eyes. 'She tried, though, because that's how much Mum cared about your happiness.' I paused. 'And I saw her crying plenty, after you left home.'

Bridget's fingers, which had been absently plucking at the loaf of bread, froze in mid-air. 'What do you mean?'

'You know how much Mum and Dad missed and worried about you. It's not like she never mentioned it.'

'I was old enough to look after myself.' Bridget's voice held a trace of old defiance. 'I didn't need them.'

'No, but you cut yourself off so completely, were so independent, it left them reeling, Bee. Especially Mum. You were her grown-up girl,' I said. 'That's what she used to call you. My grown-up girl, in the city, meeting god knows who.'

Bridget's eyes went glassy. 'I thought… because she had you…' She stopped and chewed her lip.

'It was never a competition,' I said. 'There was room for us both in her heart, but I was here and you'd gone.' Before she could respond, I leapt up. 'Wait here a minute.'

I left the kitchen and made my way to Dad's office, pausing to glance in the living room. Romy was curled in the armchair, cuddling her teddy, her eyes reflecting the glare from the television. *EastEnders* had finished and she looked engrossed in *DIY SOS*, which I figured was harmless enough.

In the office, I stood for a moment, breathing in the familiar scent of leather, books and a faint hint of Dad's 'Eau Sauvage' aftershave, which I once overheard Mum say 'drove her wild'. His trophies lined a shelf – one for heading up a successful housing redevelopment in the eighties, another for his work on a yachtsman's house making use of natural light – and the duck-egg blue walls (painted by me) were lined with framed certificates, and cards from grateful clients over the years. I felt a pang of missing him; his smile, which pulled me in like a cuddle, his gravelly laugh – never far from the surface – and the way he prefaced his sentences with *As Oscar Wilde once said…* or *To quote a man wiser than me…* Dad was well read, as evidenced by the stuffed shelves, which was probably where I'd got my love of reading growing up.

I picked up a photo from his leather-topped desk, of him and Mum sitting on the flowery sofa in our old house – where Dad's parents had lived before they moved to Canada. Mum's hair was over-bleached, and Dad's shirt had enormous lapels, but their happiness crackled from the glass. They'd fallen in love that summer, according to Mum, when she'd gone to work for his father's building company as a secretary, and had been inseparable ever since.

There was another photo of me as a young child, on a tartan picnic blanket on a stretch of grass, playing with a plastic tea set, a dreamy smile on my face, and another of Bridget dressed for a birthday party as a princess, scowling into the lens.

Turning away, I grabbed what I'd been looking for, and took it back to the kitchen. Bridget was still at the table, tracing circles in the wood with her finger, looking pensive.

'Here.' I laid down a slim plastic case with a handwritten label on the front. 'Dad edited and transferred our home videos onto this DVD a while ago. Have a look at it sometime, there's a player in my bedroom.'

'Why?' She touched the case gingerly, as if it might evaporate.

'Because you'll see that your memories have become distorted, and there *were* some happy times when you were a child.'

'Oh, I haven't got time for trips down memory lane.' She pushed herself up from the table, but her eyes stayed on the disc as though magnetised. 'And neither have you,' she added. 'What time do you have to be at the cottage tomorrow?'

'I didn't arrange a particular time.'

She huffed out a little laugh. 'Still not treating your job like a business.'

I could feel a pulse beating in my throat. 'I'll be there at ten, OK?'

'Good. I'll text you my mobile number.'

Typical that she had mine even though she'd never used it.

As I rose, and headed back up to my bedroom, jumping when Romy shouted 'HOUSE!' I sent up a prayer that Seth was ready to meet a woman with a chip the size of New Zealand on her shoulder.

Chapter Eleven

'Morning!' I held up a bag of flaky croissants I'd bought from the Old Bakery on my way to Seth's. 'Time for some breakfast before we start talking swatches?'

'Morning, Tilly.' Seth glanced over his shoulder, then came outside and pulled the door closed behind him.

'OK, I suppose we could eat out here.' I gave him a puzzled smile, and made as if to open the bag of croissants. 'What's going on?'

'There's, um, been a development.' He shoved his hands in the pockets of a grey sweatshirt and hunched his shoulders. There was a bracing wind skating across the sea and tossing our hair around. Snow was still forecast, but I'd given up believing it would happen.

'What sort of development?' I asked as I hoicked up the hood of the ancient duffel coat that had been sufficient to see me through several cold winters in Vancouver. 'You need the roof replacing, or the bathroom's sprung a leak?'

'Not that sort of development.' He looked over his shoulder again, as if checking the door was shut. 'You know I told you my mother was staying for a few days?'

I nodded, but before he could elaborate the door was flung wide and a haughty voice said, 'For heaven's sake, Ainsley, what are you doing out there?'

Ainsley? Seth interpreted my look of horrified amusement and flinched with embarrassment. 'Seth's my middle name, after my paternal grandfather,' he muttered. 'My mother's the only person who calls me Ainsley.'

'Because that's the name you were christened with.' She was clearly in possession of superhuman hearing. Peering over Seth's shoulder, the first thing that struck me was that she was wearing pearls. Who wore pearls these days, apart from the Queen and Michelle Obama? She was probably Mum's age, with ash-blonde hair swept back from a widow's peak above a faintly lined forehead. Her eyes were vividly blue like Seth's, but arctic, where his were warm, and her long nose gave her a hawk-like air. I was instantly reminded of my old headmistress at Kingsbridge Academy, who'd taken an instant dislike to me – probably because I'd been expelled from the grammar school Mum and Dad had sent me to, for being too 'daydreamy'. That wasn't the word they'd used, but it had amounted to the same thing. I didn't concentrate in lessons, always had my head in a book, homework was never handed in, et cetera, et cetera.

'What on earth are you doing out there, in this weather?' His mother passed a glacial look from me back to Seth. 'For goodness sake, where are your manners? At least invite the woman in, Ainsley.'

I couldn't stop a snigger escaping, and the woman's high-arched eyebrows came together. 'What's your name?' Her voice was clipped with shortened vowels, like an upper-crust snob in a period drama.

'Tilly Campbell.'

Once again, her eyebrows moved. 'Campbell?' she said. 'Isn't that Scottish?'

'It is.' I stepped past Seth into the hallway, where Digby barrelled into my legs and licked my hand before trotting off, casting Seth's mother a baleful look. 'A grandfather thrice-removed on my dad's side. I've never been. To Scotland, I mean.'

'You're very tall,' she said, as if being tall was akin to having leprosy, before shifting her attention back to Seth. 'Are you coming in?'

As he edged past, I caught a whiff of the shower gel I'd used a couple of days ago and flashed back to meeting his startled gaze in the steamy bathroom. 'Tilly, this is my mother, Felicity,' he said, in a neutral way belied by his apologetic smile.

'Nice to meet you,' I said, thinking Felicity would have looked more at home in the marbled foyer of a castle, than standing in a low-ceilinged hallway the colour of a used teabag. Her tailored grey woollen skirt met low-heeled leather boots at the knee, and her fitted mustard twinset was obviously cashmere. A set of dainty earrings matched the string of pearls nestled against her neat bosom, and her rather workmanlike hands bore several plain gold rings. 'What do you think of the cottage?' I asked her, to break the icy death grip of her stare.

She lifted her chin as though preparing to sack a servant. 'Not a lot.' She clearly wasn't the type to bother mincing words. 'Not when my grandson could be living in comfort with me and his grandfather.'

'Well, I think it's lovely.' I sensed she had a lot more to say on the matter, and decided to cut her off. 'I grew up not far from here, and it's perfect for children. Lots to do, plenty of open spaces and fresh air.'

'Fresh air?' She made it sound like heroin. 'There's plenty of fresh air in Surrey.'

'No beaches though.' Hearing Seth's indrawn breath, I wondered whether she'd found out about Jack's episode in the sea and I'd said completely the wrong thing.

'No, but there's a very good boarding school for boys there.' She flashed Seth a pointed look, but he was saved from replying by a shout from behind one of the doors off the hallway.

'Do you want carpet in here as well?'

Felicity gave a terrifyingly chilly smile. 'I've already told him we don't.' Shaking her head, she moved away with a surprisingly bouncy stride.

'What's happening?' I said, when she'd disappeared inside the room, noticing there were skirting boards lined up against the staircase, as well as several tins of paint in a neutral shade.

Seth curled his hand into a fist and lightly punched the wall. 'Come into the kitchen,' he said quietly, not quite meeting my gaze. 'It'll be easier to talk in there.'

As I followed him, I peered into the living room and saw some carpet swatches on the floor, and several rolls of wallpaper in a shade best described as smog.

In the kitchen, Seth was filling the copper kettle at the sink. Jack was at the table, playing on his iPad, an empty bowl by his elbow, while Digby chewed on a rubber bone by the back door. There was a radio on the worktop, quietly playing 'Once in Royal David's City', lending a cathedral-like air.

'Hi,' I said, realising they'd already eaten breakfast. I shouldn't have spent so long chatting to Big Steve at the bakery, but he'd had a good story about last year's Christmas party when he'd worked at Tesco's, and his supervisor turned up with one of her boobs decorated as a reindeer, and asked him to stroke it not realising he was gay. By the time I'd phoned to check the progress of the floorboard redelivery, and swung by the café to reassure Gwen that progress was being made, it was already ten thirty.

Jack gave a brief nod I assumed was intended for me. He didn't seem surprised that I was there, as if I'd become part of the furniture, or was someone he'd known a while.

'What are you playing?'

'Minecraft,' he said, not lifting his head.

'Oh, I've heard of that.' I realised how lame it sounded. A lot of people had probably *heard* of it. 'Never played it though.' Another dumb comment. 'What level are you on?'

'Five,' he said. 'Looking for bedrock.'

I glanced at Seth, who spread his hands as if to say *don't ask me.* 'Right.' I undid the toggles on my duffel coat. 'Good luck with that.'

Jack looked up, as if checking whether I was being sarcastic. 'It's nothing to do with luck.' He gave a little smile that revealed a cute dimple I hadn't noticed before. 'You've got to have skills.'

'I'm sure you do. I mean, I'm sure you have. Got to have skills. And that you've got them.' Seth's face twitched with amusement. 'I've no idea what I'm talking about,' I said, as if it wasn't obvious.

'I know.'

The corner of Jack's mouth lifted further at his Dad's reply. His eyes were back on his screen and his hair was falling in his eyes. He still had his dressing gown on – a wine-coloured affair that looked too grown up for him – and I wondered what he did all day, when other kids his age were at school.

'He's starting school in the New Year, aren't you, Jack?' It was as if Seth had heard my unasked question. 'We thought he needed a bit of time off to... well, to adjust to things being different.'

'He means not living with Grandma and Granddad any more.' Jack's deadpan voice made it hard to assess his mood, and I couldn't work out whether he minded or not.

'Sounds sensible.' I cringed inside when he didn't respond, and pulled out a chair to sit next to him. He didn't stop playing his game, but didn't move away either. I put down my croissants and slipped my coat off. 'So, what's with the paint and wallpaper samples?' I looked at Seth, who'd been watching Jack with a look of tender fear.

'That's the development, I'm afraid.' He held up a jar with *tea* on the side and gave me a quizzical look.

'Milk, no sugar.'

He switched on the kettle to boil again. 'My mother has taken it upon herself to get this place redecorated as a Christmas present for me and Jack.'

It took a second to sink in, even though it had been pretty obvious what was going on. 'Oh.' I deflated like a bouncy castle. 'So, you don't need an interior designer?' *Top marks for observation, Tilly.*

'I'm really sorry,' he said, pouring milk from a carton into two mugs. 'She's still set on, you know,' he gently inclined his head at Jack, and I guessed he meant gaining custody of her grandson and sending him away to boarding school, 'but thinks in the meantime that we should at least make this place respectable.' He gave the word respectable quote marks with his voice, shaking his head. 'My mother's all about what's respectable,' he said, and in those few words I could read their whole relationship. The word *rebelling* featured heavily. It was probably why he'd become a racing driver instead of, say, a barrister. I'd spoken to Felicity for less than a minute, and knew she wouldn't have approved of her son's career choice. 'I'd have loved you to do it after Christmas, but once my mother's set her mind on something there's no stopping her, I'm afraid.'

I wanted to say that he could have said no but understood that, under the circumstances, the last thing he wanted to do was ruffle her feathers. 'Well, it's kind of her to want to help out,' I said, for Jack's benefit. It would hardly be fair to criticise his grandmother in front of him – or at all, I reminded myself. I may have been thrust into the epicentre of his life, but that didn't give me the right to comment on it. 'I'm sure she'll do a good job.'

'She's got a company up from Surrey, she calls them her *team*.' Seth removed the teabags from the mugs and dropped them on the worktop. 'They did the house there.'

'The house where you grew up?'

He nodded as he handed me a mug with 'I'm a Mug' stamped on it. 'It's nice, but I prefer being by the sea.'

'Grandma thinks the cottage is too small.' Jack, who'd given no indication he was listening, was clearly absorbing every word. 'She wanted to send a gardener and a maid to help us, like at her house.'

Blimey.

'We don't need staff, and the cottage is big enough for us, and for Grandma and Granddad, if they want to come and stay.' Seth sat opposite, and plucked a croissant from the paper bag, and I knew he was thinking, like me, that he couldn't imagine his mother and father staying at the cottage – and I'd never even met his father.

'But where would they sleep?' Jack's fingers had momentarily stilled, as if he too was trying to picture it.

'I'm sure we could throw a mattress on the floor,' said Seth, and looked gratified when Jack chuckled.

'You could always send them to us,' I offered. 'We've plenty of room at our house.'

Jack looked at me. 'Are you the lady that left a message on our phone calling Dad a shit?'

'What?' I looked at Seth who'd closed his eyes and was biting his bottom lip. 'No! Of course I didn't, I wouldn't, I mean… it wasn't me,' I finished, somehow giving the impression I was lying. 'I only met your dad two days ago.'

'Do you like him?' He sounded oddly hopeful as he studied me through his tangle of dark blond hair.

'Of *course* I like him.' I gave a funny little laugh. 'He's definitely not a shit.'

'I told you, Jack, it was a lady I used to know in Italy who left the message,' said Seth. 'She got a bit cross because I didn't want to be her boyfriend any more.'

'Because of me.'

'Not because of you, Jack.' He reached across the table, but Jack shunted backwards. 'Because of me.'

Sensing Seth was wading out of his depth, I opened my mouth to say something, but before the words could emerge (and I had no idea what they would have been) Felicity swept into the kitchen, lowering the temperature by at least twenty degrees.

She looked at each of us in turn, sitting at the kitchen table in a parody of a happy family, before training her frosty gaze on me. 'So,' she said. 'I suppose you must be the nanny Seth told me he was taking on?'

Chapter Twelve

The silence that followed Felicity's question seemed to last a lifetime, and she broke it herself by saying, 'You don't look like a nanny.'

About to say *that's because I'm not* – the idea was laughable – I heard myself say instead, 'What's a nanny supposed to look like?' I met her gaze full on. 'Should I be carrying a magic bag and umbrella, like Mary Poppins, and be wearing a daisy-trimmed hat?'

'Of course not.' She gave a sniff of disdain. 'But in my day, people made more of an effort to look smart at work.' Her comment made me think of Mum, telling me her grandma had believed that women shouldn't go out without a corset and lipstick, and if they didn't 'they were no better than they ought to be'. Whatever that meant.

'Smart's not really my style,' I said. 'But that doesn't mean I'm not capable.'

'I disagree.' Felicity smoothed her sweater over her remarkably flat stomach. 'How a person dresses reflects their personality.'

Judging by her laser appraisal, I was barely a step up from being a homeless alcoholic. 'I can promise you, I'm good at what I do,' I said, thinking – in spite of myself – that she might have a point. My outfit reflected that I didn't much care about my appearance, which some might say was indicative of my attitude towards life. For some reason, this realisation rankled. 'I suppose you judge a book by its cover, too.'

'Always,' she fired back. 'How else are you supposed to know what it's about?' *Goal to Mrs frosty-knickers.* 'Do you have qualifications and references?'

'Mum,' Seth began, but I felt like challenging her. It was almost as if I *wanted* to be Jack's nanny. Or, maybe I just didn't like her making assumptions based on her own prejudices.

'Don't you trust your son's judgement?'

Her eyes shrivelled. 'I beg your pardon?'

'Surely it's up to Seth – and Jack – to decide who looks after him.'

It was a loaded statement and Felicity was silent for a moment, as if perhaps weighing up how much I knew about their personal circumstances.

'I only have my grandson's best interests at heart.'

'So does his dad,' I said. *Goal to me.*

'If that was true, he'd see that a cottage on the edge of a cliff, with a boy who's missing a female influence and needs firm and consistent guidance, isn't the right environment.'

Nor is a boarding school, I wanted to say, but knew I'd be overstepping the line even further than I already had. 'Maybe Jack has something to say about that.'

'Jack doesn't know what's best for him, he's too young.'

'That's what we're working out,' Seth interrupted, his voice thick with tension. 'It's why I've asked you to back off for a while, Mum, and give us a chance to prove we're OK here.'

'And what about *your* life?' She turned to Seth, colour riding up her cheeks. 'You gave up everything you knew—'

'I thought you'd be glad about that.'

'—and while it's *admirable*,' she steamrollered on, 'I can't help wondering how long it'll last.'

'Mum.' Seth's voice was a warning, eyes flashing in his son's direction. Jack was still looking at his screen, but his shoulders were hunched around his ears, and the sight provoked what I could only interpret as motherly concern. I guessed it wasn't the first time he'd heard this argument. 'You said you'd leave it if I let you do up the cottage, and I've already told you I'm thinking of getting a nanny so Jack has a female influence, and that I'm ready to settle down.'

'Yes, but...' She looked at me, as if double-checking I wasn't a horrible figment of her imagination. 'I just think—'

'I know what you think, Mum.' Seth's jaw was set, and I suddenly noticed the panda-rings under his eyes, and a rip in the shoulder of his sweatshirt as if he'd pulled it on too quickly that morning – perhaps in a rush to check Jack was OK and to appease his mother; show her he was a good father.

'Would you like a croissant?' I said, to diffuse the strained atmosphere, rattling the paper bag. Digby dropped his bone and trotted over with hope in his chocolate-brown eyes.

'I never eat pastry, it's full of trans fats,' said Felicity. 'And Jack's already had his porridge.'

2-1 to Felicity. 'They're from the bakery in the village.' I broke a piece off and threw it to the dog. 'They use organic ingredients.'

'I take it you're local, Miss Campbell?'

'Tilly, please.' I wish she'd at least sit down. She couldn't have been more than five foot four, but somehow gave the impression of towering over us. Her upright posture suggested a strict exercise regime, though I couldn't for the life of me imagine what sort. 'I'm Devon born and bred,' I said, playing up my accent. Feeling more was required, I added, 'I lived in Canada for a decade, but came back last year with my family.'

'Canada?' Her eyebrows elevated, as if she couldn't believe that anyone born in Devon would have the nerve to set foot outside the country. 'Whereabouts in Canada?'

'Vancouver.'

'I was in Canada a few years ago, for the Grand Prix,' Seth said warmly. 'Funny to think we were in the same country without either of us knowing.'

A fizz of curiosity sparked between us. I wanted to ask him more, and sensed he felt the same, but Felicity was still probing.

'And your parents?' she said, as if trying to establish the credentials of an Edwardian governess.

'Mum, for crying out loud.' Seth scraped his chair back, grabbed Jack's bowl and took it across to the sink. 'Tilly's not even—'

I cut in before he could finish. 'My dad's an award-winning architect, my mum sells pottery online, and my sister's a finance manager for British Airways,' I said. No need to mention my father had retired, my mum's pottery was a hobby, and my sister was a single parent hoping to date Felicity's son. 'We're what my friends' parents used to call "well-to-do" so no need to worry that I'm planning to run off with the family jewels.' I had no idea where that had come from. Or why I was trying to convince her I had some sort of pedigree, and was fit to look after her grandson – only that something about Jack was getting to me, and I wanted to know he was going to be OK.

Something flickered behind Felicity's eyes. 'And yet you became a *nanny*,' she said, making it clear she considered the job on a par with rubbish removal.

'Mum, please stop.' Seth switched off the tap, annoyance radiating from him, and Jack slid us both a look, as if he was gripped in spite of himself and wanted to know what was coming.

'I happen to love children,' I said, while an inner voice screeched *what the hell are you saying?* 'Isn't that the most important criteria for being a nanny?'

Felicity studied me, her tastefully lipsticked mouth reduced to a thin line. She looked as if she was trying to muster an argument that didn't disagree with the sentiment, but made it clear I was very far from suitable – which, of course, I was. 'We'll see,' she managed, then added to Seth, 'I'll be upstairs, if you need me. I promised to call your father, and then I'll be taking Jack shopping for new shoes.'

'I don't need new shoes,' Jack muttered, when she'd whipped out of the kitchen, leaving a trace of perfume in her wake; something heavy that made me want to cough. 'She'll get those shiny ones I don't like.'

'Keep saying they're too tight,' I offered. 'She can't buy you shoes if they don't fit you.'

Jack flicked me a look and his mouth curled up. 'Cool,' he said, and I felt a soaring sense of victory that was out of all proportion.

'Jack, you'd better get dressed,' said Seth. 'You know your grandma doesn't like to be kept waiting.'

Jack tutted, but got up from the table with his iPad tucked under his arm and left the kitchen, one hand in the pocket of his dressing gown like a mini Sherlock Holmes.

'Great advice from the new nanny, by the way,' Seth said dryly, when Jack was out of earshot. 'You do realise my mother now believes that's what you are?'

'Were you really looking for one?'

'I told her I was.' He folded his arms and leaned against the sink, visibly more relaxed now his mother had left. 'It's a condition of her holding back on custody proceedings, though I know she's just waiting for me to fail.'

'I bet she wants to vet the applicants as well.'

'Apparently, she just has.'

I picked at the croissant Seth had left on the table and Digby, lying by my feet with his head on his paws, gave a low whine. 'I'm sorry if I gave your mother the wrong impression, I don't know what came over me.'

Seth shook his head. 'I'm the one who's sorry,' he said. 'I should have made it clear straight away that you weren't here for the job.'

'Why didn't you?'

He passed a hand over the bristle on his chin. 'I don't know,' he said. 'It seemed like you were saying all the right things and I got caught up in it.' His rueful smile had a surprising effect on my pulse rate. 'I almost believed you *were* the new nanny.'

'At least you don't have to look for someone now. Not if she thinks you've found her.'

'I do think Jack would benefit from having a female around. One who's not my mother.'

'So you said.' I recalled our conversation in the car, about him being ready to meet someone. 'I suppose it depends on the female,' I said.

His face took on a pensive expression. 'I want to let nature take its course in the relationship department, but my mother breathing down my neck makes everything more urgent.'

'But it would get your mother off your back to think you'd got a nanny?'

He nodded.

'Then I'm happy to pretend I'm Mary Poppins for a bit.'

He released a little laugh. 'In other words, you're doing me another favour.'

'I won't have to do much, once your mother's gone home.'

'She might ask Jack about you. She phones him every evening.'

'I don't mind hanging out with him if it'll put her mind at rest.'
What was wrong with me? 'If he doesn't mind, of course.'

'I think he likes you,' he said. 'And not only because you saved
his life.'

'Maybe he's just glad I'm not the woman who called you a shit.'

He winced. 'That was Gina,' he said. 'I didn't know she'd left that
message on the landline, and didn't mean him to hear it. I'd put it on
speaker, thinking it was my mother.'

'Gina?'

'My ex-girlfriend.' A nerve jumped beneath his eye. 'Like I said,
she's Italian, and a bit… shall we say, temperamental.'

'Is that how you like your women?' If so, Bridget wouldn't be his
type. Cool and controlled was her default setting – except when she
was around me.

Seth vehemently shook his head. 'Maybe once, but not any more.
Jack's mum was the same—' He stopped abruptly, clearly not wishing
to bad-mouth her. 'I mean, she was a great mother, most of the time,
but I hated that she used Jack against me.'

I tried to imagine having that mindset. I'd taken for granted my
parents' loving support over the years, and the thought of them splitting
up and fighting over access was impossible to envisage. 'It can't be fair
on the child, especially when they have no say.'

Seth looked at his feet, which were encased in the sort of thick
woollen socks he'd lent me two days ago, which I'd worn in bed as they
were so warm and cosy. 'I suppose it's fair if there's just cause,' he said.
'I was a Formula One driver, which – apart from it being perceived as
dangerous – meant I was hardly ever around, probably partying and
drinking a bit too much. Maybe she thought she had reason to keep

him from me, but I think it was more of a power thing. A way to get back at me and hurt me for…'

'For?'

'For cheating on her,' he said.

Messy. The word floated into my head, followed by *complicated.* Twin traits I did my best to avoid. But this wasn't a relationship, as Meg had pointed out. *You can be his friend. It sounds like he needs one.*

'Talking of women,' I said, even though we hadn't been – at least, not in a good way. 'I've got my sister's number, if you'd like to give her a call and arrange that date.'

His face went blank for a moment, as if struggling to recall what I meant. 'Oh yes. Dinner,' he said, in much the same tone he might have used if I'd mentioned a dental appointment. 'That's on, then?'

'Honestly, you'll like her.' I fished my mobile out of my coat pocket and, after bringing up my contacts list, I passed it to him. 'Put your number in there and I'll text you Bridget's.' I knew once they'd met, Seth would be smitten.

'What should I say to Jack?' He gazed at my phone, as if he'd never handled one before. 'Shall I be honest and tell him that I'm going out with a lady?'

I thought how much Bridget would enjoy being called a lady.

'Well, you said he'd like a new mum, and although you're not going to be marketing anyone like that right away, I suppose it's good that he sees you going out,' I said. 'It wouldn't be healthy if you didn't go out now and then.'

He turned my phone over in his hands. 'It's ages since I've been on an actual date,' he said. 'I've been focused on trying to keep things stable for Jack for the past few months.'

'All the more reason to do it.' A thought occurred. 'What do you do all day, now you're not racing cars?'

'Well, I'm learning to be a better cook.' He nodded to a pile of cookbooks by the Aga. 'And I like gardening, as much as you can at this time of year, and I'm supposed to be writing my autobiography.'

I sat up straighter. 'Sounds intriguing.'

He pulled a face. 'I hate the thought of writing about myself.'

'So, don't do it.'

'I've been given a substantial advance, so I kind of have to.' At last, his fingers were moving across the screen of my phone, presumably entering his number.

'Maybe write something else?'

'Funny you should say that,' he said. 'I—'

My phone starting ringing and he almost dropped it, before handing it back to me.

'I'd better take this,' I said, seeing the café's number. 'Hi, Gwen, I'll be on my way shortly, I'm just—'

'You'd better come right now, mate,' she said. 'You'll want to see this.'

Chapter Thirteen

'Who would do something like this?'

'Someone who don't like us?' Gwen's face was blotchy with annoyance. 'I didn't see it sooner, 'cos I know you don't like no one comin' in 'ere, what wiv the floor bein' damp and anyway, what is there to see?'

'So, what made you look?'

Gwen hefted up her shoulders. 'I've got a sixth sense,' she said. 'I take after me nan, she 'ad the gift. Swore she saw me granddad not long after 'e'd gone, standin' outside the window, and there 'e was, large as life in the garden.'

'His ghost?'

'Oh, 'e weren't dead, 'e'd cleared orf with the milkman's wife, but forgot to take 'is pyjamas – silk they were, don't arsk me why, 'e weren't a bleedin' toff – so 'e came back in the dead of night, but daren't go in the arse 'cos me nan would 'ave 'ad 'is balls.'

I dragged my gaze back to the windows. 'And you didn't see who did it?'

'I reckon it must 'ave 'appened last night. Probably someone 'oo'd been drinkin' and fort it'd be a larf.'

My heart gave an unpleasant bump. On the way over, leaving Seth with a promise that I'd be in touch, I'd thought perhaps Jerry hadn't turned up for work, or Meg had baked a more-spectacular-than-usual cake of the day. What I hadn't expected was to find several of the windowpanes smeared with purple paint.

'You got any enemies?'

I looked at Gwen. 'Me?'

'Well, it 'ain't me, mate,' she said. 'Everyone loves me.' I couldn't argue with that. 'An' I doubt anyone's got a grudge against the Maitlands, 'cos everyone loves them too.' I couldn't dispute that either.

'It's unlikely to be drunken holidaymakers at this time of year,' I said. 'And it's not as if the café's in competition with any other businesses around here.'

'I dunno,' said Gwen. 'The landlord at the Smugglers Inn's a bit peed off that we've got a license to serve alcohol on Christmas Eve.'

'But Bill's coming to the party,' I pointed out. 'And I really can't see him doing something so… so *shitty*.'

'Nah, me neither,' Gwen conceded, scratching her chin. 'S'gotta be personal then.'

'Personal?' I jabbed a finger at my chest. 'To me, you mean?' Gwen widened her eyes a fraction, and my attempt at a laugh fell flat. 'Nobody dislikes me *that* much.'

'Even that bloke you was talkin' to the other day?'

Rufus. 'Of course he doesn't dislike me, just the opposite,' I said. 'And, apart from anything, he's a teacher, Gwen. He wouldn't do something like this.'

'I fort you was breakin' up wiv 'im.' Her voice was loaded with suspicion. 'I swear 'e was almost in tears when you was gettin' 'im some cake.'

'Of *course* I wasn't breaking up with him, I was trying to make a decision about… something,' I said. 'And how could you tell he was crying from behind the counter?'

''Cos I've got eyes in me 'ead.'

About to challenge this, something occurred to me. 'Actually, I think I recognise the paint,' I said. 'It's Perfect Pansy.' My stomach plunged. 'I helped Rufus choose it when he was redecorating his dining room and he bought too much.'

'So 'e thought 'e'd use it up by slingin' it over our windows, did 'e, the bleedin' 'alfwit? You'd better 'ave a word wiv 'im, Tilly.'

'I'm not saying it *was* him.' *But it was a hell of a coincidence.* 'Probably lots of people have used that shade of paint.'

'Not if they've got good taste.' Gwen adjusted her waistband, where she'd adapted a leather tool belt and stocked it with cloths, a spray gun, notepads and a pen. 'Tell 'im we could get the police involved. Either that, or I'll pay 'im a visit meself.'

'But I don't understand why he'd do something like this.' Could Rufus have misinterpreted our conversation on the beach? I didn't see how he could have, but he hadn't been in touch yet, despite saying he'd call. Maybe I'd misunderstood, and he'd been waiting for me to call him, and when I hadn't... but no, it was unthinkable he'd be so angry he'd come to the café in the dead of night and chuck paint over the windows. Why not come to my house, if he wanted to make a protest? Why not just talk to me? 'Has anyone else noticed?' I shivered into my coat. It was probably psychological, but it felt as if the wind was pushing against the windows, trying to get in.

'Just me and Jerry.' Gwen's eyes burrowed into me. 'You'd better get out there and 'ope it washes orf,' she said.

Part of me wanted to argue that I shouldn't be the one cleaning up, but if Rufus *had* gone rogue with a tin of paint, I couldn't deny I'd had some part to play – however unintentional and bizarre.

Supplied with a bucket of soapy water, a sponge, and a pair of rubber gloves, I trudged outside and, before I set to work, I snapped a couple of pictures of the mess with my phone, eyes watering in the wind. It was upsetting to see the manifestation of someone's frustration – assuming that's what this was, and not a would-be Banksy expressing their creativity – and I couldn't get my head around Rufus doing something like this.

I'd just about got the glass clean again, after emptying and refilling the bucket three more times – at least it was emulsion which was easier to clean and it hadn't stained the wooden frames – when I saw someone rounding the building, his golden-brown hair lifting off his forehead.

'Danny Fleetwood!' I lifted a dripping, rubber-gloved hand in greeting, pushing Rufus to the back of my mind – for now. 'Howdy.'

'Nice look, Tilly.' His eyes twinkled at me in their customary friendly fashion. 'What are you doing?'

'Isn't it obvious?' I squeezed out the sponge, which had turned the water in the bucket a lurid aubergine.

'It should be obvious, but I've never seen anyone clean windows with purple paint before. I normally use plain water.'

'Ha ha,' I obliged. 'It's…' I hesitated, and dropped the sponge in the bucket. 'I don't really know what it is, to be honest.'

He regarded me for a moment, but didn't push it. 'If there's anything I can do, let me know.'

'Thanks,' I said.

'Is Cassie around?'

'Not as far as I know.' I tugged off my rubber gloves. 'She's with the mayoress again today, trying to finish her portrait. Didn't she tell you?'

'She did.' He gave a dramatic shudder as an icy blast of air blew his woolly scarf across his eyes. 'I just wanted to double-check she wasn't going to suddenly turn up here.'

'Did you ask Gwen?'

He fought his scarf down. 'Actually, it was you I wanted to see. Gwen said you were out here.'

'Oh?' I smiled at him, because it was hard not to smile in Danny's company, even when the weather was arctic and I was standing by a bucket of purple water. When I came back from Canada, Danny had been one of the first people I'd bumped into, after Meg. We'd attended the same high school, and I'd had a tiny crush on him – until it became obvious that he'd had feelings for Cassie. Plus, our outlook on life and work was far too similar, neither of us driven by money and, as Bridget had once opined, I needed a man who would shake me up a bit. Or 'not put up with your crap' as she'd put it, though I hadn't understood what she'd meant at the time, considering myself not so much low-maintenance as *no*-maintenance in the girlfriend department, which was surely what men preferred. And she'd no room to talk, with her terrible taste in men. 'So, what can I do for you?'

Danny threw a look over his shoulder, as if scoping the area for undercover cops, and before he even spoke, I guessed what his next sentence was going to be. 'I wanted to ask whether the function room's going to be ready by Christmas Eve.' I *knew* it. 'Cassie mentioned you were having problems with the flooring, and that the electric still needs sorting out for the lighting.'

'Why are you asking?' I kept my tone neutral in case he didn't know that I knew about the baby, and that Cassie had already approached me about their big announcement.

'Promise you won't say anything?'

'Of course.' I prepared to arrange my expression into surprised delight, wondering why Cassie hadn't mentioned to him that I knew about the baby.

Danny looked at the sky and inflated his cheeks, and when he brought his sparkling gaze back to mine, I almost wished I was about to hear the news for the first time.

'I'm going to ask Cassie to marry me,' he said, with ill-concealed excitement.

'What the *fudge*?'

'I know!' He was clearly enjoying my look of (genuine) surprise. 'I mean, we haven't been together very long, but it just feels right and what with…' he paused and looked briefly at the toes of his boots, then murmured '… the baby.'

His voice so was jam-packed with emotion that tears caught at the back of my throat.

'It's amazing, Danny.' I touched his sleeve with my freezing fingers. 'I'm so happy for you both.'

'You haven't…?' He flicked a look at the café.

'I haven't told anyone, no, of course not. I promised Cassie I wouldn't.'

'And you won't mention this to anyone?'

'No!' I almost shouted, suddenly as close to hysteria as I'd ever come. First Gwen, plotting to claim Jerry like a raffle prize, then Cassie announcing her pregnancy, and Meg organising a wedding for her parents… and now this. It was going to be one hell of a party.

'Are you OK?' Danny suddenly looked alarmed, as if my face had changed shape.

'Are you sure Cassie won't mind you proposing in front of everyone?'

'I won't do that, although I'm fairly confident she'll say yes,' said Danny. 'I just think the setting will be perfect, with our loved ones here, but I'll ask her outside, or away from everyone, just in case she wants to turn me down.'

'She won't.' I spoke with absolute confidence. It was obvious that Cassie had found someone who would always put her at the centre of his life, and she knew it. 'It'll be perfect, Danny. I'm not even going to pretend to gag, like I normally would at such a display of *feelings*.'

'Pleased to hear it.'

We laughed a bit, half-embarrassed, half giddy at how *huge* this was. Cassie was going to be the first of us to get married and have a baby.

'It's enough to bring a tear to a glass eye,' I said, quoting my dad for some reason. 'Her parents might not survive the shock. They've only just got over the excitement of having one grandchild, and now there's another on the way, plus a wedding.'

'I nearly went the whole hog and asked Cassie's dad for her hand in marriage before they went away, but I thought she might not like that.'

'She wouldn't,' I agreed. 'She's not into the idea of being *given* to a man, or any of those patriarchal traditions.'

'Outrageous!' Danny adopted the tone of a 1950s husband. 'I expect her to agree to obey me, and be fully made up with a ribbon in her hair when I get home from work once we're wed.' He puffed on an imaginary pipe. 'Woe betide her if she hasn't run a duster around the house, or lit the fire so I can unwind with my crossword and a glass of whisky.'

I laughed and, picking up the sponge, flicked water at him, clapping my hand to my mouth when I saw that his windcheater was covered in purple flecks. 'Oh god, I'm sorry, Danny.'

'I quite like it.' He brushed at the splodges with his hands. 'Very Jackson Pollock.'

'It's emulsion, so it'll come out.'

'That was very thoughtful of your vandal.'

'Exactly,' I said. 'That's what I thought.'

'So, the room will be ready?'

'It's all in hand,' I said, aware I still hadn't heard back from my broken-armed electrician.

'Tilly, wot the bleedin' 'ell are you doin'?'

I wheeled round to see Gwen, bundled into a black quilted coat that made her look twice as wide, walking round from the terrace. 'I was just talking to Danny,' I said. 'I've finished cleaning the windows.'

She was looking at me as though I'd blown my nose into my hands. 'You 'avin a larf?' she said. 'There ain't no one there.'

I turned. Danny had disappeared, and I wondered for a moment whether I'd been daydreaming – until I saw him peering round the side of the building. He mimed a scream before vanishing for real. 'He was here,' I said. 'We were just—'

'I know 'e was, mate,' Gwen said. 'I was windin' you up.'

'Well, that's kind of you, thanks.' Maybe it was Danny's news, combined with the shock of the paint on the windows that might have something to do with Rufus, but I felt tears pricking the backs of my eyes again.

'Go and get yourself an 'ot chocolate before you do anyfink else,' said Gwen, pulling a stick of chewing gum from her pocket. 'I reckon you've earned it.'

Her tone was gruff, which meant she was being kind, so I nodded, not trusting myself to speak until I'd picked up the bucket. 'Are you coming in?'

She shook her head. ''Avin' me break out 'ere, to give Jerry a chance to miss me,' she said, flicking a chunk of chewing gum into her mouth. ''E needs to know what a catch I am.' She winked. It didn't suit her and, in spite of myself, I mustered a smile. Poor Jerry hadn't a clue what he was letting himself in for.

'Oh, and Tilly,' she called as I walked away.

I turned, trying to hold the bucket so that the water didn't slosh over my feet. 'Yes?'

'Call that bloke of yours sooner rather than later,' she said. 'You need to know what 'is game is.'

Chapter Fourteen

'I'm at home, if you want to come round now.' I'd forgotten the college had closed for the Christmas holidays, and hadn't expected Rufus to answer his phone. I'd planned to leave a message telling him to expect a visit from me later on, and felt myself floundering for something to say. 'I'm waiting,' he said. Confusingly, he was using what I'd come to recognise as his 'sex' voice.

'I've seen the paint, Rufus. Gwen wanted to call the police.'

'Oh, Christ, Tilda—'

'It's *Tilly*.'

'Tilly, please don't call the police—'

'So it *was* you.' My stomach sank. Up until then, I hadn't really believed it.

'Well, obviously.' That threw me. 'Unless you've been seeing someone I don't know about.'

'Of course I haven't.'

'Look, after our little chat, I wanted you know how strongly I feel about you,' he said. *What*? 'It probably wasn't the best way to go about it, but I knew you'd see it when you got there this morning, and that you might…' His words faded. 'I thought you might be calling to tell me you felt the same way.'

'The same way as what?'

'As I do about you.'

I struggled to make sense of his words. 'You smeared leftover paint from your dining room on the windows at the café, to tell me how you feel?' In that case, he must hate me.

'Of course I didn't *smear* it.' He sounded hurt. 'I know it sounds a bit soppy, and it's not really you, but I still think we have a strong connection even if you won't admit it.'

'And that's why you chucked paint at the windows?'

'What? Why would I do that?' His tone sharpened. 'That would be vandalism.'

'Graffiti *is* an act of vandalism,' I said.

'Not when it's a declaration of love.'

'What are you talking about?'

'I painted *I love you Matilda Campbell* about twenty times, and loads of love hearts.'

Sounds of the café rushed in as I stared into my almost empty cup, letting his words settle. I'd taken Gwen's advice to have a hot chocolate, before calling him. 'I'm going to send you a photo.'

I texted Rufus the picture I'd taken, and when I brought my phone back to my ear I heard him groaning like a man who'd been given twenty-four hours to live. 'It wasn't raining when I went up there, but it must have started again in the early hours,' he said. 'Tilly, I'm so sorry, that wasn't at all what you were meant to see.'

'So, you didn't mean to make that awful mess?'

'Of *course* I didn't. What do you take me for?'

'I didn't think you would, but when I recognised the paint—'

'You recognised my paint?' He sounded as pleased as if I'd announced I wanted to have his babies, and when he added, 'Look, come round and let's talk properly. I bought some of that tomato and herb sourdough you like from the bakery over there,' I found myself agreeing.

❄ ❄ ❄

'I feel terrible that you ended up cleaning the paint off, not realising it was a message,' Rufus said, fifteen minutes later, when I'd plonked myself on his distressed leather sofa with a plate of toasted sourdough. 'I really didn't think it through, did I?'

He looked so tormented, I assured him it was fine, trying to picture him creeping up to the café in the dark and cold, with his tin of paint and a brush. It seemed so… *extreme.* No one had ever done anything like it in my name, and I couldn't work out what I felt.

'Honestly,' I said, 'I'm over it.'

He instantly brightened, and endearingly said, 'Help yourself to cheese and olives.' He indicated the spread on the glass-topped coffee table, which he must have either laid on while I was driving over, or earlier, when he was anticipating me calling to express joy at his artistic endeavours. 'I know you like the strong stuff, so I got some Stinking Bishop.'

'Lovely,' I said, though I'd only professed a liking for strong cheese because Rufus did, and it had seemed to be a grown-up thing to like. I actually preferred mild cheddar, and The Laughing Cow cheese triangles, which tasted great on crackers. 'I might have some later.'

'So, you haven't changed your mind about the wedding on Saturday?' He seemed to be holding his breath.

'No,' I said, popping an olive in my mouth. I was starving. 'I told you, my word is my bond.'

'*Great!*' Before I could work out what was happening, Rufus had flumped beside me, holding an open laptop. 'Here she is!' On the screen was a man with a hulking frame and a luxuriant ginger beard, squinting at the image of us that had popped up in the corner. 'This is my brother, Grant,' said Rufus, tossing an arm around my shoulder and pulling me close so that I tilted sideways, spilling my bread on the floor. 'He wants to say hello.'

'Hey!' The man lifted a hand in a friendly wave. 'You weren't lying, bro', she's gorgeous.'

He was Skyping his brother? Swallowing my olive whole, I tried to pull away, but Rufus was strong from his hours in the gym and had an iron grip.

'I *told* you,' he said, a note of triumph in his voice, and I didn't know whether to be flattered or furious that he'd gone to such lengths to show me off to his brother without warning. 'She's definitely real!' He was grinning, but an undercurrent in his voice suggested years of competition with his brother, who was younger and better looking (from what I could see under the beard), with smiling eyes, and a head of red-gold hair that probably drove Rufus mad with jealousy. 'She'll be at the wedding on Saturday and you can meet her for yourself.'

'I'll look forward to that,' said Grant, his friendly face looming large. 'It's good to meet you, Matilda.'

Rufus shifted slightly and I managed to move away, reconstructing my face into a pleasant smile. 'Good to meet you too,' I said politely.

'Have you sorted out your best man's speech yet?' Grant's eyes swivelled back to his brother.

'Oh yes,' said Rufus, and I remembered him saying something about having a few anecdotes up his sleeve to embarrass his brother with on the big day.

'Anything you'd care to share?' Grant's tone was lightly teasing.

'That you wet the bed until you were twelve?' Rufus winked at me. 'I wouldn't be that cruel, mate.'

'Thank Christ for that.' Clearly, Grant hadn't spotted the wink. 'Although it's no secret that I had a weak bladder that had to be fixed in my teens.' I loved how matter-of-fact he was about it.

Rufus clearly wasn't on the same wavelength. '*Right*,' he said in an exaggerated way that meant he thought Grant was lying. 'Good job I won't be mentioning it then.' He tried to nudge me playfully, but I'd moved too far away.

'Well, I'd better be off,' said Grant, glancing at his watch. 'Good to talk to you, Roof.' He sounded completely genuine.

'See you Saturday.' Rufus's voice was loaded with meaning, and not in a good way. Did he even *like* his brother?

'Nice to meet you, Matilda,' said Grant, his gaze meeting mine once more, and I thought I saw something like pity in his eyes – unless it was a trick of the light. 'Don't take any nonsense from my brother. He can be a bit—' Rufus slammed the screen shut.

'He's an idiot,' he muttered, his expression unusually sullen. It was suddenly easy to see the twelve-year-old boy he'd once been, and I felt a burst of pity. There was obviously a lot of history between him and his brother that I didn't know about, but I could relate to having a difficult sibling relationship. 'Just because he saved Dad's life once, and went on to become a heart surgeon, and runs marathons for charity, and is marrying the daughter of a woman he brought back to life on a flight to New York and is adopting her two children, it doesn't make him better than me.'

'I didn't realise your brother was a heart surgeon, he looks—'

'Like a trucker, I know,' Rufus said, though I'd been about to say a friendly lumberjack. 'He loves the element of surprise when people meet him for the first time.' *Or, he's just comfortable in his own skin.* 'I could have been a doctor, only I'm not very good with blood, but he looks down on me for being a teacher.'

I wasn't sure that was true and couldn't believe that Rufus hadn't mentioned any of this while we'd been seeing each other – then again, he'd probably been presenting his best side. He was obviously a mass of insecurities, at least where his brother was concerned. 'Being a teacher's amazing,' I said, bending to pick my bread off the oatmeal carpet. 'I couldn't do it.'

'No, but you don't like working. It's one of the things I like about you,' he added, when I opened my mouth to protest. 'I love the idea of coming home to find a gorgeous woman in my kitchen. Or bedroom,' he blustered, when I opened my mouth again. 'Or anywhere in the house.' He must have sensed my protests were reaching bursting point. 'What I'm saying is, Tilly, that I want you in my life.'

'Let's just start with the wedding,' I said, before he dug himself in any deeper.

'Is that a proposal?' One of his sandy eyebrows twitched, and I realised he'd made a joke – the first since we'd met.

Biting back the words *absolutely not*, I smiled and said, 'Nice one, *Roo*.' I meant the nickname ironically, but his cheeks pinked with pleasure.

'Keep saying it until it catches on.' He leaned over and grasped my hand. 'What do you think of the decorations?'

I looked around his orderly living room, with its matching pale-wood furniture and fake-coal fire, and the giant television he liked to watch rugby and cricket on, and noticed he'd draped garlands of gold tinsel around everything, in a rather desultory fashion. There was a Christmas tree in front of the window, precisely arranged with red and gold baubles, as if it had sprung out of the box already decorated. Which it probably had, if the tinsel arrangements were anything to go by.

'It's… nice,' I said, unable to summon a more enthusiastic description.

128 Karen Clarke

'I know it won't meet your design standards,' he said with a chuckle, squeezing my fingers. 'You have my permission to work your magic here, any time you like.'

'Oh no, you've… honestly, you've done a good job,' I assured him, spotting a pair of beady-eyed elves, sitting on the bookshelf. 'The way people decorate reflects their personalities, and I like that.' I couldn't tear my gaze from the grinning elves.

'They came out every year when we were kids,' he said, following my line of vision. 'Jollybum and Merrybottom.' His laugh was tinged with nostalgia. 'Grant wanted to call them KITT and Goliath, from *Knight Rider*, but I cried so much that Mum let me have my own way.'

His brother had obviously been the cool one, but I could hardly say so. 'I wasn't expecting to meet him today.' I disentangled our fingers. 'You should have warned me, Rufus.'

'I thought you'd like the element of surprise.' Based on what, I wasn't sure, but it barely seemed worth protesting when he clearly hadn't meant any harm. 'Listen, we're going to have a great time.'

'Does it really mean that much to you?' Bridget had married her Frenchman in secret – a spur-of-the-moment union with two strangers as witnesses – and although Mum had cried when she found out, presumably at having missed her firstborn's wedding, I'd been curiously ambivalent. Maybe because I'd known what he was really like, but Rufus seemed almost fanatical about attending his brother's nuptials… with me.

'It really does.' He placed his laptop on the cushion beside him and shuffled round to face me. 'I can't wait for everyone to meet you.'

I studied his sensitive features, and tried to imagine meeting his family, and what they would make of me. Would they see me as a suitable match – as my grandmother would have said – for their youngest son, or were they secretly hoping he'd bring someone more... sensible? Another teacher, perhaps, or a nice nurse? Perhaps they'd be disappointed that I was taller than him. 'I'm looking forward to it, too,' I said brightly, hoping they were all as nice as Grant had appeared to be.

'I saw you, you know.'

'Saw me?'

'Save that boy from drowning,' Rufus said unexpectedly. 'I heard you shouting on my way to the car park, and when I looked round you were running towards the sea. There was a mongrel on the beach,' I remembered he didn't like dogs, 'and a boy in the water, and I realised you were going to save him.' His face came alive, as if he was describing the plot of a film he'd seen and loved. 'You were amazing, Tilly. I think I knew then that I was going to have to work very hard to keep you.'

Ignoring the last bit, I said, 'Did you call for help?'

'What?' His gaze refocused. 'Help?'

'The coastguard, an ambulance?'

He drew his head back. 'I didn't need to,' he said. 'You'd obviously got things perfectly under control.'

'But, what if I hadn't?'

'Well, obviously I would have called for help if you'd been struggling, but do you know how much it costs to mount a rescue?' He'd turned a bit huffy, and his cheeks reddened. 'They wouldn't have thanked me for calling them out, only to get there and find they weren't needed,' he said. 'That man seemed very grateful. Was it his dad?'

'How long were you watching?'

'I saw him hugging you.' Was that what had prompted this outpouring of... I couldn't call it love. *Was it love?* I had nothing to compare it with, but it didn't *feel* like love.

'He was very grateful,' I said.

'I should have called the local paper.' Rufus became enthused. 'I still could,' he said. 'You deserve a bravery award for what you did.'

'Please don't.' Seth would hate that. 'I don't want an award.'

'My students would be impressed.' The uncharitable thought that he wanted to bask in some reflected glory popped into my head, and I felt instantly guilty when he added, 'You'd be a good role model for them.'

'I really don't want you to.' I spoke more sharply than I'd intended, unsure why I didn't just tell him the man was Seth Donovan. I had a feeling if I did, he might want me to introduce them. 'Promise me you won't.'

'I promise,' he said sincerely. 'You're too modest though, Tilly.'

'Listen, I've got to go.' I stood up, suddenly keen to escape the over-heated room and Rufus's puppy-dog eyes. A puppy-dog who was a bit over-excited and looked like he might bite me. 'I have to, er…' Luckily, my phone obliged by ringing. 'I have to get this, I'm expecting a call about the café.'

Phone pressed to my ear, I gave Rufus a distracted smile and hurried out, leaving him standing awkwardly in his living room, a hand outstretched as if to restrain me.

'I've had a call!'

'Bridget?'

'Seth Donovan rang me this morning.' She sounded oddly breathless. 'He's taking me out for dinner this evening, and I need you to help me find something to wear.'

Chapter Fifteen

No sooner had Bridget imparted her news than Romy shouted 'POO!' and needed her bottom wiping. I'd barely promised Bridget I'd be home by five at the latest when she hung up and my phone vibrated again.

'Hi, Seth.' I waited for him to relay the same bulletin that my sister had, and was taken aback when he said, 'Tilly, I know this is asking a lot, but my mother is keen to see you in action with Jack before she goes home, and I wondered whether you might be free to come over.'

A knot tightened in my stomach. 'When is she going?' There was no way I could convince Felicity that I was a bona fide nanny – or magically gain a qualification in childcare overnight.

'Around five,' said Seth.

'*Today?*'

'My father just called her to say there's a problem on the work front she has to get back for.' His tone conveyed an apology, mild despair and a touch of irritation. 'I hate asking, but since we've set this particular ball in motion…'

'Aren't you taking my sister out this evening?' I said. 'She just phoned me.'

'Oh, Christ.' It sounded as if he'd already forgotten. 'I'd assumed my mother would be here to babysit Jack.' He made a frustrated noise. 'I'll have to call her and cancel.'

'Don't do that,' I said quickly, imagining Bridget's disappointment – which she'd no doubt blame me for. 'I'll look after him.'

'You will?' I couldn't work out whether he sounded hopeful. 'But I've already asked you to come over and pretend to be Jack's nanny, it's too much to expect you to babysit for real.'

'I don't mind,' I said, deciding quickly. There was nothing I could do at the café for the moment, other than hang around. 'Just give me half an hour and I'll be there.'

I scrambled into my car, pretending not to notice that Rufus was watching from his living room window, and drove past the tightly packed houses to the end of the street, where I stopped and pulled on the handbrake. It felt as if there wasn't enough oxygen in the car, but when I opened the window cold air rushed in, so I closed it again and called Gwen to tell her I wouldn't be coming back. Jerry answered the phone. 'She's having a one-to-one with Dickens while it's quiet,' he said, relief seeping into his voice. 'I told her I'd heard him miaowing as if he was missing her, and she shot off to give him a cuddle.'

'Nice one.' I smiled as I imagined his shock when Gwen made her move on him at the party. 'You are coming on Christmas Eve?' My smile faltered as I pictured everyone turning up to find the function room cold, damp, empty and dark.

'I expect so.' He gave one of the world-weary sighs I'd frequently overheard since he started working at the café. 'Gwen's asked me to help serve drinks, and I don't have anywhere else to be so I thought, why not?' It struck me he could have invented somewhere else to be, and I wondered again whether he was as impervious to Gwen's 'charms' as he made out.

'Tell Gwen I've got some things to sort out for the function room, but that everything's in hand, will you, Jerry?'

'Will do,' he promised, and released another hefty sigh. Maybe he was short of oxygen too.

'Thanks,' I said, and after calling my broken-armed electrician, to be told he was still trying his best to find a replacement, I resisted the temptation to Google *how to behave like a nanny,* and drove to Seashell Cove with an image in my head of Mary Poppins sliding down a banister, holding her umbrella aloft.

'Thanks for this.' Seth held the car door open as I got out. I'd parked beside his car on a patch of flattened grass at the side of the cottage. There was a silver Land Rover there that I guessed belong to Felicity, and I had to make a mental adjustment as I'd pictured her being chauffeured around, rather than driving herself.

'Thanks for asking my sister out to dinner.'

'I said I would.' He didn't seem too thrilled in the flesh, but I knew that once he clapped eyes on Bridget, he'd realise I'd done him a big favour.

'Nice outfit.' I eyed his furry trapper hat and fleece-lined parka with slight envy. I'd almost forgotten that a British winter could be just as unforgiving as a Canadian one. 'Or is it another disguise?'

He gave a sheepish grin. 'I've been for a walk,' he said, glancing around him. The sky was a chalky-white that seemed to go on for miles, and the sea was thrashing the empty beach below. 'I needed to get out of the house.'

'No Jack?' I followed his gaze back to the cottage.

'My mother's giving him a haircut.'

'I didn't realise she was a hairdresser.'

His smile was fleeting. 'She actually runs an equestrian centre,' he said. I could easily see her bossing around young, posh girls on ponies. 'She's not as hands on these days, which gives her more time to interfere in my life,' he went on. 'And I don't think she realises there are hair salons in this part of the world.'

'Don't you have any say in that sort of thing?'

'Not if I want Jack to stay with me.'

'Does *he* have any say in the matter?'

'Hang on, you have *met* my mother?' He tilted his head, his expression warily playful. 'Nobody has a say when she's set her mind on something.'

'Well, maybe they should.'

'Oh boy.' Seth dropped his head down in mock-despair. 'Don't go thinking you can change her,' he said. 'Many have tried and been wounded in the process.'

'How did Jack's mum get on with her?'

'Don't even get me started.' He dug his hands deep into his coat pockets. 'She never thought Charlotte was good enough for me, and she only met her once.'

'At your wedding?' I had no idea why I was asking, especially while standing outside with freezing toes and glowing ears. At least, it felt like my ears were glowing. A benefit of growing my hair out was that they weren't always visible.

'At our wedding,' he agreed, and seemed to shudder. 'Let's just say, Mum wept through the ceremony, and they weren't tears of happiness.' My bubble of sympathy for his wife popped when he added, 'Mind you, Charlotte didn't do herself any favours by telling my mum her outfit made her look fat, then announcing that she'd found out that morning that she wasn't really pregnant.'

I stared. 'You married her because she was pregnant?' I was focusing on the least bad part of his admission. 'That's a bit old school, isn't it?'

'Don't get me wrong, I was madly in love and thought I was ready to settle down,' he said, moving from foot to foot in a subconscious attempt to keep warm. 'She was gorgeous too, she'd appeared on *America's Next Top Model*—'

'Oh, what a cliché,' I couldn't resist saying. 'Sports star meets model and they *don't* live happily ever after.'

To his credit, he looked a bit shamefaced. 'I know,' he said, mouth turning down. 'I was a living cliché back then and the terrible thing is, deep down, I knew it.'

'So… Jack?'

'He came along the following year.' His face softened. 'Things were really good after that for a while, he brought out the best in us both, but I was hardly ever at home, and… another cliché alert… Charlotte ended up having an affair and so did I and—'

'What the blazes are the pair of you doing out here?'

We started violently as Felicity hurried over, sporting a pair of green wellies, her expression as flinty as if she'd caught us dancing naked. It hit me that she was the reason we'd been reluctant to go indoors, and why I'd been grilling Seth about his marriage – and probably why he'd responded.

'You shouldn't be over-familiar with the staff,' she admonished Seth, and it took a second to realise she was referring to me.

'Tilly isn't *staff*,' he said – which was at least true. 'And it isn't nineteen twenty-two, Mum. People don't have staff, at least not in their homes.'

'Of *course* they do,' she snapped. 'What else do you call cleaners, cooks, gardeners and so forth?' I assumed she was referring to her own army of helpers, and wondered who the *so forth* were. Maybe she had a butler, and someone to operate the remote control for the television. 'I wouldn't call them friends, it blurs the boundaries.'

'*Staff* sounds stuck up and snobbish,' Seth persisted. 'It's embarrassing, Mum, and I won't have you talking like that around Jack.'

It sounded like an old argument, and one Felicity didn't seem keen to participate in. 'Come on, Miss Campbell,' she said to me.

'Please call me Tilly.'

'You'll be no good to my grandson if you catch your death of cold.' She scanned my duffel coat – the coat I'd been wearing the last time we met – and I supposed, in her world, there were a multitude of coats to be worn on different days, and in different situations. I wondered whether she'd have approved had I turned up in a grey, button-up jacket and ankle length skirt, and wished I had a more up-to-date reference than Mary Poppins. 'What are you waiting for?'

A miracle. 'Just letting you lead the way,' I offered, extending my arm for her to go ahead. 'There *is* rather a nip in the air.' My voice sounded different. Was I starting to *talk* like Mary Poppins? Seth gave me a look, as if to say *what the hell was that?* but Felicity tightened the belt of her heavy cardigan and merely nodded. 'Jack's waiting,' she said.

My heart juddered. 'Does he know about all this?' I whispered to Seth as we followed Felicity's jaunty stride to the cottage.

He lowered his head close to mine without breaking his pace. 'I asked him whether he'd mind you looking after him now and again and he said it's fine.'

'He did?' I remembered his presence in the kitchen while we'd been talking. 'Do you think he understands what's going on?'

'I'm sure he does.' Seth slowed down. 'He doesn't say a lot, but I think he takes everything in. Even though we've not spoken about my mother having custody in front of him, I've a feeling he gets the gist.'

'You don't think she might have talked to him behind your back?'

He looked stricken. 'God, I hope not,' he said. 'But I think he would have said something if she had.'

'And you haven't spoken to him openly about it?'

Seth shook his head. 'I wouldn't know where to start, to be honest, and I don't want to confuse him any more than he probably already is.'

'But what if he'd like to stay with your parents?'

He stopped abruptly. 'As long as I've breath in my body, I'll fight to keep my son with me.' His voice was low and urgent. 'There's no way he's going to end up living with my mother.'

'*Now* what are you two talking about?' Felicity was in the doorway, her tone bristling with impatience. 'Anything that needs to be discussed can surely be done where it's warm?'

We looked at each other a moment longer, Seth's face a determined mask, before turning as one and heading into the cottage. Inside, Felicity's team of workmen were banging and hammering, and a smell of emulsion wafted from the nearest downstairs room. I sniffed appreciatively and Felicity gave me a funny look. At least, I assumed it was a funny look. It was hard to tell in the dingy hallway – though I guessed it wouldn't be so dingy once her *team* had worked their magic.

After she'd removed her wellingtons, and Seth had taken my coat and hung it with his on the banister – to his mother's narrow-eyed disapproval – she said, 'Jack's in the drawing... I mean, living room.' She flapped her hand and tutted. 'I can't get used to this place not having a drawing room,' she said, flicking the overhead light on and glowering at the bulb.

Seth rolled his eyes in such a teenage way, I had to hide a smile. 'Most normal houses don't have a drawing room, Mum.'

'That's rich, coming from you, when you had a... what did you call it?' She puckered her cinnamon-lipsticked mouth. 'A mezzanine floor

at your place in Italy, not to mention a games room and a cinema.'
She directed a snooty gaze my way. 'A mezzanine is a raised platform
that creates additional space, dividing the floors—'

'I know what a mezzanine is.' I was about to add that I'd worked
in a new-build in Vancouver with a mezzanine floor (one of the few
projects I'd committed to while I was there) when I remembered I
was supposed to be a nanny, not an interior designer. 'It's… quite a
common word around here.' It was clearly a ridiculous statement. No
one would drop the word *mezzanine* into conversation unless they
happened to have one, or to be building one.

Seth's eyebrows rose and his lips clamped together, while Felicity
studied me closely, perhaps trying to work out whether or not I was
taking the mickey out of her.

'Your place in Italy sounds amazing,' I said to Seth, after a long
stretch of silence broken only by one of the workmen whistling 'Jingle
Bells' over and over. 'Not at all the sort of place I'd expect a champion
racing driver to live.'

To my surprise, Felicity picked up on what I'd intended to be a
lightly teasing tone and gave a bark of laughter. 'Everyone can see your
playboy lifestyle for the shallow pool it was,' she said to Seth.

'*Was* being the operative word,' he replied, and I realised with a
lurch that I'd given the impression I was being sarcastic; looking down
on him like Felicity was, and in much the same way that Bridget
looked down at me. '*This* is my life now.' He jabbed a finger at the
floor. 'Where I'm staying.'

'But for how long?' Felicity placed a well-manicured hand on the
wall, as if to support herself. 'That silly ex-girlfriend of yours called
the landline while you were out. I expect you'll be back in Italy with
her soon.'

'Dad?' We turned to see Jack, framed in the doorway of the living room, in dark blue jeans and a top with a *Star Wars* ship on the front. Beneath his newly cut fringe, his face was pale and tense. 'I don't want you to go away,' he said.

Chapter Sixteen

'I'm not going anywhere, Jack.' Seth gave his mother a hard stare. 'Your grandmother was being silly.'

I willed him to go to Jack, get down on his level and say it again with conviction while looking his son in the eyes, but the moment had already passed. Jack returned to the living room, dragging his blue-socked feet.

'Now see what you've done.' Felicity returned Seth's stare with added ferocity. 'If you'd finished with that woman properly, she wouldn't keep trying to get hold of you.'

'I *did* end it properly, but she's clearly not getting the message.' Seth spoke with forced patience. 'I'm not going to throw flames on the fire by responding.'

'Then change the number.'

'I shouldn't *have* to change my number. I've already blocked her on my mobile.'

'Which is why she's calling you here.'

'I'm not changing my number.'

'No, because then the rest of your harem wouldn't be able to get hold of you.'

'I don't know where you've got this idea that I have a harem.' He shot me a look. 'It's not true.'

Felicity made a *pah* sound. 'Anyway, I'm sure Miss Campbell doesn't want to hear about her employer's love life.' I refrained from saying I was actually quite intrigued. And that Seth was *not* my employer. And from asking her to call me Tilly… again. 'At least that's one good thing about living here,' she went on. 'There aren't any women.' Catching my expression, she added, 'Not my son's type, I mean.'

I stole a glance at Seth, who appeared to be grinding his teeth. Bridget was undoubtedly different from his usual type – the thought of her appearing on *America's Next Top Model* was hilarious, and although she was bad-tempered (around me) it was more British bulldog than fiery Italian – which meant that Felicity might approve of her. Then again, Bridget was a single mum so maybe it was as well Felicity would be gone before Seth's date with my sister.

When he didn't respond, Felicity said, 'Perhaps you could make some tea, while Miss Campbell—'

'It's Tilly,' I couldn't stop myself saying.

'While Miss Campbell attends to Jack,' she continued, refastening her cardigan belt. The workman had stopped whistling and was now, to the tune of 'Jingle Bells', singing *Rum-tum-tum, rum-tum-tum, rum-tum-tum-TUM-TUM,* and Felicity directed an irritated look at the door. 'In the meantime, I'll go and have a word with Mr Berryman.' She brushed past and vanished into the room, and on hearing her demand that Mr Berryman run through the itinerary for the rest of the week, Seth lifted his eyes to the ceiling.

'I'm so, so sorry,' he said, with a helpless gesture at odds with his size and presence. 'You must think you've landed on a totally bonkers planet.'

'I said, go and make some tea!' As Felicity's tone rang out, Seth brought his eyes back to mine.

'You can make a run for it, if you like,' he murmured, raking a hand through his hair. 'I wouldn't blame you.'

'Actually, I'm fine.' I was surprised to find I meant it. It was an unorthodox set-up, and Felicity was clearly living in a different century, but it made a change from fending off questions from Gwen, or sparring with Bridget at home. And – I was loathe to admit it, even to myself – it was more relaxing than being with Rufus, trying to work out the rules of a 'grown-up' relationship. 'I'll go and chat to Jack while you make the tea.'

'Thank you.' Seth expelled a long breath. 'I'm never going to be able to repay you for any of this.' While he made his way to the kitchen with shoulders so hunched he gave the impression of being headless, I straightened my back and entered the living room.

Jack was on his belly on the floor beside a snoozing Digby, looking at his ever-present iPad. The television was on with the sound turned down, cars whizzing around a circuit like noisy toys.

'Do you like Formula One?' I said, hovering by the sofa. It sounded horribly stilted, like something a distant auntie would say, and I couldn't blame him for merely shrugging a shoulder in response. 'What sports do you like to watch?'

'I don't like watching sports. It's lame.'

'What about playing them?'

'I don't like watching, *or* playing sports.' He twisted his head. 'Just because my dad used to be a racing driver doesn't mean I have to like it too.'

'Of course you don't.' I gripped the back of the sofa to steady myself against a rise of uncertainty. 'I just… a lot of boys like football, that's all.'

Both his shoulders lifted. 'I don't.'

'Me neither.'

Silence.

Digby lifted his head and smiled at me. At least, that's what it looked like.

'Are you playing Minecraft?'

'Trying to.'

Releasing my hold on the sofa, I moved slowly round it, wondering what Mary Poppins would say. 'Supercalifragilisticexpialidocious' probably, which wasn't exactly helpful. 'Did you enjoy swimming yesterday?'

Another shrug. 'Dad went down the slide three times, after me.'

'He did?' I was inordinately pleased. 'Did he like it?'

'He went too fast the first time and his shorts came down.'

'Yikes.' I remembered the middle-aged women at the pool. They must have thought they'd died and gone to heaven. 'I bet that was awkward.' I edged further round and sat cross-legged on the floor beside Jack, while Digby rolled onto his back and displayed his tummy for rubbing. 'That happened to my dad once, on holiday.' I obligingly stroked the dog's soft fur, and his tail brushed the floorboards. 'He jumped off the diving board, and when he climbed out of the water everyone saw his bare bottom.'

To my relief, the edge of Jack's mouth curved up. 'Dad says we can go swimming again soon.'

'That's good.' I battled for inspiration. 'Did you get your new shoes?'

Eyes still fixed to his screen, Jack shook his head. 'I said they were too tight, and Grandma gave up because there weren't enough shoe shops in Kingsbridge.' *1-0 to Jack.* 'We did Christmas shopping instead.'

'You did?'

He nodded. 'I got Dad a shirt without a collar and a book, and some socks for Granddad, and Grandma helped me wrap them up.'

I hid my surprise. 'That was nice of her.' It hit me that she and Seth's dad had been taking care of Jack for the past three years, and obviously loved him very much. 'Did you buy her something too?'

'I got some chocolates that she likes, and she didn't look while I paid for them, and Dad will help me wrap those.'

'Good plan.'

'She's got lots of horses.' His words were coming more easily, as if I'd broken through an invisible barrier. 'She said I could learn to ride.'

'Would you like that?'

'I might fall off.'

'I'm sure she wouldn't let that happen.'

'She said if Dad had learnt to ride a horse he could have played badminton.' He darted me a look, brow furrowed. 'I don't get it.'

'I think she meant he could have ridden a horse at Badminton,' I explained, wondering whether Seth had deliberately chosen a sport with four wheels instead of four legs to annoy his mother. 'It's a place, and there's a prestigious competition there for riders that lasts three days.'

'What does prest... igious mean?' He pronounced it carefully.

'It means...' *ludicrously posh*? 'It's the sort of event the royal family would go to, and only the very best horse riders from around the world can compete.'

'Like the Grand Prix, where my dad won?'

'*Yeees*,' I said slowly, feeling on shaky ground. I had no idea whether Felicity – or Seth for that matter – had spoken to Jack about his dad's former career, or what impression they'd given; whether the dangers of driving at speed had been highlighted, or disgust expressed (Felicity probably hadn't held back) or whether Jack had been encouraged to be proud of his dad's achievements.

'I don't think Dad likes horses very much.'

Feeling like I'd dodged a bullet, I said, 'Do you?'

'They're a bit smelly and high up, but I don't mind,' he said. 'I like Grandma's house, and Granddad lets me polish his car.'

Surprised at his show of faith, I said, 'What about your other grandparents?'

'They died before I was born,' he said. 'Dad told me they're in heaven, with my mum.' He slid me an anxious look. 'If I'd drowned in the sea, would I be there too?'

My breathing stalled. Digby, tiring of me rubbing his tummy, stood up and shook himself. 'It wasn't time for you to go,' I said. My voice sounded funny, as if I'd swallowed something hard. 'Your mum wouldn't have wanted you to. That's why I was there, to help you.'

'Like an angel?'

My eyelids heated up. 'I'm not an angel,' I said, wondering how we'd got here so quickly. I looked at the curve of his cheek and sweep of eyelashes, and felt an urge to fold him against me and stroke his shiny hair. Instead, I tried to remember what Mum had told me when Nanna Hopkins died. I must have been around Jack's age, but hadn't known her that well because she'd developed Alzheimer's when I was three. Mum had said she was 'at peace' and I'd had a comforting image of her sleeping in a long white nightgown, surrounded by dancing butterflies.

Realising Jack's iPad had powered down while he waited for a response, I said, 'Like a friend,' feeling the weight of the words settle on me as I spoke. I was in no position to counsel a boy who'd tragically lost his mother. What if I said the wrong thing? 'You've got your whole life to live, Jack.' *Stop right now, Tilly.* 'That's what your mum would have wanted, and it's what your dad wants too, more than anything in the world.'

He nodded once, seeming to accept what I'd said, and touched his screen to bring it back to life. I felt light-headed and tearful, like I had when I was recovering from a flu virus during the summer, and ransacked the room with my eyes for a distraction.

'Hey, shall we decorate the tree?' I spotted a rather stumpy pine in a pot in the corner, with a cardboard box spilling decorations nearby.

'Dad thought we should leave it until the paint's dry in here.'

I noticed the walls were a pleasant buttery shade that complemented the dark oak floorboards. 'I'm sure it's dry by now, and I bet we can do it in...' I looked at my watch. 'Five minutes.'

'Five minutes?' Jack pushed himself to his knees and made to push his fringe away before remembering it had been cut. 'Not possible,' he said, folding his arms, but there was a spark in his eyes.

'I bet it is.'

'Can I help too?' Seth came in with a tray of steaming mugs, followed by Felicity, and I wondered whether they'd overheard my conversation with Jack. Seth's blandly smiling face gave nothing away, and Felicity wore what I was beginning to realise was her default expression of vague disapproval. I wondered whether she'd always looked like that – if so, Seth must have been relieved to escape to boarding school.

She came to rest on the arm of the sofa, as if it was against her nature to sit on it and get comfortable – perhaps put her feet up. I tried to imagine her cuddling Jack, or telling him a bedtime story like my parents used to – and like my grandparents had when they were still capable of travelling over from Canada – but could only picture her astride a stallion, ordering a stable hand to fetch her a whip.

'Ready... steady... GO!' said Seth, after settling the tea tray on the floor, and we hurtled towards the tree and began digging into the cardboard box. Digby clattered over and delicately stopped a rolling bauble with his paw. Jack gave an infectious chuckle, and I met Seth's gaze and smiled.

'You really ought to buy some proper decorations, instead of using that old jumble you asked me to fetch from the attic at Oaklands,' said Felicity. I guessed Oaklands was the family home. 'I don't even know why I kept it.'

'Because Dad made you.' Seth clumsily attached a one-eyed angel to one of the branches. 'I guess he knew I'd want to use them, one day.'

I wound some lantern-style fairy lights around the tree, beginning at the bottom, close to the trunk and swiftly working upwards, wishing Felicity would join in instead of criticising.

'Hey, you've done this before,' said Seth, eyebrows gathered as he tried to hang two silver baubles simultaneously.

'Every year,' I admitted. 'I've been helping decorate our tree since I was six.' It had been Bridget's job before that but, aged sixteen, she'd lost interest – plus I 'had an eye for detail' even then, according to Mum and Dad, who had photos to prove it and weren't shy about showing them off. 'Where's the socket?' Seth pointed and I pressed in the plug, watching Jack's face as the lanterns lit up: red, blue, gold and green.

'Wow,' he breathed, his eyes reflecting the light, and watching Seth watching his son made my heart feel as though it had doubled in size.

'Only two minutes left.' I flashed my watch. 'Quick, quick.'

Jack foraged some silver tinsel out and draped it over the lower branches, while Seth practically hurled assorted decorations at the tree, some missing and falling on the floor. Jack copied his movements – his iPad forgotten – and I hunkered down and joined in, resisting the urge to even things out and colour-coordinate, though I couldn't resist moving some glittery baubles to the top of the tree as it was looking a bit bottom heavy.

'I remember making this with Granddad Norman.' Seth held out a wooden robin with a splodge of red paint on its chubby breast and an unnaturally long beak. 'I clearly wasn't destined to be a carpenter,' he said, and I saw a spasm of emotion cross Felicity's face before she leaned down to pick up her mug of tea.

'Put it at the top, Dad!' For the first time since I'd met him, Jack sounded like a normal, happy six-year-old. 'It's better than a fairy.' Digby barked his agreement, making us all laugh – apart from Felicity.

'What would you like for Christmas?' I asked him, as Seth tried to balance the robin at the top of the tree by winding tinsel around it.

'I keep asking him that,' said Seth.

'I don't know.' Jack dropped to his knees and pushed around a Christmas decoration in the shape of a racing car, driven by a jolly-faced Santa. Catching Felicity watching him, I imagined her buying it for a young, car-mad Seth, not realising that one day he'd grow up to drive one for real. 'I might want a lightsaber and a Lego *Star Wars* game.'

Seth dropped him a glance full of pleased wonder. 'I'll have a word with Father Christmas,' he said. 'I don't think it's too late yet.'

Jack looked up and gave a quick smile, his gaze grazing mine, and I had the feeling my presence had somehow given him the confidence to ask for what he really wanted. And when Felicity stood up and spoke, I understood why.

'We've already talked about this haven't we, Jack?' She brushed her hands down her herringbone skirt before turning to look at Seth. 'There are some wonderful educational gifts that will help Jack to learn,' she said. 'He spends enough time on that silly computer as it is, and needs to broaden his horizons if he wants to do well.'

'Doing things you like is just as important as learning,' I said, before I could stop myself. Trying to bring back the laughter, I added, 'If Santa had bought me an educational toy, I'd have sent it back.'

'And that, right there,' she poked a finger between Seth and me, as if we were somehow in cahoots, a dangerous look in her eyes, 'is what's wrong with today's youth.'

'Mum,' Seth began, but she'd already turned and dipped to scoop up the tea tray. 'You haven't even got a coffee table for heaven's sake,' she snapped. 'And the tea's gone cold while you've been messing about.'

The last bit was directed at me, accompanied by a frosty glare as she swooshed out of the room, calling back, 'You'll need to come out of there, by the way. The skirting boards need glossing.'

In silence, Jack shuffled across to pick up his iPad, followed by a subdued-looking Digby, while Seth studied a patch of fairy-lit floor by his feet. Watching them while Felicity issued an order to the decorators, I was overcome by the strongest sensation that I mustn't – at any cost – let her gain custody of Jack.

Chapter Seventeen

'You said you'd be back by five, and it's nearly half past.'

'Sorry, I got held up.' The electrician had called to say he couldn't find a replacement after all, and I'd had no luck either, despite offering double the amount of money for just a few hours work. It seemed no one was available this close to Christmas.

'Oh yes, it was your first day working for Seth, I nearly forgot.'

I briefly froze, hoping Bridget wouldn't ask for details, then sloughed off my coat and entered the kitchen. Romy was sitting at the table, about to upend a bowl of baked beans.

'No!' roared Bridget, reaching a hand out to stop her a second too late.

'BEANS!' Romy emptied the bowl, before dashing it to the floor and began smearing the juice over her cheeks.

'Oh, Romy, for heaven's *sake*,' cried Bridget, dashing to the sink where she grabbed a cloth and wrung it out under the tap.

Grateful for the distraction, I zoned in on an empty tin on the worktop, beside a heap of chopped carrots and leeks. 'I didn't realise Heinz had moved into the natural, organic food business.'

'I couldn't get the bloody blender to work, and Romy said she was starving, and beans have lots of the amino acids so I figured it wouldn't hurt this once.'

'BLOODY, BLOODY, BLOODY!' chanted Romy, twisting her head back and forth so that Bridget kept missing her target with the cloth.

'Romy, please keep still,' she implored, throwing me a murderous look when she caught me grinning as I pulled out a chair and sat down. 'I'm supposed to be meeting Seth at eight, which means I've only got two and a half hours to get ready.'

'Blimey, Bridget, you don't need that long.'

'In case you haven't noticed, Tilly, I've got a child to look after. I haven't had time to wash my hair, or do my nails, or even go for a wee.'

'What *have* you been doing?'

'What have I been *doing*?' She gave up aiming the cloth at Romy and dropped on a chair opposite, as if my question was so shocking she needed a minute to comprehend it. 'Only a non-parent could ask a question like that,' she said at last, chucking the cloth on the table. She was wearing a checked shirt I recognised as Dad's and had pulled her mass of hair into a lopsided bun. 'Let me see now... I tried to teach Romy her alphabet, but she kept putting her hands over her ears, then we went to the park – you know, the one where I used to take you – and that took ages because Romy wanted to bring *all* her toys, and then she kept poking her tongue out at a boy on the swing, and his mum told me off for not noticing right away, and then we went to the supermarket where Romy knocked a jar of pickle off the shelf and it smashed. I say knocked, she actually picked it up and threw it because I wouldn't let her have a Curly Wurly because it was too close to lunchtime, and then she didn't want a banana so I ended up giving her some Smarties I found in my handbag.' As she finally ran out of steam, I noticed her eyes were red and puffy as if she'd had a good cry at some point.

'Have you tied your hair up with a pair of knickers?' I said gently.

'I couldn't find a hairband.' Her chin trembled. 'They don't even fit me any more.'

'Knickers!' bellowed Romy. She scooped up a handful of beans and slopped them onto the floor. 'Beans!'

'Why don't you go and have a bath?' I said to Bridget, who'd dropped her head into her hands and was rocking gently back and forth. 'I'll keep an eye on Romy and clear up the kitchen.'

'I don't know.' Rallying a little, Bridget lifted her head and cast a wary look at her daughter. 'She'll probably cry for me as soon as I leave the room and you won't know what to do.'

'Give me a chance, Bee.' I wondered why I was bothering when she clearly didn't trust me, even when she was desperate – but she was obviously more desperate to meet Seth because she nodded.

'Fine, but you must call for me straight away if you feel you can't manage, Tilly, I mean it.' She stood up, swaying a little. 'Promise?'

'Promise.' I pressed a hand on my heart, deciding not to berate her for her lack of faith. She'd had a tough day, and it wouldn't do for her to turn up to her date looking as if she'd been mugged. 'Go on,' I urged. 'Have a nice soak.'

'And you'll find me something to wear?'

I was already regretting offering to help on that front, but I'd promised so I nodded. 'Shout me when you're out of the bath.'

She blew a kiss to Romy, who was delicately squashing a baked bean between her finger and thumb, and when she'd gone, my niece fixed me with her clear blue eyes and her mouth dimpled into a smile, and the sight of her orange cheeks and tiny teeth made my chest tighten up.

'Hello, you.'

''lo,' she said, suddenly shy, peering at me through her fingers. It was the first time we'd been left alone, and released from the pressure of Bridget's critical gaze it was easy to lift Romy off the chair and transport her to the sink. She was weighty for such a small person, but when she flung her arms around my neck and held on, I found I didn't want to put her down. She smelt of shampoo and beans, and the feel of her soft, small body and her silky hair made it hard to breathe.

'Let's get you cleaned up, little monkey.' I sat her on the draining board, and she let me wipe her face and hands with a dampened tea towel, watching me with great solemnity – like a royal visitor allowing a native to anoint her with holy water. 'You're a scamp,' I said, which was what Dad used to say to me, though – by all accounts – I'd been nowhere near as difficult as Romy. Not that she was being difficult now. In fact, she was like a different child. 'That's better,' I said, once her cheeks had been restored to her natural rosy hue. 'Now, you sit at the table while I make some toast.' I was suddenly starving. I hadn't eaten since the bread and olives at Rufus's house.

Seth had seemed disappointed when I'd told him I had to get home for dinner, and suggested I eat something at the cottage as I was going to be babysitting Jack, but not wanting to give away that Bridget had asked for help getting ready for their date, I'd pleaded some errands I had to run first. Felicity, ushering a harassed-looking workman with a tin of gloss paint into the living room, had said archly, 'Had enough already, Miss Campbell?' leading Seth to remind her I'd done them a favour by taking time out of my day to be vetted by her. Jack – on his way upstairs with Digby – had stopped to say, 'Bye', without being prompted, and I'd found myself reluctant to leave, in spite of Felicity, and was already looking forward to returning.

'Would you like some toast?' I asked Romy, aware that she hadn't eaten her beans and was probably hungry too.

She nodded. 'Toast!' she beamed, clapping her hands. She seemed to like repeating words.

'A, B, C, D, E,' I said, as I slid four slices of bread into the toaster.

'AY, BEE, CEE, DEE, EEEEE,' she echoed, and clapped her hands in delight.

'Well done,' I said. 'Say that to Mummy when she comes down.'

'Mummeeee!'

I spread the toast with butter, making Romy giggle by pretending to feed her teddy bear, which I'd rescued from under the table where she must have lobbed him. 'TEDDY!' she shouted. She took him from me and squashed him to her face, planting noisy kisses all over his fur, and by the time Bridget shouted that she was out of the bath we'd finished our toast, I'd eaten six ginger biscuits, and we'd got up to M in the alphabet. 'Coming!' I called back.

'Could you bring me a glass of wine?'

I pulled an astonished face. 'Mummy wants some *wine*?' I said to Romy. Bridget must be nervous about her date, because she didn't drink as a rule – she hated the feeling of being out of control.

'Wine,' echoed Romy, patting Teddy on the head.

I found a half-open bottle in the fridge and poured a large glassful, then hoisted Romy up and carried both upstairs.

'She can walk, you know.' Bridget emerged from the bathroom in a fog of steam, wrapped in a lemon towel, another around her head. 'She has to learn to use her own two legs.'

'You sound like Felicity,' I said, putting Romy down. She immediately scampered across the landing, shoved open the door to Mum and Dad's bedroom and dived onto their bed.

'Felicity?' Bridget took the glass of wine and had a long swig.

'Seth's mother.'

Her eyebrows flew up. 'You met his mother?'

'She was at the cottage today while I was… working,' I said. 'She's been staying a couple of days.'

'So, how did it go?' Bridget's eyes were already brighter than they'd been half an hour ago. 'Is the cottage nice?'

'It's, er, yes, at least it will be once it's been decorated.' No need to mention I wasn't the one doing the decorating.

'Was he pleased with your work? Seth, I mean.' It was obvious who she'd meant, but I had the feeling she was enjoying saying his name – as though anticipating how it would sound when she told people who she was dating.

'I… I think he was.' I hadn't got round to mentioning to Seth that Bridget thought I was doing up his cottage. The moment hadn't presented itself. I'd caught him looking at me once or twice, while we were decorating the tree; as if he couldn't quite believe it was happening. That, not only were he and Jack in the same room, they were doing something together and Jack was having fun. Just thinking about it ignited a glow that spread through me, warming my face and damping down a worm of anxiety about finding an electrician.

'And what's he like?' Bridget held up a hand before I could open my mouth. 'No, don't tell me.' She glugged some more wine, then whipped the towel off her head, shaking out her hair in a way that reminded me of Digby on the beach. 'I want to find out for myself, and you probably didn't get much of an opportunity to talk.'

'Not really,' I said, recalling Felicity's overbearing presence. If she hadn't been there, would Seth and I have talked more? But if she hadn't been there, neither would I, I reminded myself. And why was I even thinking about Seth? I tried to replace his image with one of Rufus, but ended up with a scary combination of them both. 'Let's get you dressed.' I picked up the towel that Bridget had dropped on the floor and draped it over the banister. 'There's nothing in my wardrobe that would fit you, but I'm sure there'll be something in Mum's.'

'Are you kidding?' A look of dismay spread over Bridget's freshly-scrubbed face. She looked almost a decade younger than nearly forty, her freckles only adding to her youthful appearance. I wondered how Seth felt about freckles. 'Mum's nearly seventy!' she cried, waving her half-empty wine glass.

'You've been practically living in her cardigans and Dad's shirts,' I pointed out.

'But that's around the house.'

'You're the same height and shape as Mum, and she's got loads of good stuff she hardly ever wears.'

'But…'

'Trust me.' I lowered my voice and pointed through the doorway to Romy, fast asleep on our parents' bed, still clutching her teddy, one thumb jammed in her mouth. 'She's so gorgeous, Bee.'

'When she's sleeping,' stage-whispered Bridget, and knocked back her glass of wine as though it was medicine.

Entering Mum and Dad's bedroom, with its soft pile carpet, built-in wardrobes, and pale candy-striped wallpaper was like stepping back in time. Even the air smelt the same; Mum's jasmine perfume mingled with the leathery scent of the Italian shoes Dad always wore for work.

'I still don't understand why you made every room look like the ones at the old house.' Bridget followed with great reluctance, as though entering the tiny cell of a convicted felon. 'It gives me déjà vu.'

'I told you, we were happy at the old house.' I moved across the room and carefully pulled the curtains closed against the inky-black night. The threatened snow still hadn't arrived, proving – yet again – that weather forecasters always got it wrong. 'We'd have moved back there if we could, but the house was gone, so we recreated it here.'

'Creepy.' Bridget joined me at the walnut dressing table that had been shipped back from Canada, along with the rest of our furniture, and picked up one of the many-framed photos that cluttered its surface. It was a picture Dad had taken of Mum, caught off guard, coiling a strand of hair around her finger, her lips slightly parted. ('I look a bit gormless,' she always said, but she didn't – she looked beautiful.) 'Weren't these taken on their honeymoon?' Bridget pointed to a photo a holidaymaker had taken of them hand in hand, paddling in the sea.

I nodded. 'Seems funny to think of them newly married in Egypt.' They looked happy, smiling into each other's eyes. They'd been smiling at each other for over forty years now, and showed no signs of stopping. 'Where did you and Frenchie go on your honeymoon?'

Bridget swiped my arm. 'Don't call him that.' The wine must have mellowed her mood as her lips didn't tighten at the mention of her ex-husband. 'We went to stay with his parents in the south of France. He got pissed every day, and tried to shag a waitress at a café he'd taken me to.'

I pulled a face. 'I could have told you he was no good.'

'Mum wrote to me, you know,' Bridget said unexpectedly. 'She told me you'd mentioned him trying it on with you the day I introduced him, and that's why you left in such a hurry.' She gazed at a photo of the two of us, eating fish and chips on a beach, a brooding seagull close by. It was the last day out we'd had as a family, before Bridget left home for good. 'They forbade me from ever bringing him to the house again.'

I looked at her. 'I didn't know.' Was that why Mum had cried when Bridget married him? Not because we weren't invited to the wedding, but because she'd gone ahead with it, knowing what he'd done?

Bridget shrugged. 'I think deep down, I knew what he was like.' She picked up a bottle of perfume and absently sprayed her wrist. 'I just didn't want to admit I'd picked a wrong 'un.'

'He *was* really good looking.' I wished I'd plied her with wine a lot sooner so we could have talked like this. 'And his accent was...' I kissed the tips of my fingers. 'Ooh la la.'

'Ooh la la!' Bridget tittered. 'No one in France says that.'

'Good job we're not in France then.'

'To the wardrobe!' She pointed a sergeant major-ish finger, dropping her towel as she swivelled around. Luckily, she'd put on underwear – a black and cream satin-and-lace combo that showed off her ample assets as she tiptoed past the bed with exaggerated care, blowing kisses to a gently slumbering Romy, before miming a scream as she stubbed her toe on the bed frame. 'That fucking well hurt,' she hissed, thudding onto a velvet-topped stool to massage her foot in a very un-ladylike pose. Now, I was starting to wish she hadn't had any wine. It was so rare for her to drink – and probably on an empty stomach – that she was already tipsy, and I wanted Seth to see her at her best. Fortunately, the pain in her toe seemed to have had a slightly sobering effect.

'I don't want to look mumsy, or frumpy,' she said. 'I've had a look at his exes online, and they all look like supermodels. In fact, his dead wife *was* a supermodel.' She prodded the roll of fat above her knickers with a disconsolate pout. 'I looked like I was having a litter when I was pregnant with Romy. I'll never get rid of this muffin top.'

'You're gorgeous, Bee, and he's done with women who look like supermodels.' I slid open Mum's wardrobe, which probably rivalled

Victoria Beckham's with deep drawers for handbags and shoes, and shelves of sweaters and tops. I started riffling through the hangers. Some of her clothes were eighties vintage, but I bypassed the sequins and ruffles and pulled out a cropped, black blazer, and a fire-engine red wrap-dress that I knew would complement Bridget's spectacular hair.

'Put these on,' I instructed. 'And these.' I took out a pair of black velvet shoes with high heels. 'You're only half a size bigger, you should be able to cram your toes in.'

As her head popped through the dress's soft material and it fell smoothly across her curves, she stood up and hobbled over to the full-length mirror. 'Not bad.' She smiled at my reflection.

'It's perfect.' In comparison, I looked like a lanky youth on day release from a remand centre, and wondered whether it was time to rethink my own wardrobe. I seemed to be living in jeans and sweatshirts these days, and could hardly believe I'd turned up at Rufus's house and then Seth's looking so… *scruffy*. Maybe I should get changed before going back over there. It was one thing trying to channel Mary Poppins, another to resemble a suspect on *Border Patrol*.

'Would you mind popping Romy into her own bed?' Bridget's voice jolted me out of my critical self-appraisal.

'Sure,' I said, surprised. It seemed a shame to disturb her. 'Now?'

'I don't want her waking up in here later, on her own.' Bridget pivoted and studied her rear in the mirror. 'She should brush her teeth, but I suppose I can let it go this once.'

A thought occurred. 'Who's babysitting?'

Bridget stopped preening and a wrinkle appeared on her brow. 'I'd have thought that was obvious,' she said. 'You are.'

Chapter Eighteen

It was a measure of how much wine was in Bridget's bloodstream that she didn't completely freak out when I told her I'd promised to look after Jack, as Seth's mother was going home.

'You put Seth Donovan's son before your own niece?' She sounded more hurt than annoyed, which was rich considering she hadn't asked me to babysit. If I'd thought about it, I'd have expected her to hunt down a childcare expert, not trust her useless sister to look after her daughter.

'He was going to cancel,' I said, handing her the blazer to try on with the dress. 'I didn't want you to miss your date, so I offered my services.'

'Well… that was nice of you, I suppose.' She spoilt it by adding, 'But you don't know anything about children.'

I managed not to roll my eyes, or say *why do you want me to babysit Romy then*? 'I've got to know Jack a little bit. I'll be fine.'

'Fancy you looking after Seth Donovan's son.' Her eyes saucered wide, as if the absurdity had just hit her. '*Seth Donovan*!'

'He's just a man,' I said drily. 'He bleeds like the rest of us.'

'Oh god, what am I going to do?' Clutching the blazer, she glanced at Romy who was beginning to stir, making soft whispery sounds as if in the grip of a dream. 'I'm supposed to be meeting him at the restaurant at eight. Should I take her with me?'

'Why don't I take her?' I said impulsively. 'I can look after them both at the cottage.'

Bridget's expression hovered between hope and indecision. 'Oh, Tilly, I don't know.'

'Seth trusts me with Jack, so…' I let the words hang for a moment.

'But will Seth mind? It seems a bit much for him to meet my daughter before he's even met me.'

'I'll text him.'

She chewed her bottom lip – a gesture I remembered from watching her do her maths homework at the kitchen table, before she got fed up of her kid sister asking her what she was 'drawing' and flounced up to her bedroom.

'But Romy's so much younger, and it'll be confusing for her.'

'It'll be a lovely, mind-broadening adventure,' I said, in a no-nonsense tone Mary Poppins would have approved of. 'And she'll get to meet a really nice boy who has lots of toys that she can play with.' I had no idea whether Jack had toys that would be suitable for a two-year-old, but Romy's face lit up.

'TOYS!' she shrieked, immediately awake. She leapt up and bounced on the bed, hair drifting with static, and Bridget peered at the alarm clock beside the bed and bolted out of the room, muttering about needing a stylist to sort her out.

By the time I'd texted Seth and whipped around the house, gathering things that Romy might need – according to Bridget's shouted instructions – and Bridget had transformed into a semblance of her former self, with glossy waves, smoky eyes and red lips, it was time to leave.

'Will I do?' She paraded downstairs with Mum's velvet blazer hooked over one shoulder, but it was obvious from her posture that she knew she did, and all I had to do was whistle and nod. 'Seth won't know what's hit him,' I said, which was clearly the right response as she gripped my shoulders, kissed my cheek and said, 'Thank you,' in a heartfelt way that left me speechless.

Romy seemed bemused when Bridget crouched to help her on with her coat, and kept touching her hair, open-mouthed. 'Queen,' she said reverentially, as if her mother was a fairy tale character who'd sprung from the pages of a book. She beamed at us when we laughed. 'Not Mummy!' she pronounced.

'It *is* Mummy, but nicer.' Romy laughed loudly at my comment, despite not understanding, while Bridget tutted and smoothed the skirt of Mum's dress. 'I told you it would suit you,' I said.

'OK, Stella McCartney.' She straightened. 'Let's get Romy into the car.'

After throwing on Dad's overcoat to combat the cold outside, she transferred Romy's car seat into my Picanto and made sure her daughter was securely fastened in. Romy protested that she wanted to sit in the front – by kicking the passenger seat and shouting 'FRONT!'

'She'll be fine, don't worry,' I promised. In the brightness of the security light spilling over the driveway, Bridget was starting to look fraught, and her freshly-styled hair was being pushed around by the wind. 'Go back inside. We'll see you later.'

'Drive carefully,' she called, as if I was planning to emulate one of Seth's races. She watched as I pulled away in second gear, and was still watching as I carefully turned the corner, and I wondered whether she'd be able to enjoy her date, knowing her daughter was with someone who'd never babysat in her life.

❄ ❄ ❄

'She's cute,' said Seth as he let us into the cottage. When he'd texted to say it was fine to bring my niece, I'd wondered whether he was just saying yes to everything in the interests of 'repayment' but he seemed genuinely charmed by Romy, who was clutching my hand and looking around, her teddy tucked under one arm.

She'd been silent on the way over, but as I was considering engaging her in a nursery rhyme sing-off, I'd checked the rear-view mirror and found her looking chilled, as if she was enjoying the peace and quiet, and looking forward to an evening out.

'DOGGY!' she squealed as Digby trotted out of the living room and came to investigate the visitors with a couple of throaty woofs. ''S a doggy,' she repeated, looking at me for confirmation, while Digby sniffed at our feet.

'It is,' I said, enjoying her simple joy, thinking it might be nice to get a pet at home – except Bridget would only complain that it was something else to look after.

'His name's Digby,' Seth informed her, and we shared a smile as she passed her fingertips gently over his head. 'Do you know what colour he is?'

'Black,' she said. 'Silly.' She chuckled, as if tickled by the idea that Seth didn't know what colour his own dog was.

'He's three years old,' Seth persisted. 'How old are you?'

'Twenty-eleven,' said Romy, and ran after Digby who'd finished his snuffling and was on his way back to the living room.

'I wish I was twenty-eleven.' Seth grinned at me. 'It sounds sort of magical.'

'It actually does.' I returned his grin, thinking how nice he looked in his 'going out' clothes – a midnight blue shirt, open at the collar, and dark jeans that showed off his thighs without being too tight. Rufus had worn skinny jeans once, that left nothing to the imagination, and I'd had to fight back horrified laughter at the sight. Apparently, his sixth-formers had convinced him to get some, saying they'd make him look 'hench'. They'd made him look like a court jester, and he'd swiftly reverted to the slightly baggy blue jeans he wore when he wasn't teaching.

'You look nice.' Seth raised a brow and I immediately coloured up. I'd changed out of my sweatshirt at the last minute, into a jumper I'd spotted while finding Bridget an outfit – one that Mum rarely wore because she said the colour made her look like a blob of mustard, but somehow toned nicely with my skin and hair.

'Thanks,' I said, tugging it over the waist of my jeans, conscious my bosoms didn't make much of an impression in the kitten-soft wool. 'It's my mum's actually.' *Great piece of information, Tilly.*

'No disrespect to your mum, but I'm guessing it looks better on you.' I could feel my cheeks burning scarlet. Was this how he flirted with women? Was he practising for when he met Bridget? 'I'm guessing your mum wasn't available for babysitting duties this evening.'

'My parents are away at the moment.'

'Oh?' I hadn't taken much notice before, but his eyes were inquisitive. The sort that could make a woman feel fascinating. A different woman. Not me. 'Somewhere nice?'

'I'm sure my sister will tell you all about it.' I sidled past, avoiding his gaze. He'd put on cologne and smelt how I'd imagine an exclusive men's club would smell – all wood and leather with a top note of expensive brandy. It almost eclipsed the lovely whiff of paint hanging in the air. 'I should go and check on Romy.'

'Jack was looking forward to meeting her.'

I turned. 'He was?'

'Well, he came down from his room, which I took as a good sign, and hasn't run back up there.'

'Was your mother…?' I hesitated. 'Did she say anything after I'd gone?'

'It's hard to tell with Mum, but I think she was…' He paused, and screwed up his eyes. 'Not impressed, exactly, but I think she *nearly* liked you.'

I couldn't help laughing. 'Nearly?'

'As much as my mother likes anyone outside her immediate circle, who hasn't been educated at Oxford or Cambridge.'

'Hey, how do you know I wasn't Oxbridge educated?'

'Because you still have a local accent, and lack an air of entitlement?'

'Ooh, that's mean.' I was still smiling. 'I'm sure not everyone who went to Oxford feels a sense of entitlement.'

'Hey, how come you don't have a Canadian accent if you lived over there for ten years?'

'You've lived abroad,' I countered. 'How come you don't have an Italian accent?'

'*Per favore, penso di no, alla prossima, mi dispiace,*' he replied, with an exaggerated flourish, eyes smouldering in the manner of a passionate Italian.

'You speak the language?' I was impressed, in spite of myself. The only accent sexier than a French one was an Italian one.

'Actually, they're just a few basic words and phrases I picked up over there,' he admitted. 'Please; I don't think so; 'til next time; I'm sorry.'

'Ah.' I nodded. 'Sounds like you spent a lot of time apologising.'

'A lot,' he said wryly. 'Not that it did me much good.'

Something I couldn't find a word for flowed between us, and I jumped when thunderous music erupted from the living room.

Rushing through, I saw Romy – big-eyed with fright – gripping the television remote, the volume deafening, Jack on the sofa in his pyjamas and dressing gown, hands clapped over his ears, while Digby spun in circles, barking with excitement.

'Give it to me, Romy.' I took the remote from her outstretched hand and stabbed at the buttons, somehow switching channels several times. There was a horrible moment when skimpily-clad females were thrusting their pumped up buttocks at the screen, while a rapper in leather and sunglasses droned, 'Ma bitches, I love ma bitches. I really love dem bitches.'

'BITCHES!' Romy bellowed, and I finally jabbed the off button before she started twerking. In the silence that followed, I looked round to see Seth in the doorway, a hand over his eyes, shoulders shaking with laughter, and Jack started giggling; a wonderful gurgling sound that made Digby cock his head. Romy shunted her coat onto the floor and scrambled up beside Jack, her plump legs, encased in woollen tights, barely reaching the edge of the sofa.

'Tree!' She pointed to the hastily decorated Christmas tree, which hadn't been touched since our efforts earlier, but looked somehow charming, especially with the lights casting a rainbow of colours across the wall. 'Pretty,' she mused, and it struck me as funny that she liked it just as much as the perfectly decorated one at home.

'She's got good taste,' Seth murmured, eyes twinkling almost as brightly as the lights. 'Hey, buddy,' he said to Jack, coming over to the sofa. 'I'll see you later, OK?' He ruffled Jack's hair. 'You be a good boy for Tilly, and go to bed when she tells you to.'

'I'm not a baby,' Jack protested, shifting away from Seth's touch, and I felt a pinch in my heart as the laughter drained from his face.

'I'm not a baby, too,' said Romy – the longest sentence I'd ever heard from her.

'We'll be fine,' I assured Seth, wanting to bring back his smile. 'No partying, no alcohol, no eighteen certificate films.'

'Sounds a bit dull.' His mouth lifted, but some of the brightness had left his eyes. He'd be no good to Bridget if he left the house feeling bad.

'Hey, how many marks out of ten would you give your dad's outfit?' I said to Jack. 'Give him a twirl.' I motioned to Seth, who looked mortified. 'Go on!'

He obliged, doing a slow spin on the spot, hands out to the side, his eyebrows raised while Jack watched, as if he couldn't help himself – as if he'd never imagined his dad doing something playful.

'Maybe… eight and a half?' he offered. 'You should wear a suit for going out.'

'I should?' Seth looked down at his jeans. 'I was going for smart casual.'

'It's OK,' Jack conceded, turning his attention back to Digby who'd climbed up on the sofa. Romy was trying to pull him onto her lap. 'Careful,' Jack said to her, adjusting the lapel of his dressing gown. 'He's quite heavy.'

'Go,' I whispered to Seth. 'Have fun.'

He stood for a moment, watching the children, as if he wanted nothing more than to throw himself down beside them, and I sensed the effort it took to turn and head for the hallway. 'You've got my number?' he said, over his shoulder.

'You know I have.' I tutted. 'I texted you earlier.'

'Oh, yes.' He looked distracted as he pulled on a black pea coat with a purple lining and patted his pockets. 'Well… call if you need me.'

'Go.' I made a shooing motion. 'Don't keep my sister waiting.'

He held up his hands. 'OK, I'm gone.' With a final glance at each of us, he took his keys off the table by the door and left, and I stood for a moment, feeling somehow bereft.

Chapter Nineteen

An hour later, I was wondering why I'd never babysat before, when it was proving to be such fun. Romy was full of beans after her earlier nap, and excited about being somewhere new, so after locating some popcorn in a kitchen cupboard I microwaved a bowlful and we all settled down to watch *Paddington 2* – which was so good, I made a mental note to watch the first *Paddington* (again) at the earliest opportunity.

Seth and Bridget texted twice to ask how things were going, and I replied *Swimmingly!* along with a selfie of us bathed in the glow of the television screen, tongues out, Digby's tail in blurry shot as he attempted to get in on the action. I considered texting Bridget to ask how the date was going, but decided against it. It would be awkward for her to reply in the middle of dinner, and my mind got stuck on an image of them, staring at each other over plates of spaghetti, lost for words – which was silly when they both had enough baggage to fill any conversational gaps.

When the film finished, no one wanted to move, so I suggested a game I'd loved playing as a child, when Dad would give me the first line of a story to carry on, and we had to take it in turns to keep it going. Usually Mum would join in, and things would quickly descend into silliness. Jack embraced the idea with surprising enthusiasm.

'Once upon a time there was a boy who…' I began, unoriginally.

'… was made of seaweed…' he continued, bare feet curled beneath him, one arm slung over Digby who was lying across us, while Romy snuggled against me, absently stroking my arm.

'*Seaweed*?' I grinned. 'OK… was made of seaweed, which meant he lived on the beach…'

Romy's head shot up. 'He made a sandcastle!'

'It was a *ginormous* sandcastle.' Jack demonstrated with his hands. 'And he decided to live in it…'

'… but then the tide came in, and…' I made big eyes and looked at Romy.

'WHALE!' she yelled, and Digby's ears twitched.

'The boy climbed on the whale's back and it swam into the ocean…' Jack gave me an expectant smile that made my heart fill.

'… where they met a mermaid…'

'Mermaid!' Romy loud-whispered.

'… who had a beard and sticky-out ears…' said Jack.

I laughed. '… and was driving a Lamborghini, then…'

'… they drove to the moon…'

'Moon is made of cheese!' declared Romy.

I stroked her hair back. '… where they saw three blind mice…'

Jack wriggled upright. '… and one of the mice had a sword and said…'

'Bitches!' Romy looked gleeful as she and Jack descended into hysterical giggles.

There then followed a game of I spy, which Jack proved particularly good at, suggesting 'Something beginning with C' which turned out to be 'claw'. Digby looked shy as we examined his paw and Jack flushed with pleasure when I exclaimed how clever he was, and that I'd never have guessed.

'Spy beginning wiv TREE!' Romy pointed at the Christmas tree and Jack rolled onto Digby, helpless with laughter, and when she shouted POO! for the comedy value, I knew it was time to calm things down.

I suggested I make some hot chocolate and while we sipped it, Romy – using her trainer cup for safety – said she was going to ask Father Christmas for a dog like Digby, and Jack told her about the horses when he'd lived with his grandmother; in particular one called Velvet, who blew steam out of his nose like a dragon, which made Romy's mouth drop open in awe. 'Want a dragon for Christmas, *and* a unicorn.'

Jack explained kindly that unicorns weren't real, and Romy said they were because she'd 'seened one in the toyshop'. By this time, her eyelids were drooping, and Jack was doing face-splitting yawns, and when I suggested it might be time for bed, neither offered any resistance.

Romy balled herself on the sofa, a cushion under her head, and by the time I'd pulled down the chenille throw off the back and placed it around her she was almost asleep.

'I'll brush my teeth in the morning,' Jack announced, and I didn't push it. He let me enter his room and watch him throw off his dressing gown and climb into bed, and when I scrunched his duvet around him, he didn't struggle – just eyed me drowsily, his pupils enormous in the glow from his rocket lamp.

'Curtains open or closed?' I was fighting an urge to press my lips to his forehead, guessing he wouldn't like it.

'Open,' he whispered, eyes drifting to the window. 'I want to see if it snows.'

It struck me out of nowhere that his mother would never share the moment her son saw snow for the first time – or any of his milestones

– and I couldn't help hoping she somehow knew how hard Seth was trying to do the right thing for their child.

'I really hope it does,' I whispered back, tears filming my eyes. 'You'll be able to build a snowman with your dad.'

'A sand snowman,' he murmured.

'Sand snowman?'

'A snowman on the beach,' he said. 'My dad said we can make one together when it snows.'

'Perfect.' I blinked hard as he shuffled onto his side, palms tucked under his cheek like a boy in a picture book.

'Lamp on or off?'

'Off.'

I obliged, and the room was bathed by the light of the moon outside, sparkling through the darkness.

'Night, Tilly.'

'Night, Jack.' I couldn't resist, after all, kissing my fingers and pressing them to his forehead. 'Sleep tight.'

Downstairs, Romy was snoring softly, one arm curled around Teddy, and I switched off the overhead light and beckoned to Digby, figuring he might need to go out. I'd barely got the back door open before he shot into the garden and cocked his leg, and I shivered, hugging myself as I walked round to look at the globe of the moon, silvering the sea in the cove. It was obvious Seth had been hard at work in the garden, transforming it into a space I could imagine Jack playing, though it was impossible to pick out the colours in the moonlight.

I called Digby back and he obediently returned, slipping past me and running upstairs, where I guessed he'd nose Jack's bedroom door open and head for the rug by his bed.

Yawning, I made some coffee, and wondered again how Seth and Bridget were getting on, and why I was having such a hard time visualising them getting to know one another. I could only picture Bridget slumped at the table at home, her braless boobs sagging beneath whichever top of Mum's or Dad's she was sporting, and Seth's face as he ruffled Jack's hair, filled with hope that his son would turn and look at him adoringly.

Filled with a restlessness I couldn't explain, I quickly replied *No worries!* with a smiley face to Rufus, who'd apologised again for the mess the paint had made, then searched some trade websites as far away as Plymouth and left some enquiries.

Deciding to check out the workmen's efforts from earlier, I clicked the brass light-switch in the room next door, and the recessed lighting sprang to life. Three of the walls had been painted a warm shade of primrose, which complemented the pale grey wallpaper on the fourth, and the floorboards were sanded and waxed a rich rosewood colour. I had to hand it to Felicity, if she'd chosen the colour scheme herself – she had good taste. Not over the top, but not too neutral either. The only bum note was the rather formal dining table surrounded by high-backed chairs in the centre of the room, that looked expensive but well-worn, as if they'd come from her own house. Too ceremonial for my taste. I preferred the table in the kitchen, but could easily imagine Bridget in this room, presiding over a healthy well-cooked meal. Not cooked by her, of course, but I would imagine she and Seth could stretch to employing a chef – or maybe Seth would cook as he'd mentioned it was something he was learning to do.

An image nudged into my head: Seth persuading Bridget to sample his pasta sauce, holding a silver spoon to her lips, his hand underneath to catch any drips, their eyes meeting, then dinner quickly forgotten as passion overtook them, and Bridget began reaching for Seth's belt…

My thoughts took a sideways dive, and put Jack in the picture, arms folded, a sullen set to his face, and Romy slinging handfuls of rice at the pair from her potty as she demanded to have her bottom wiped.

Immediately ashamed, I switched to an image of Seth and Bridget wrapped lovingly in each other's arms. Not post-coitally – maybe watching a sunset, or sunrise, or perhaps the six o'clock news, or maybe having a quick cuddle before Seth put the bins out and Bridget went off to work – a long commute that would take her away for weeks at a time, leaving Seth lonely, prowling the cottage, raking his hair back, longing for a woman's touch and driven to calling…

ENOUGH! I ordered my raging thoughts, wondering what was wrong with me. Maybe I should have invited Rufus over to babysit with me – though try as I might, I couldn't see him playing I spy or making up silly stories; but whose fault was that? To date, we'd only ever been out for meals and drinks on our own, where I'd spent most of my time rebuffing Rufus's eager attempts to 'draw me out'.

Sighing, I tipped what was left of my coffee down the sink, and ran my hands under the cold water tap, feeling a need to go swimming – which was pretty inconvenient considering it was after ten, and I was in charge of two young children.

I jumped as the landline on the worktop rang, and snatched it up, before it woke the children. 'At last-a! Seth-a, my darling, please-a do not-a hang-up-a. I just want to say one thing-a.' It was a woman, her strong – almost comedy – Italian accent adding an 'a' to nearly every word, and I realised at once it was Gina – his fiery ex.

'Seth's not here,' I said politely, conjuring a seductive Monica Belluci lookalike. 'Can I pass on a message?'

'Oh yes, please-a do,' she said, all husky-voiced. 'I tried-a to tell-a the woman who answered before-a, but she was… how you say? *Un vecchio barbone*… an old-a bat-a. No. A bitch-a.'

'She was just looking out for her son,' I said, surprising myself by defending Felicity. 'You called him a shit in the message you left, and his son heard.'

Her gasp was off the scale theatrical. 'I'm-a *so* sorry about-a that. I don't-a want-a to hurt either of them!' she cried. 'I know how much he want-a to be with his son. I was so frustrated that I could not tell him this-a, because he blocked-a my number,' she said. 'I went-a to a lot-a of trouble to get-a hold of this-a one, to try to tell-a him that-a I understand-a why he had-a to go, that I wish-a him all-a the very best. That I'm so glad-a he's found-a a new mamma for little Jack-a.'

How did she know he was out with Bridget? *New mamma* was a bit strong. But no one knew about their date, apart from Seth and he obviously hadn't spoken to Gina.

'Couldn't you just have told him this in the first place?' I said. 'Then he wouldn't have blocked your number.'

'I was so angry then,' she admitted, her voice now soaked with tears. 'I loved-a him *so* much, and couldn't accept-a that he did-a not want-a me… the most-a beautiful woman-a in all of Italy.' Wow, she was full of herself. 'It's a title the media gave-a me, a long-a time ago, after my first-a film,' she said silkily, and I wondered whether she *was* in fact Monica Belluci, using a pseudonym. 'But is true.'

'Right,' I said. 'Well, I'll certainly pass on your message, and thank you for calling.'

'Tell Seth I won't-a trouble him again, *angelo*.' Angel. I immediately thought of Jack, when he'd spoken about going to heaven. 'My heart is at-a peace now.'

'I'm glad to hear it.' *Could I sound any more British?* 'Cheerio.'

After she'd hung up, I stood for a moment, her voice ringing in my ears, feeling as if I'd just nodded off and had a peculiar dream. Then I found a pen and notepad in a drawer and scribbled *Gina called to say she's very happy for you and Jack's new 'mamma' and said she won't call again, her heart's at peace now.*

Then I went through to the living room and picked up my mobile to message Cassie and Meg.

I'm babysitting tonight. Thoughts?

Meg replied right away. *Ha ha, you nearly had me there!!*

Cassie's response was a crying-with-laughter emoji, and a gif of a woman in a cab, advising her toddlers to call 911 if they needed anything.

Laughing softly, so as not to disturb Romy, I typed, *Thanks for believing in me* and added a crying face.

Oh my god, has Bridget entrusted you with her offspring?? I could almost hear Meg's disbelief but knew it was directed at my sister, not me.

She and Seth are on their date. I'm minding Jack too, at the cottage.

Cassie's response made my eyes prick. *I bet they love you* she wrote, alongside a big red heart. *How's it going?*

Suspiciously well.

Seth Donovan's on a date with your sister? Meg's eyes were probably bulging. *How did that come about???*

I filled them in as best I could, fingers flying over the screen while Romy slumbered beside me on the sofa, and the television played soundlessly in the background.

I'll pop into the café tomorrow for a proper catch-up Cassie wrote back, and Meg said she'd hang around after delivering her cake of the day because *I need to know whether it's the start of an amazing love story – or whether Bridget has put him off women for life.*

After promising them all the details, I put my phone down and looked around the room. It was still pretty minimalist, but I figured Seth might not have had anything – apart from his personal items – to bring from Italy, and was more or less starting from scratch. There weren't even any Christmas cards, but that wasn't too surprising considering they didn't know anyone local – and I doubted the crowd that Seth had known were the type to send them. I didn't write many myself these days, though Mum loved the routine of a Christmas card list, and usually sent out a pile to arrive on the first of December.

There were no pictures on the walls yet, and no framed photos anywhere, but I spotted what looked like a brown leather wallet wedged down the side of the sofa where I was sitting and tugged it out. It was a small album with plastic pages for pictures to slot inside, and was stuffed with images of Jack, from baby to boyhood, that I guessed Felicity must have put together. There were a few of Seth too as a boy, faded with time, looking a lot like Jack did now. I smiled at the sight of him astride a horse, aged around seven, wearing a riding hat that was much too big and a scowl on his face.

Another showed Seth in a smart school uniform, solemn-faced, but in another he was smiling as he kicked a ball to a tall man with floppy blond air I assumed must be his dad. The same man – older – appeared again, with Jack on his shoulders, grinning at the camera towards the end of the album. There were no pictures of Jack with his mother, other than the one I'd seen in his bedroom, but I supposed that Seth might have some to show him one day. If Felicity had ever had any, she'd probably destroyed them.

Putting the album back where I'd found it, I pushed a curl of hair off Romy's cheek, before slipping upstairs to check on Jack. I could just make out his shape under the duvet in the moonlight, but he was clearly sleeping soundly. Digby, coiled on the rug, didn't stir.

I'd intended to go back downstairs, and perhaps find a film to watch, but found myself in the bedroom next door instead. I wasn't snooping, I told myself. I was curious that was all, looking in from the doorway. There wasn't much to see. A lamp on a table by the bed was switched on and the bed was neatly made, a couple of shirts flung across the plain duvet cover, as if Seth had tried on a couple before settling for the one he was wearing. An oak wardrobe and matching chest of drawers were the only other furniture, both with a sheen of newness, but there was a framed photo on top of the chest that I couldn't resist creeping in to take a look at. It was a black-and-white shot of Seth, holding a tiny baby Jack, kissing his forehead even though Jack's mouth was wide, exercising his lungs. I smiled, somehow reassured by the picture, and was about to back away, when I glanced through the window and saw a sweep of headlights coming from the road leading down to the cottage. I hurried out to the landing, where I had a clear view of Seth pulling up and getting out of his car. He moved round to the passenger side, and opened the door and Bridget emerged, laughing at something he'd said. She stumbled a little in her heels and he caught her arm, and looked to be smiling too, and then her arms were around his neck, and they were kissing, and I didn't have time to dart away before Seth glanced up and saw me.

Chapter Twenty

Heart thumping, I ran back down to the living room in time to hear Seth's key in the front door, and suddenly they were inside, and Bridget was trying to smother laughter and saying, 'Shhh!' in an exaggerated whisper.

I threw myself on the sofa as she came in, face aglow in a way I couldn't remember seeing since Romy was born, though the glow had been short-lived and she'd merely looked exhausted. Chad had live-streamed the birth to us in Canada.

'You didn't drive?' I said, as though I didn't already know.

'Had a teensy drink, so left the car at the restaurant.' She pointed, all gooey-eyed. 'There she is! My beautiful, beautiful girl.'

'Why, thank you,' I said.

Bridget giggled for an unsettlingly long time. 'I was talking about Romy.'

'I know, I was joking.' I glanced at Seth who'd followed her through, smelling of wine and good food, and the cold air outside – surely tonight it would snow – but he seemed to be avoiding my gaze. I noticed his hair was rumpled, as if Bridget had run her fingers through it; though it could have been the breeze. 'I hope you weren't bombarded with fans, and requests for selfies,' I said to him.

'Lovely food.' Seth pushed his keys into his coat pocket, still not looking at me. 'And no one seemed to recognise me or, if they did, they left me alone.' His face was harder to read than Bridget's. 'How was Jack?'

'Perfect.'

At last, his eyes landed on mine. 'Honestly?'

'Cross my heart.'

Bridget had lurched to the sofa to gaze at a still sleeping Romy, but now straightened and grabbed Seth's hand. 'I want a grand tour,' she said. Her slightly glazed eyes flashed around the room, taking it all in. Despite her assertion that living in a cottage by the sea was 'romantic', I knew she'd have expected something grander because of who Seth was, and the images she'd seen online of his villa in Italy. 'Bit bare,' she concluded, though her Notting Hill house – from what I recalled from my very infrequent visits – was hardly stuffed with furniture, just expensive 'pieces' that spoke more of her ability to be able to afford them, than her own, personal taste. 'And what's *that*?' She recoiled from the sight of the Christmas tree before sweeping Seth out of the room, heels clacking like a shire horse.

'Can we do this another time?' I said, as Seth threw me an unguarded look of helplessness over his shoulder, but she was already dragging him to the room next door and I got up and hastily followed.

'Hey, you've done a nice job in here,' she said, after crashing the light on and tottering over to the gleaming dining table. 'I was telling Seth how good you were at interior design and that he was lucky to have you.'

'You were?' I found it hard to imagine Bridget bigging me up to anyone, let alone Seth.

'She was,' Seth confirmed in a meaningful way, and I realised he was letting me know that, as far as my sister was concerned, I was still doing up the cottage – that he'd guessed I hadn't told her Felicity had beaten me to it.

'Oh. Well, thanks,' I muttered, a hot wave of guilt moving through me.

'And you think you'll get it all done before Christmas?' Doubt clouded Bridget's features, as if what she'd seen had convinced her I'd need at least a year to make the place look habitable.

'She's got a team in to help,' Seth said.

'Ooh, I didn't know you had a *team.*' Far from being sarcastic, Bridget sounded impressed as she sized up the room through narrowed eyes. 'Good for you, Tilly Campbell,' she slurred. 'I always knew you had it in you to be successful, once you stopped being a lazy cow.'

There was the Bridget I knew. 'How much has she had to drink?' I asked Seth. He was looking intently from Bridget to me as if trying to work out how we could possibly be related. I guessed I wasn't coming out of it well.

'Oi!' She wagged a finger at me. 'You know I don't drink.' She hiccupped gently. 'I might have had a couple of glasses of vino, but I'm not battered.' She was definitely battered. She'd never have used the word battered otherwise, and definitely not with a hint of her old Devon accent.

'It was just a couple of glasses, but she did mention she doesn't normally drink, so…' Seth shrugged, seeming amused, and I could tell he was completely taken with her – and why wouldn't he be? Apart from her ferocious intelligence, she could be warm and witty, and looked stunning – even with faded lipstick, and a hint of curl returning to her straightened hair.

She leaned on one of the dining chairs, presenting her cleavage like a gift, and I noted Seth's gaze was drawn there, as if her breasts were magnets.

'I expect I'm driving you home, then.' My voice was too loud.

'I wanna see the rest of the house.' Straightening up, Bridget crossed her arms, hoisting her bosoms even closer to her chin. 'Can we go upstairs?' she asked Seth.

'Erm…' He rubbed his cheek, darting me a look I couldn't decipher. 'I'd rather not disturb Jack,' he said.

It dawned on me what Bridget was really asking.

'What about Romy?' I'd gone the full Mary Poppins now – only sterner, and more disapproving. 'And what am I supposed to do, while you two…?' I flapped my hand between them. 'Do the business?'

'The business?' Bridget looked befuddled.

'*Business?*' Seth sounded vaguely appalled.

'You know I like checking out bathrooms,' said Bridget. I didn't, but I'd clearly misunderstood. She was merely hoping the decor upstairs was a touch more luxurious than what she'd encountered so far.

'I thought…' I began, but Seth leapt in.

'The bathroom's the least appealing room in the house, and I promise you won't like it one bit.' He cocked his elbow for Bridget to hold onto. He still had his coat on, as if he wasn't planning to stay. 'Next time, you can have the grand tour.'

So, there was going to be a next time. *Of course there was.* Which was brilliant, obviously.

'I'll hold you to that.' Bridget slipped her arm through his and let him escort her into the hallway, where she screwed up her eyes at the carpet as if seeing it for the first time. 'Christ, that's hideous,' she said. 'It's like looking through a kaleidoscope only… much worse.' She squinted up at Seth. 'I got a kaleidoscope for Christmas, once. It did my head in.'

'I'm sorry to hear that.' Seth smiled at her, clearly enchanted. 'I can't imagine any child being satisfied with a kaleidoscope these days.'

'I wasn't satisfied *then*,' Bridget declared. 'I wanted a Rubik's cube.'

'She was only five.' I'd heard the story before. 'When I was five, I wanted a doll's house.'

'Dad made one for her.' I immediately wished I hadn't brought it up. Apparently, he'd spent hours designing and building it – had insisted on putting in a spiral staircase and a working lift – leading to accusations of favouritism from fifteen-year-old Bridget, even though she'd got the violin she'd asked for that Christmas (she gave it up six months later). 'It was am*aaaaa*zing.'

'Which is why you set it on fire.' The words were out before I'd even thought about saying them.

'I didn't mean to.' Bridget checked Seth's reaction out of the corner of her eye. 'I'd been secretly smoking in Tilly's room, and accidently dropped a lit match.'

'Uh-oh,' he said, seeming fascinated.

'She did put it out, to be fair,' I explained, grabbing my jacket off the banister where I'd left it earlier. 'By throwing a glass of Coke all over it.'

'Dad only went and "renovated" it for you, anyway,' said Bridget, which was the closest she'd ever come to admitting she'd done it on purpose.

'I don't think Seth wants to hear about our childhood squabbles.' I pointed to the door. 'Why don't you wait in the car, and I'll fetch Romy out?'

She pointed at herself. '*I'll* get Romy, and *you* wait in the car.'

'You're a bit drunk, Bee. It would be easier if I carried her out.'

'She's right,' said Seth, flashing me a bland smile. 'I'll walk you to the car, Bridget.'

No doubt he was planning to thoroughly snog her again.

'Okey-doke.' She shot him a lopsided grin. 'So nice to meet a real gennelman.'

Seth glanced towards the living room. 'You might not be able to get Romy's coat back on if she's asleep,' he said, directing the words somewhere over my shoulder. 'Take the throw. You can drop it back sometime.'

'Tomorrow.' Bridget was fumbling with the door latch.

'Sorry?'

'She's workin' here, yeah? Gotta finish the job.'

'Oh.' Seth grimaced at me. 'Of course, I meant tomorrow.'

It looked like the last thing he wanted was me at the cottage, and I couldn't help wondering whether Bridget had said something about me that had made him wary – perhaps even convinced him I wasn't a fit person to be around Jack, after all.

As he manoeuvred her outside, I plucked Romy's coat and shoes from the living room floor and, making sure the throw was firmly tucked around her, picked her up and carried her outside. She barely stirred as I strapped her into her seat, while Seth did the same to Bridget in the front.

'Thanks for a lovely evening,' she was saying, pronouncing her words very carefully. 'I had a very nice time, and hope we can do it again.'

'I hope so too,' he said.

I tried to ignore the little drop in my stomach, and told myself I was glad they'd hit it off.

'Tilly's lucky getting to see you every day,' she grumbled, snatching at the lapels of his coat. Yanking his head close to hers she planted a smacker on his lips, and I looked away as I got in the car and started the engine, turning the heating up.

'Thanks again for taking care of Jack,' Seth said.

'No problem.' I sensed him looking at me, but couldn't meet his gaze, and was glad when the interior light went off.

As he closed Bridget's door, I drove off quickly, and even though I didn't check my mirrors, I knew he was watching us go and wondered what he was thinking.

'Such a nice man,' murmured Bridget, sounding sleepily happy. 'Thank you for setting me up with him, Tilly. I know I'd never have met him if it wasn't for you.'

'That's OK.' I was suddenly ashamed that I'd thought she might have bad-mouthed me to Seth. She'd even praised my design skills to him.

'Why didn't you tell me you'd saved his son from drowning?'

My head whipped round. 'He told you that?'

'Hey, watch the road!' She flapped a floppy finger at the windscreen before her head lolled back against the seat. 'Of *course* he did,' she said. 'He's so grateful, Tilly. He talked about you a lot, actually.'

'Oh?'

'He obviously feels like he owes you big time, even though he's let you loose on his cottage as a favour.'

Ignoring the last bit, I said, 'Oh.' *What had I expected?* He was still hung up on trying to repay me for saving Jack's life, which was the only reason I was still around.

'It was funny hearing someone talk about you like that,' she mused.

'Like what?'

'As if he's got a lot of respect for you, but then he would,' she went on, as if talking to herself, 'considering he'd watched you drag his son from the sea.' Now her finger was wagging in front of my face. 'Trust you to make a big splash.' She paused and chuckled. 'Splash! Do you get it?'

'Yes, Bridget, I get it.'

'You weren't stalking him, were you, and that's why you were on the beach at that precise moment?'

'Of course I bloody wasn't.' *I was having a 'grown-up' conversation with Rufus.* 'I just happened to be taking a walk.' I threw her a look. 'Why do you always think the worst of me?'

'Because I know you,' she said with a drowsy chuckle, as if I had a history of criminal behaviour, rather than a lack of ambition. Though, in Bridget's book, they amounted to the same thing. 'I expect Seth's going to pay you well for doing up the cottage.'

I focused on a tricky bend. There were no lights on this stretch of road, and the moon had vanished behind some clouds.

'You could have just accepted some money, without doing any work, but you didn't and I really admire that, Tilly. Great idea to showcase your talent instead.'

'Why would I take his money, Bee? Apart from anything else, I don't need it.'

'Well, you could have asked him to make a donation to charity,' she said. 'You know he's a patron of Save the Children, and he supports war heroes too?'

'I didn't know that.' *Why* hadn't I accepted his suggestion of a donation to charity, instead of persuading him to date my sister?

Suddenly Bridget was upright and I slowed a little, certain she was going to ask whether Seth's invitation to dinner had been a favour to me, but instead she said, 'Tilly, do you fancy him yourself?' She clutched at my arm. 'I know he's not your usual type, and you don't like being around children, but he's *soooooo* handsome and famous, and Jack sounds amazing—'

'I'm not sixteen,' I said coolly. 'I don't *fancy* Seth Donovan.' My hammering heart said otherwise, but I wasn't listening to it. 'Why would you even think that?'

'Er, because of everything I just said about him being handsome, et cetera.' She let go of me and sank back. 'I know you're with Rufus, but it wouldn't be surprising to have a crush on someone like Seth,' Bridget continued. She turned to me, her eyes illuminated in a flash of headlights coming the other way. 'I really like him.'

'Well, that's good,' I said crisply. 'Because he obviously likes you too.'

'I know.' She twisted to check on Romy and, before I could begin to process my train of thought, she said, 'I told him about you and Rufus, and how it's your first proper relationship and that you're really making a go of it.'

My grip on the steering wheel momentarily loosened, and the car did a little swerve. 'You talked to Seth about Rufus and me?'

'He was really interested.' She paused to yawn. 'Asked me what he was like.'

'What did you say?'

'That he was a teacher, came highly recommended by our father and that you're going to a wedding with him on Saturday, which might give you ideas.'

'Ideas?'

'About walking down the aisle.'

'For god's sake, Bee, can you honestly see me walking down an aisle?' I felt furious all of a sudden. I hated the idea of her discussing me with Seth behind my back. Or, at least, discussing Rufus and me, when I wasn't even sure where our relationship was going. 'We've only been seeing each other for a month or so. I've never even met his family.'

'You'll meet them on Saturday.' She tried to cross her legs, but there wasn't enough room, and she gave up. 'Good idea to see them all together under one roof.'

The thought of it made my scalp itch, and I was grateful that we'd finally arrived home and I didn't have to respond.

'Better get Romy into bed.' I whipped my seat belt off, and before Bridget had time to react I was out of the car and releasing my niece from her seat.

'Tilly,' she murmured, her breath sweet and warm on my cheek as I lifted her out. 'Want a doggy.'

'Of course you do,' I whispered, hoping Bridget hadn't overheard, but she was on the drive in her stockinged feet, shoes dangling from her fingers, gazing up at the sky.

'It's snowing,' she said, with uncharacteristic awe.

Sure enough, white flakes were whirling down, melting on my upturned face. 'Look!' I made to show Romy, but she was sleeping again, her cheek pressed into my shoulder, so I made a wish for Jack to open his eyes and look out of the window, and for Seth to be with him when he did.

'Snow!' Bridget twirled on her tiptoes, arms outstretched, as if briefly transported back to childhood. 'A perfect end to a perfect evening,' she said.

Chapter Twenty-One

'It really snowed?' Cassie glanced through the café window, to the distinctly unsnowy view outside.

'It really did,' I said gloomily. When I'd got up, after a fidgety night, I'd looked out to see that the world looked much the same as it had the day before – overcast and cold. It was as if Mother Nature had backtracked on a magical promise... or something. Or maybe the fact that I hadn't slept much accounted for my low mood. 'Bridget saw it too, so I couldn't have dreamt it.'

'Well, they're still forecasting a white Christmas.' Cassie fixed me with her big, grey eyes. 'Wouldn't it be lovely if it snowed for the party on Christmas Eve?'

'It would be inconvenient if it meant people couldn't get here.' I ignored the pointed way she'd said *party on Christmas Eve;* a subtle reminder that the function room wasn't finished. And no one had got back to me about the electrics.

'I still can't believe your sister kissed Seth Donovan.' Meg had returned with a plate of adult-only mince pies bursting with brandy-laced fruit, and planted herself at the table, next to Cassie. 'The papers would have a field day if they knew.'

'I don't think they'd be that interested, to be honest,' I said. 'I mean, he's not David Beckham famous. If you're not into Formula One, you probably wouldn't even know who he was.'

'I'm not into Formula One, but I've still heard of Damian Lewis.'

'You mean Damon Hill,' I corrected. 'Damian Lewis is that ginger actor who was in *Homeland*.'

Meg's forehead furrowed. 'I don't know who Damon Hill is.'

'Maybe you meant Lewis Hamilton?'

She looked blank. 'I've heard of James Blunt.'

Cassie giggled.

'He's a *singer*,' I said. 'And everyone's heard of James Hunt. He was the bad boy of racing, back in the day.'

'That's who I meant.' Meg looked pleased. 'I watched a film about him, once.'

'Your references are really old,' I grumbled.

'Someone's got out of bed the wrong side this morning.' She arched her eyebrows. 'Either babysitting has drained you of your life force, or you're a teensy bit jealous.'

'I actually liked babysitting,' I said. 'And why would I be jealous? Bridget's a really good match for Seth, and if seeing him keeps her in a good mood, I'm all for it.'

I'd expected her to be at least a little bit hungover at breakfast, but had found her fully dressed (albeit in a pair of Mum's stretchy trousers and one of Dad's sweaters) sitting at the kitchen table with a giant mug of tea, softly singing 'Let it Snow!' as she watched Romy eating mushed up banana on toast.

'I woke up to a very lovely text,' she'd said, but wouldn't be drawn on the contents. 'All in good time.' Tapping the side of her nose, she'd got up with a sparkly-eyed smile and made me some tea. Once I'd got over the shock of her good humour, I'd spent too much time pondering what Seth might have said in his text that couldn't have waited until they next saw each other. It must have been more than *Thanks for the lovely*

snog, or she wouldn't have been acting so secretive. I knew better than to
probe, and resisted asking as I drove her and Romy to the restaurant to
collect her car. She'd enjoy holding back, and I didn't want her to know
how curious I was.

'Anyway, Tilly's with Rufus,' Cassie was saying. I'd filled her in on
my trip to his house while we were waiting for Meg to bring her mince
pies over, and I began to explain about his botched declaration of love
on the café windows.

'He wrote, I love you Matilda Campbell in purple paint—'

'Oh my god, that's so romantic!' Meg flashed her eyes at Cassie.
'Remember when Danny wrote that message in the sand, saying he
liked you?'

'I'd hardly forget it.' She smiled, her eyes going far away. 'Nobody
had ever done anything like that for me before.'

'Me neither,' I said, wondering why I didn't feel as thrilled about
Rufus's gesture as Cassie still did about Danny's. Probably because she
hadn't had to clear up the mess afterwards.

'So, do you think he might be the one?' Meg prodded, as Cassie
crumbled a chunk of mince pie on her plate instead of eating it. 'I can't
imagine you agreeing to go to his brother's wedding if you didn't,' she
answered her own question.

'How do you even know if someone's "the one"?' I scratched speech
marks in the air.

'Well, I'm not the best person to ask.' Meg shook her shiny hair
back, and I wondered how she managed to look so gorgeous all the
time. I thought I'd made an effort, dressing in clean jeans and a loose,
cream sweater after my shower, but next to Meg, in her fitted white
jumper and stripy voile skirt, and Cassie's dungarees and zebra-print

top, I felt like a faded photo. 'I was all set to marry Sam, a few months ago,' Meg went on. 'I thought he was the one for years.'

'I didn't know right away that Danny was the one.' Cassie discreetly pushed her plate aside. 'He grew on me.'

'Very quickly,' I said.

She grinned. 'That's how it happens sometimes, I suppose. Or, there's a catalyst like, maybe you nearly lose someone and it makes you realise how important they are.'

'And other people know right away,' offered Meg. 'It's like a chemical thing.'

It was obvious I wasn't going to get the clear-cut answer I'd been hoping for – because there wasn't one. On the other hand, it was reassuring to know my slightly befuddled feelings weren't entirely unnatural.

'Just go to the wedding, and see how you get on,' Meg said soothingly. 'Maybe the magic will happen during the couple's vows, or while you and Rufus are having a smoochy dance.'

Cassie mimed an adoring look at an invisible partner. 'You'll gaze into each other's eyes during a Celine Dion number, and that'll be the moment you know.'

'If you hear that I've smooched to Celine Dion, you'll need to stage an intervention,' I said, pausing at the sight of Gwen behind the counter, in a pair of reindeer antlers, their jaunty bobbing at odds with her stony face.

'Do you remember when we got you to try those dating tips we saw on *Perfect Match*?' said Cassie, eyes bright with amusement.

Meg swallowed her mouthful of mince pie. 'I remember that show, it was awful, but we loved it.'

'We made you try them out on that boy you liked in year six...
what was his name?'

Meg snapped her fingers. 'Lennie Jamieson.'

'Hold his gaze for three seconds, touch your hair, then smile,' I
chirped, in the manner of the perky dating 'expert', who'd had the
unfortunate surname, Cox.

'Only, for some reason, you did them all at once, three times in a
row,' said Cassie.

Meg giggled. 'You looked like you had a really itchy scalp, and
Lennie came over and asked you if you'd got nits.'

'And you two almost wet yourselves laughing.'

'You weren't cut out for flirting, even then,' said Cassie. 'Not that
you had to. All the boys liked you anyway, you just didn't notice.'

'Always got your head stuck in a book.' Meg's impression of our
Maths teacher was terrible, but she'd got his expression spot on – like
a court official serving a summons.

'Books were *way* more interesting than most boys,' I said. 'Anyway,
it was Lennie Jamieson's loss.'

'Apparently he's wanted for embezzlement now and has fled to
Spain,' said Cassie. 'Danny knows someone in the police who happened
to mention it.'

'Brilliant.'

'Good job you never got together.' Meg finished her mince pie and
took a bite of Cassie's. 'You might both have been on the run.'

'A modern-day Bonnie and Clyde,' said Cassie.

'How's your portrait going?' I was keen to get off the subject of
Lennie – and men in general.

'She's given up on the lingerie idea, thank goodness.' Cassie's cheeks
were peaky, and she pushed aside her coffee. Definitely morning sick-

ness. 'She wants something Picasso-style, picking out certain features, which gives me a bit more freedom.'

A commotion at the counter drew our attention. Gwen was presiding over Meg's cake of the day: a giant Christmas pudding, dark, rich and sticky, which was gently steaming on a plate.

'What's she doing?' Meg stood up. 'She's taken the icing off it. It took me ages to make it look like snow.'

'I think she's going to set it on fire,' I said.

'No way.' Cassie's eyes were wide as we moved to the counter to join the audience that had gathered.

'Tip some on then,' Gwen was instructing a visibly trembling Jerry, who was gripping a small saucepan, a bottle of brandy at his elbow. 'A nice big dollop to get a good flame goin'.'

'Gwen, you can't,' said Cassie, in a tone that dared Gwen to disagree.

She didn't disappoint. 'It's traditional,' she said, a mutinous tilt to her jaw. 'Warm brandy, hot puddin' an' a lit match. What can possibly go wrong?'

'What about health and safety?'

'Says the woman wot filled the café with cats six months ago.'

'You wouldn't have adopted Dickens if I hadn't.'

'Exactly,' said Gwen, which immediately made us giggly.

'You only need a spoon full of brandy,' said Meg, one hand shielding her eyes as if fearing an explosion.

'Rubbish,' said Gwen, nudging Jerry's arm. 'Go on then, before it goes bleedin' cold.'

Jerry did as he was bid, while Gwen struck an extra-long match she must have brought in specially.

Around us, nervous laughter rose, along with a few gasps and murmurs of *she wouldn't*.

Oh, she would.

There was a collective intake of breath as a shaking Jerry sloshed out the contents of the pan, and Gwen leaned over the pool of liquid on the plate with the flaming match. I shouted a warning and screams broke out as blue flames leapt around the pudding and flared up. Gwen dropped the match and jumped backwards, and when she looked up, her eyebrows had disappeared.

'Bleedin' 'ell.' She snatched off her antlers and scratched her head, and the sight of her puzzled face, combined with Jerry's horror, and the smell of singed hair had us collapsing with laughter. Jerry sprang into action and tossed a sopping wet tea towel over the flickering pudding, while Gwen grabbed the bottle of brandy and took a hefty swig.

'Absolute legend,' someone said, wet-faced with mirth. 'That's totally made my Christmas.'

'My poor pudding,' Meg wheezed, wiping her eyes. 'But it was totally worth it.'

After checking no real damage had been done, to the café or Gwen – I suspected from the gleam in her eyes she was hugely enjoying herself – the customers dispersed, replaying the scene on their phones. As if nothing had happened, Gwen snapped her eyes onto me.

'Where's them floorboards then?' she demanded. 'You need to be gettin' a wiggle on.'

'On their way,' I said, hoarse from laughing, but her suspicious look suggested I was fobbing her off with excuses. 'I'll go and see what else I can do, if it'll make you happy.' I flipped my eyes up for Meg and Cassie's benefit. 'You're not very good at being patient, are you?'

'Patience is my middle name,' she said, pressing her fingertips to the reddening strips where her eyebrows had been, before following me through the plastic divider into the function room. 'After my great-grandma, Patience Green, a suffragette.'

'Is that true, Gwen?'

'On me cousin's grave.'

'Maureen's still alive.'

'Me 'uvver cousin, Brett,' she said. ''E fell over puttin' 'is socks on and 'it is 'ead on the garage door. 'E were only seventy-five.'

'Seventy-five's quite old.' I had no intention of asking why he'd been putting his socks on in the garage.

'Not these days, it ain't.'

Her eyes – somehow smaller and naked without their furry pelmets – were probing the room as though picturing it finished. On impulse, I reached for one of the paint tins. 'I might as well make a start on the walls myself.'

'I fort you 'ad to do the floor first, or you get dust on the paint, or summink.'

'It'll be fine as long as I'm careful,' I said.

'What about the decorators?'

'I'm capable of slapping some on myself,' I said. 'On the walls,' I amended when Gwen's invisible eyebrows rose. Every time I looked at her, I had to bite back a giggle. 'The decorators will be pleased. They weren't happy about the schedule being mucked about.' I didn't mention they'd warned they might not be able to squeeze the job in this side of Christmas.

'Not bein' funny, it's just I'm in charge while Ed and Lydia are away and I don't want nuffink goin' wrong.' Said the woman who could have burnt down the café.

'Neither do I.' I stood up, cradling a tin of paint. 'Trust me, Gwen, I want the room to be ready for Christmas Eve just as much as you do, if not more. You just focus on sorting out the drink and food and entertainment, and leave the rest to me.'

'It's already done,' said Gwen. 'Cassie's bruvver and 'is mate Fletcher's agreed to do the music.'

'Oh, that's good.' Cassie's brother had been quite famous before leaving his band to settle in Seashell Cove and become a dad. 'That'll be the first time he's played in ages.'

'Some of us is organised.'

'So was I,' I protested. 'I didn't know a pipe was going to spring a leak, did I?'

Gwen looked like she might be about to argue, but the sound of a cup smashing on tiles drew her attention away. 'He's a right but-terfingers.' She was no doubt referring to Jerry. 'That's the second time this mornin'.' Her face broke into a devilish grin. 'I reckon 'e's doin' it to attract my attention.'

It was a measure of how enamoured she was that she didn't rush off and demand he pay for a replacement, like she had when I'd dropped and broken a saucer during my ill-fated 'helping out' session.

'It might have been a customer,' I said, and she disappeared so fast I wouldn't have been surprised to see sparks shoot off her heels.

After fetching the paintbrushes and rollers I kept in the boot of my car – I'd been known to get hands-on with painting before – I rolled up my sleeves and made a start, laughing softly as I thought about Meg's poor Christmas pudding. On cue, she popped her head round to say she was heading back to the bakery, and Cassie had gone as she wasn't feeling too good.

'You're doing a great job,' she added. 'It's just a shame the floor isn't down yet.'

'It will be.'

As I painted, I relaxed and got into a rhythm, enjoying the precision of reaching into the corners, careful not to smudge paint on the wooden ceiling beams.

'Good job you're seven feet tall,' said Gwen, coming in with the phone in her hand to find me on tiptoes, paint splattered down my arm as I nudged the very edge of the brush into the final corner. 'Not bad.' She cast a critical gaze round, her naked forehead crinkling. 'What's the shade again?'

'Sea Mist.' I wiped the back of my hand across my cheek, where a strand of hair had got stuck. 'Looks OK, doesn't it?' I stood back to admire the effect, loving the way it reflected the colours outside – just as it would when the sun was out, or when it was snowing, or raining. 'It's designed to blend with whatever's happening outdoors, like a trick of the eye,' I explained.

'It's what I'd imagine pollution would look like, if it was a colour.' Gwen's head was cocked, and I could see she was making a genuine point and had to hide a smile.

'But could just as easily be a cloud, or a puddle, or a rainbow,' I enthused. 'That's what I love about it.'

'S'only bleedin' paint.' She held out the phone. "S'your sister.'

'Bridget?' Surprised into almost dropping the paintbrush, I laid it across the open tin and wiped my hands down my jeans.

'Unless you've got another sister, then yes.' Rolling her eyes, Gwen passed me the handset. 'I'll get you some coffee,' she said on her way out. 'I'll put a bit of brandy in it.'

'How come you're calling me here?' I said, pressing the phone to my ear, realising as I spoke that I'd left my mobile in the car.

'Because you weren't answering your mobile.' Bridget's voice sounded oddly compressed. 'I thought you'd be at Seth's, but he said he hadn't seen you yet,' *shit*, 'so I guessed you'd be at your other job.'

Other job. I never thought of what I did as *jobs.* Have a job was being paid for regular employment: working in an office, commuting to work, putting in forty hours or more a week; doing something you didn't enjoy very much. 'Yes, I'm, er, here,' I said. 'I left my phone in the car.'

'You should keep it with you at all times, Tilly, especially if you're hoping to get more work. If potential customers can't get hold of you straight away, they'll simply go elsewhere.'

'I'll take that on board, boss,' I said, aiming for levity. 'Everything OK?'

I guessed it must be, or she wouldn't be blathering about phones and jobs, but I couldn't imagine she'd be ringing for a chat either. 'How was Seth?'

'Hmm? Oh, fine,' she said quickly. 'He sounded distracted.'

Distracted. What did that mean? Was Jack OK? Had Felicity been on the phone? Maybe Digby wasn't well, or *the team* hadn't turned up, or something had gone wrong—

'Tilly!'

'What?' I realised I'd tuned out. 'Sorry, Bee, I was just, er... checking the fuse board with the electrician.' *Chance would be a fine thing.*

'Oh, right.' She did a laugh that sounded as if it was for someone else's benefit. 'Well, I was just saying that Rufus is here if you'd like to take a lunch break and pop over.'

Chapter Twenty-Two

I drove home wondering what Rufus was doing at my house. He must be at a loose end, though I couldn't imagine it somehow. Didn't he have Christmas shopping or something to do?

More importantly, why was I a bit put out at the thought of him turning up out of the blue? Because he hadn't been invited? It wasn't as if he'd never been to the house before, and if we were in a relationship, I'd have to get used to it. I could hardly keep seeing him without ever bringing him home.

'That's what people with boyfriends do,' I said out loud. Danny was like part of the family at Cassie's house, and Meg's mum had practically adopted Nathan, who sadly didn't have a mother of his own.

Would Mum and Dad eventually see Rufus as the son they'd never had? I couldn't quite conjure a set-up where we were all sitting around the table, enjoying a Sunday roast, or watching something together on the television – probably because it was something I'd never done. I had no idea whether Rufus watched anything but sport on TV and, if he did, what he liked. Or what his favourite music/colour/animal/star sign was. No, that was a lie. I did know his star sign, because his birthday was three days after mine, which meant we were both Virgos; though Rufus had more of the traits than I did, being meticulous, practical and reliable – though his recent outburst of love wasn't exactly typical.

Still, his brother's wedding was an hour's drive away, which meant I could fill in the gaps on the way there and back. Maybe I should draw up a list of things to ask – favourite childhood memory, first kiss, would he rather be a ninja or a pirate? (Ninja for me – much cooler, plus I get seasick.) I could ask the big things too – did he want children? Who did he vote for in the last election? Did he believe in the right to die? What was his favourite snack?

I was starting to feel sweaty and nauseous and opened the car window a notch. I was probably hungry. All the hilarity at the café, and then the painting, had worked up an appetite, and I hadn't had a chance to drink Gwen's brandy-coffee.

After parking behind Rufus's shiny, economical, hybrid car, I burst into the kitchen to find him ensconced at the table, opposite Bridget, who'd made an effort with her hair, and was wearing lipstick, and one of Mum's nicer cardigans – cream with pearly buttons – with a pair of narrow-cut jeans that enhanced her curves. Obviously meeting Seth was having a knock-on effect. Maybe they'd arranged to see each other again.

'What are you doing here?' I turned to Rufus, who was rising from the table, smoothing his hands down his trousers, and I noticed a festive bouquet on the worktop, scarlet and green with pine cones, their scent rather overpowering.

'Just thought I'd pop in and say hi.' He came over to press a kiss on my cheek and squeezed my upper arm. 'I brought Christmas flowers.'

'So I see,' I said. 'They're lovely, thank you.' *No one had ever bought me flowers before.* 'I thought you'd be busy.' Steering clear of the bouquet, which was inducing a headache, I plucked a clementine from the fruit bowl and peeled it.

'I got fed up of practising my speech.' He sat back down, clearly at home in our kitchen as he picked up the mug of black coffee that Bridget must have made. 'I was wondering what you'd like for Christmas.'

'Oh, you don't have to get me anything.' His face fell and I was pricked with guilt that I hadn't considered buying him a gift. 'The flowers are enough,' I said. 'Maybe we can have a look at the sales in the New Year?'

He brightened – whether at the idea of shopping, or because I was planning ahead, I couldn't tell. 'Good idea,' he said. 'There's some nice leather goods in Tanner Bates, but they're a bit pricey. Bound to come down after Christmas.'

Still in my jacket, I crossed to where Romy was leaning over a book, painstakingly colouring in. 'Ooh, a blue Minion, that's unusual.' I felt a stab of affection as I spotted the wax crayon clutched in her chubby fist.

'I like blue.' She paused to swipe a curl of hair off her forehead and threw me an angelic smile.

'She keeps saying more than one word.' Bridget's tone was a mix of bemusement and wonder as she moved from the table to the worktop.

'Blue!' shouted Romy, and we laughed.

'Blue's a good colour.' I sat beside her and ate a segment of fruit, smiling in Rufus's direction. 'I haven't got long,' I said. 'I'm supposed to be working.'

'Your sister was telling me you've quite a lot on at the moment.' He put down his mug and rested his forearms on the table, lacing his fingers together. He looked as if he was about to interview me; very teacher-like in his pale pink shirt. It was gripped in the waistband of his trousers with a brown leather belt that matched his shoes. 'You didn't let on that you were so busy these days.'

I glanced at Bridget, watching us from the worktop where she'd been attempting to make a pie, judging by the heaps of greyish pastry lumped around, and bags of opened flour. The fact that she kept on trying, despite all evidence telling her she ought to give up, made fondness swell inside me. Catching my gaze, she gave a tight shake of her head, and in a moment of complicity, I understood that she hadn't mentioned to Rufus that I was 'working' for Seth Donovan.

'Well, you know me,' I said. 'I don't want it getting out that I've joined the rat race.'

He choked out a snorting laugh that made Romy's head whip up.

'Pig!' She chortled and went back to her colouring.

I watched a tide of red wash up from Rufus's neck.

'Sorry,' said Bridget, in a slightly strangled voice. 'She didn't mean… it was just the sound you made…'

'Oh, it's fine.' He waved his hand with a rather weary smile. 'I've been called a lot worse by my sixth-formers. You'd think with the education they've had by this stage, they'd come up with something better than pillock.'

'Oh, I get it,' said Bridget. 'Because your surname's Pinnock.'

A laugh bolted out of my mouth before I could stop it. 'Sorry,' I said, when Rufus turned disappointed eyes my way.

'Pillock,' Bridget murmured. I caught a glimmer of amusement in her face and had to stem another flow of laughter. 'My English teacher was called Miss Bullwinkle, which was funny enough on its own.'

'She was still there when I started school,' I said. 'Everyone called her Miss Winky, because… well, I don't know, really. I suppose it was easier to say.'

'It's bullying really.' Rufus folded his arms and leaned back in his chair. 'Imagine someone shouting *Pillock!* every time you walk past, or in class, and pretending they were coughing when you ask them what they said.'

'It can be affectionate, though.' Bridget sounded conciliatory. 'Or a harmless way of getting back at the establishment.'

'I hadn't thought of it like that,' he said, shooting her a grateful look.

'I already told you,' I couldn't resist pointing out. 'You shouldn't respond.'

'So, what are you wearing for this wedding on Saturday?' said Bridget.

I looked at Rufus, then realised she was talking to me.

'Oh, I hadn't really thought about it.' I mentally ran through the items in my wardrobe and tossed them all on the floor. 'I might have to buy something.'

'A dress.' Rufus instantly revived. When he smiled, he really was very cute. I had a minor flashback to him kissing my neck in his bedroom, and remembered that things were nice in that department. The earth might not have moved, but who wanted earthquakes?

'I don't really do dresses,' I said, through another mouthful of clementine, handing a segment to Romy, who placed it gently in her box of crayons. 'I'm not the right shape.'

'You're definitely the right shape.' Rufus's eyes travelled over me appreciatively. 'Something above the knee would suit you.'

Bridget fastened the top button of her cardigan. 'She doesn't like showing her legs, I don't know why.' I sensed a compliment in there somewhere and threw her a smile.

'I know, it's a pity.' Rufus sounded sorrowful – as if he'd discovered that Santa didn't exist. 'I've told her they're stunning, but she just shrugs it off.'

'Hello, I'm right here.'

Rufus apologised. 'I'm being a bit of a dinosaur,' he said. 'But that doesn't mean I'm not on board with feminism. I fully support your right to wear whatever you like.' He adjusted his shirt collar. 'But a dress would really suit you.'

'I'll find something suitable, but prepare to be disappointed.'

'Never.' He said it so fervently that Bridget's eyes widened.

'Have you ever been married?' she said. 'I don't think I've asked Tilly that.'

She hadn't shown much interest at all, beyond the fact that I was 'dating' Rufus, and he had Dad's seal of approval.

'No.' He scratched the back of his head. 'I was in love, once, but then I found out she was seeing my brother.'

I looked at him in surprise. 'That must have been awful.' I remembered Grant, with the luxurious beard and gentle smile. Hard to imagine them liking the same woman, somehow. 'What happened?'

'They're getting married on Saturday.'

'*What?*'

'Won't that be a bit awkward?' Bridget sounded equally uncomfortable.

'I shouldn't think so.' Rufus looked surprised. 'She never knew I liked her. It was one of those "love from afar" things.'

'Right.' I was unsure whether what I was feeling was relief or annoyance. Why hadn't he said that in the first place?

'Silly,' said Romy, as though she'd absorbed everything and distilled it into a single word. She'd finished colouring her Minion blue, and had surrounded it with big red kisses.

'Looks good.' I stroked a hand over her hair, and she nodded without looking up. 'I've got to go.' I made a thing of looking at my watch and grimacing. 'Work to do, et cetera.'

Taking the hint, Rufus stood up and removed his coat from the back of the chair; the same coat he'd worn the day we'd talked on the beach – the day I'd saved Jack. 'I'll pick you up at ten Saturday morning.'

'Seven, eight, nine, ten,' recited Romy.

'Oh, good girl!' Bridget's smile was so wide and warm as she picked up her daughter and kissed both cheeks, I couldn't help smiling too, and started when Rufus laid his hands on my shoulders and pressed his mouth to mine.

'Well, that was… interesting,' said Bridget, when Rufus had driven off and Romy had scampered up to her room to find Teddy.

Something about her tone made me look at her twice. 'Interesting, as in…?'

She picked up a lump of pastry and dropped it in the bin. 'As in, weird.'

I'd been about to get up, but stared at her instead. 'I thought you approved of him.'

Another clump of pastry vanished into the bin. 'I've only really glimpsed him before but from what Dad said, he seemed nice.'

'And now he doesn't?'

'I don't know.' She undid the top button of her cardigan. 'He was different in my head.'

She'd been so adamant that Rufus was the sort of man I should be having a 'grown-up' relationship with, I'd expected her to sing his praises the second he left the house. 'Different, how?'

'Nicer.' She dusted her hands down her jeans and met my gaze. 'I think he might be a bit of a wanker.'

'A wanker?' If she'd said she was giving up finance to become a DJ I'd have been less surprised. 'Why?'

'I got the impression when he arrived that he wanted to check you weren't having doubts about this wedding, and if you were, whether I might change your mind.' A shaft of light poured through the window, rinsing her hair red-gold, so it looked like it did in a photo of her on the dresser, cradling me as a baby. 'I told him, if you'd said you were going, you would.'

I widened my eyes, as if to more fully absorb the look on her face. 'He's worried because I didn't say yes right away, that's all,' I said. 'I really don't think he's a wanker.'

'Are you sure?' Her eyes were avid, as if my answer mattered.

'Well, how would you define wankery?'

She thought for a moment. 'If I looked it up in the dictionary, I'd expect Rufus's face to be there.' Her impression of his earnest expression was so accurate, I dissolved into laughter.

'That's mean,' I said, once I'd recovered. 'He's honestly not that bad.' I told her about the misunderstanding over the paint on the café windows and the humour left her face.

'That's not romantic, whatever your friend says, it's wrong,' she said. 'It's actually a criminal act.'

'Don't be dramatic, Bee, he'd probably had a drink and didn't think it through.' I remembered his stricken face when I told him I'd had to clean up the mess. 'He was definitely being romantic.'

Bridget's frown was back in force. 'Does he drink a lot?'

'No, at least…' I hesitated. 'I don't think so,' I said. He hadn't drunk that much whenever we'd been out together, but I had no idea whether he drank at home. 'No more than anyone else.' I broke away from her gaze. 'He brought me flowers,' I pointed out.

'Yes, and those pine cones are giving you a headache.' Her face loosened into a smile. 'That's why I put the bouquet over there.'

'Thanks.' I was smiling too. She'd moved them because she'd remembered I didn't like the smell of pine.

'The point is, if he knew you properly, he'd never have brought them in the first place,' she said.

'But we're still at the getting-to-know-each-other stage.' I felt an urge to impress her with how 'adult' I was being. 'Remember, Dad recommended him, so he can't be a total wanker. Rufus, I mean, not dad.'

She flopped back in her chair and studied me for a moment. 'Well, it's good that you're giving him a chance.' She drummed the tabletop with her fingertips and pulled a face. 'And I'm hardly fit to be giving relationship advice.' She'd never referenced her own track record before – at least not in a self-deprecating way. If this was the result of an evening with Seth Donovan, I had a lot to thank him for. 'I suppose the wedding will throw you together for a day, and you'll have a better idea at the end of it whether you're right for each other.'

'Wow,' I said, faking amazement to disguise the fact that I was genuinely moved. 'You've just given me some advice that makes sense, and isn't designed to make me feel crap about myself.'

To my surprise, her eyes glazed with sorrow. 'Is that what I do?'

'Oh, Bee, you know it is.' It felt like the right time to say it, but I kept my voice gentle. 'It's the way it's always been.'

'Oh god.' She covered her face with her hands. 'I'm a terrible human being.'

Unsure whether to jokingly agree, or to offer some reassurance, I jumped when she snatched her hands away. 'Just kidding,' she said, but there was a telltale wobble in her voice. 'I suppose a therapist would say I have issues.'

'Probably.'

'Too late to say sorry and start over, I suppose?' Her face blurred in a haze of tears.

'Never.'

She reached for my hand. 'I'm sorry, Tilly.'

Chapter Twenty-Three

'What do you think brought it on?'

'I'm not sure.' I watched Meg pull a tray of gingerbread robins from the oven the following morning and set them down to cool. 'It must be the Seth Donovan effect.'

'I can see how that would work.' Meg's smile was mischievous. 'Being in love can have a transformative effect.'

'Yuk,' I said. 'She's been in love before and still been a bitch.' My stomach squeezed with hunger at the sight and smell of the freshly baked bread, cakes and pastries in the Old Bakery kitchen. 'And she *can't* be in love. They've only been out together once.'

'Remember, we're talking about Seth Donovan,' said Meg, as though he'd won some eligible bachelor of the year title. (Maybe he had.) '*And* they kissed.' She paused, one hand wedged in an oven glove. 'A lot can happen during a single kiss.'

I rolled my eyes, feeling skittish since receiving an email that morning from one of the electricians I'd reached out to, saying the only time he could fit the work in was Saturday evening at seven. I'd gushingly accepted, not caring how much it would cost. 'I know you and Nathan imploded the second your lips met, and you saw rainbows and fairies, but it's not like that for everyone.'

'It can happen, though.' She gave an emphatic nod. 'For me, for Cassie and Danny... for anyone. Even your scary sister.'

'I suppose.' I tried to remember my most significant kiss, but could only recall my worst; a tongue, darting in and out of my mouth like a lizard after a fly, from a fellow design student I'd avoided for the rest of the year. *Why* hadn't I had a significant kiss?

'Isn't Rufus a good kisser?'

'I suppose so.' I indulged a memory of his lips moving on mine. 'Not earth-shattering, but pleasant.'

'*Pleasant?*'

'Believe me, pleasant is a step up from someone sneezing in your mouth, getting snagged on your braces, chewing your bottom lip, and telling you that if you moved your mouth a bit more, you'd be a better kisser.'

'Wow.' Meg shuddered. 'You've had some horrible experiences.'

'All with the same person,' I deadpanned. 'He's doing life for murder now.'

She giggled. 'Seriously, though, if Bridget's being nicer to you and it's all down to Seth, then maybe it's his way of repaying you for saving Jack.'

'What do you mean?'

'Well, hearing about you from a new perspective might have made Bridget think about you differently.'

I remembered our brief conversation in the car on the way home, when she'd said something similar. 'So, you're saying Seth said nice things on purpose. For *me?*' It made a sort of sense, considering how indebted he still felt – but didn't tally with the way he'd avoided my eyes on his return.

'Who knows?' Meg shrugged. 'But you told us you mentioned to him that you don't get on with your sister and that's why you weren't at home much these days, so maybe he thought he was doing you a favour.'

Her words stayed with me as I left the bakery with a bag of bread rolls and a couple of (undecorated) gingerbread robins, and on impulse I pulled out my phone to call him, but spotted a text from Gwen.

Floorboards here, where r u??

Almost there I texted back. *At last*. I ducked into my car and called Ted, to ask if he could come back to the café.

'Sorry, I'm tied up,' was the short reply.

'Not literally, I hope.'

He didn't laugh. 'It'll have to wait until after Christmas now, Tilly, I'm sorry.'

'But, Ted, it can't.'

'You'll have to find someone else, then.' I'd forgiven his dour manner in the past, having heard his wife had left him for a plumber, but suddenly I didn't blame her. 'Fine,' I said, sounding churlish. 'I will.' The words *good luck with that* seemed imminent, but he managed not to say them.

Ending the call, I was gripped by panic. The Maitlands were going to return to find their lovely new function room no closer to completion than when they'd left, and although I knew they'd be lovely about it – and would probably suggest holding the party in the main café – I'd promised it would be ready and couldn't face letting them down.

Maybe I could ask Cassie if Danny knew someone who could help. I'd already gone through Dad's list of building contacts the previous evening, while Bridget read *The Night Before Christmas* to Romy, to no avail. Unable to face Gwen right away, I texted her to say I'd be in later on, and finally called Seth.

He answered right away. 'That's odd, I was about to ring you.'

I remembered Bridget saying he'd seemed distracted. 'Everything OK?' I said, relieved I hadn't blurted out *what was in the text you sent my sister yesterday*? 'Is Jack all right?'

'He's actually pretty good.' There was a smile in Seth's voice. 'He was telling me about the story game you played the other night.'

'It was fun,' I said. 'He's pretty good at I spy, too.'

'I wouldn't have imagined him playing games like that.'

'Sometimes, you have to just start,' I said. 'Not that I'm telling you what to do.'

'Please do.' His tone was dry. 'It's obvious you're channelling Mary Poppins.' I started at the mention of my aspirational nanny. 'Only with better clothes and hair, obviously.'

'Hardly.'

'Honestly, Tilly, I don't know where I'd be now if you hadn't come into my life.' His words came out in a low rush, with none of the hesitancy I'd sensed when he'd come home with Bridget. 'Though obviously I'd have preferred it to have been less dramatic, without any near-drownings.'

'Let's not go there again.' I purposely kept my voice light. 'You've made it clear how grateful you are, you don't need to keep on thanking me.'

'About the other night—'

'Bridget loved it,' I said. 'She's been in a brilliant mood since, and has been very nice to me.'

'She has?' He sounded pleased. 'I'm glad.'

'Whatever you said about me, it worked.'

'She couldn't believe you hadn't told her about saving Jack,' he said. 'I couldn't believe it either.'

'Well, she knows now.'

'I did go on about you a bit.' He gave a self-conscious laugh. 'But I got the impression she didn't want to talk about family, so I shut up in the end.'

'Family's a bit of a sore point, I'm afraid.'

'So I gathered.'

'I was expecting her to be hungover after your date, but your text perked her up no end.' *Why had I mentioned the text?*

'It did?'

'Whatever you said, I think she needed to hear it.' Now I was fishing for details.

'That's good.' He sounded relieved. 'She's a wonderful and interesting woman,' he said. 'I've never met anyone like her, and—'

'Romy and Jack got on well, too.' It was rude to butt in, but hearing him sing Bridget's praises felt a bit weird – though, obviously, I was glad that they'd got on.

'I hope they'll see more of each other. I think it'll be good for Jack to see someone apart from me.'

'Have you heard from your mother?' I wondered idly what he was wearing, and remembered I still had the clothes he'd lent me.

'That's why I was going to call you.'

'Oh?'

A sigh wafted down the line. 'She's coming back tomorrow, and I know it's to try and persuade Jack and me to stay at Oaklands over Christmas, which she says is a time for families to be together, and I'd prefer Jack not to be here, in case things get heated.'

'Are they likely to?'

'Do you really need to ask?'

'Fair point,' I said. 'Shall I ask Bridget to have him over at our house?'

'I'd rather he was with you.' His words were instant and heartfelt. 'What with you being his official "nanny".'

In the rear-view mirror, I saw that my eyes were shiny and my cheeks were peony-pink. About to say yes, and that I might need to take him with me to the café, I suddenly remembered. 'Oh *shoot*, I can't, Seth. I'm going to a wedding tomorrow.' *And I need to find a floor fitter.*

'Ah yes,' said Seth. 'With Rufus. Your sister mentioned it.' I recalled how he'd seemed a bit off with me back at the cottage, and wondered what else Bridget had said. She'd probably told him that this was my first 'grown-up' relationship, and how I'd never gone out with anyone for longer than a month before. Perhaps he disapproved. 'I promised I'd go,' I said, wondering at the pang of regret that tugged at my insides.

'Not to worry.' I had the sense he was holding back from saying something different. 'I'll make sure things stay calm here, and do something nice with Jack before she arrives.'

'Sounds like a plan.' It was nice to hear him more relaxed about doing things with his son. 'There's a pantomime on at the Little Theatre near Salcombe,' I said, remembering going to see *Dick Whittington* there with the school when I was six, and being vaguely terrified by all the shouting of *He's behind you!* 'I think they do a matinee.'

'Good idea.'

'You could start a yearly tradition.'

A short silence followed. Customers continued to dip in and out of the bakery, and a waving, big-bellied Santa drew up on a full-size sleigh with flashing lights, pulled by a big yellow van instead of reindeers, drawing excited glances from passing children.

'What's that noise?' Seth said, as a tinny, and rather ghostly rendition of 'Little Drummer Boy' filled the air.

'Father Christmas collecting money for charity.' I became aware of competing male voices, singing 'Silent Night' on the other end of the line. 'Sounds like the *team* are auditioning for *The Voice*.'

'The team are painting the staircase and landing today.' For a second, I thought about asking to borrow the team for the café, except they were on a deadline too. A Felicity Donovan deadline. I could only imagine the wrath it would incur if the work wasn't completed on schedule, to her exacting standards. 'I'll be glad when they're done to be honest,' Seth continued. 'It's intrusive having people in the house, and Digby's not up to going for another walk.'

'At least you're letting them get on with it.' I recalled a couple of jobs where clients had badgered me constantly, changing their minds about what they wanted, and another who'd fired the decorator because he'd had the cheek to take a tea break. 'A couple more days and they'll be done.'

'If you've any advice about tables and stuff like that, I'd appreciate your input,' he said. 'I don't have much of a clue about that sort of thing, but my mother's stuff is a bit old-fashioned.' I guessed he was referring to the big, shiny table and high-backed chairs in the dining room. 'That's if you wouldn't mind.'

'Of course.' I felt a slight sinking sensation. He was obviously still scrabbling for scraps to throw me, and before he was halfway through saying, 'I'll pay you for your time,' I said, 'I don't need paying, thank you.'

Another pause hung between us, broken by Jack's voice. 'Dad, can we go to the smugglers' caves on the beach?'

'Smugglers' caves?'

'He means the ones further down from you,' I said. 'There's a little network of caves past the headland, where the cliff juts out, but it's easy to get caught by the tide so you need to check the times before you go.'

'I don't think so, Jack,' said Seth. 'They sound dangerous.'

'I've got a map on my iPad. I know where they are.'

'It's too dangerous.'

I didn't fully hear Jack's response, but caught the words *hate you.*

'He doesn't hate you, he's lashing out,' I said. 'Kids do that when they don't get their own way.'

'I bet you didn't.'

'I always got my own way,' I joked. 'I wasn't a very demanding child by all accounts. Not that I'm saying Jack is,' I added quickly. 'He really isn't.'

'I know.' Seth sounded a bit defeated. 'Why do I feel like I've just taken a giant step backwards?'

'Give him time,' I said. 'I know it's a cliché, but you have to be patient.'

'Yes, Miss Poppins, but I don't have the luxury of time,' Seth reminded me. 'Not if my mother wants her own way.'

'I still don't see how a judge would determine he's better off with her, than with you,' I said. 'I honestly think you just need to ride this out.'

'My mother's best friend is a judge, and Mum can be incredibly persuasive.'

'Right.' I felt his frustration. 'Listen, check out times for the panto-mime, then get Jack in the garden,' I said. 'Plant something together.'

'Gardening?' He sounded aghast. 'In this weather?'

'A bit of cold weather won't hurt,' I said. 'Did you see the snow the other night?'

'It snowed?'

I sighed; imagined him checking on Jack before getting into bed (did Seth wear pyjamas?) and staring at the ceiling, worrying as he waited for sleep to claim him. Or maybe he'd been thinking about his kiss with Bridget, and wishing she'd stayed after all. 'Only a bit,' I said. 'Jack would have liked it.'

'I wish it had settled. I'm dying to build a snowman with him on the beach.'

He sounded wistful, and I remembered Jack sleepily talking about making a sand snowman with his dad.

'It'll snow again,' I said. 'Probably.'

'I hope so.' After another brief pause he said, 'I've started writing a children's story, about a boy and his dad and the adventures they have together.' He groaned. 'God, that sounds so trite, and it's probably been done better a million times before, but it's preferable to writing my autobiography. I'm actually enjoying it.'

'That sounds great.' I smiled. 'Try reading it to Jack, see what he thinks.'

'What if he says it's crap?'

'You won't know, unless you try.'

'I'm definitely going to start calling you Mary.'

'Please don't.'

The silence this time was comfortable. Our conversation appeared to have run its course, but I was oddly reluctant to get off the phone.

'Sure you don't want to come over?' Seth sounded equally reluctant, but I resisted the pull of temptation. He probably wanted a bit of backup with Jack, but they needed time to themselves. 'I've got work to do,' I said brightly. 'This function room won't finish itself.' *Unfortunately.*

'Maybe Jack and I could pop over to the café.' Seth's voice warmed up. 'I'm assuming they do a nice line in hot chocolate with marshmallows at this time of year?'

My heart bumped. 'Aren't you worried you'll be recognised at the café?'

'I've done enough skulking about,' he said. 'If Jack and I are going to live around here, the locals need to get used to us.' I couldn't argue with that. 'I'm probably doing more harm than good by hiding us both away.'

It was a pretty miraculous turnaround in just a week. 'OK,' I said, thinking quickly. 'Make it around three o'clock.'

'Great!' Seth sounded invigorated. 'Can we bring the dog?'

Chapter Twenty-Four

'I'm still a bit cross you invited me to the café under false pretences yesterday.' Bridget plonked two mugs of coffee by our parents' bed, while I rummaged through Mum's wardrobe for a suitable outfit to wear to a winter wedding.

'It wasn't really false pretences.' I pulled out a salmon-pink pleated skirt and matching bolero jacket and held them against me. 'I wanted you to see what I've been doing there. You haven't set foot in the café since you came home.'

'To be fair, I hadn't been further than the shops and the park before that meal with Seth.' She sat on the bed and pulled the quilted cover over her nightshirt like a shawl. 'I'd practically forgotten how to drive.'

'Well, I'm flattered you made the effort.'

'Only, you left out the bit about Seth and Jack being there.'

'I told you, I thought it would be a nice surprise for you all.'

'While you scarpered off, once you'd made me check the floorboard batches matched.'

'I told you, I needed to go to Kingsbridge to find something to wear for today,' I said.

'You clearly didn't find anything.' She gave Mum's outfit a thumbs down.

'Nope.' I didn't mention that I hadn't tried very hard.

After I'd promised a glowering Gwen the floorboards *would* be down for the party, I'd retreated to my car to call Cassie, who promised to ask Danny whether he knew anyone who could help.

'It's urgent,' I said, deciding not to beat about the bush, and there was a pause during which I imagined her biting her lip, trying not to extract any more promises.

'I've been throwing up all morning,' she said at last, sounding almost proud. 'It's getting harder to keep being pregnant a secret. I had to tell the mayoress I'd eaten some dodgy shrimp.'

'Why shrimp?'

'It was the first thing that popped into my head.'

After that, I'd gone to Kingsbridge with the intention of buying an outfit in Boutique 144, but after trying on a couple of dresses and trouser suits that made me feel more giraffe than human, I gave up and went swimming instead, and emerged from the water feeling, if not reborn, then at least less frazzled.

'You can't wear that,' said Bridget, as if she was on the front row at London Fashion Week. 'Too frumpy.' She had a glow about her again that I doubted was purely down to Romy having a lie-in. When I'd got back after swimming, they'd been snuggled together on the sofa watching *Miracle on 34th Street*, while a decent-looking casserole bubbled on the stove. She'd told me off for 'setting her up' with Seth, but admitted they'd had a nice time.

'Even the dog was cute,' she'd said, though apparently Gwen hadn't been thrilled at having to shut Dickens out the back, *in case 'e gets 'is 'ead bitten orf.* 'She's hilarious,' Bridget had declared. 'She burnt her bleedin' eyebrows off, trying to light a Christmas pudding.' Her impression of Gwen's cockney accent and gimlet-eyed stare had made me chuckle.

'Witch!' Romy had piped up, provoking more laughter. It wasn't the first time a child had mistaken Gwen for one of Grimms' fairy tale crones.

According to Bridget, they'd walked through the village with Seth and Jack after their hot chocolate (she didn't like the beach in winter) and bought some cranberry and orange cookies from the bakery. No one had mobbed Seth, though he'd got a few curious looks, and Romy had insisted that Jack hold her hand. 'He's really sweet,' had been Bridget's verdict. 'A credit to Seth.'

I'd supposed it was natural to say that, as Seth was Jack's father, but considering he hadn't spent much time with his son until recently, I'd wondered privately how much Jack's influences with his grandparents had shaped him. It was clear the effect of living with them still had a grip – and that wasn't necessarily a bad thing – but hopefully a slackening of Felicity's rules, and being around his dad, would bring a simpler joy into his life. I was sure it already had, even if neither of them had quite recognised it yet.

I'd longed to quiz Bridget on what she and Seth had talked about, and to ask whether he was surprised when I didn't join them (clearly he hadn't minded too much) but had managed to hold back.

'What about this?' I pulled a charcoal pencil skirt over my pyjama leggings. It was so tight around the hem it altered my gait to an undignified mince as I did a circuit of the room.

Bridget choked on her coffee. 'Do it again,' she ordered.

I did, faster this time, and she doubled over with laughter.

'Let me find something to go with it.' Putting down her mug, she leapt up and took one of Dad's waistcoats from the wardrobe.

I put it on back to front, over my pyjama top. 'With these?' I shoved my feet into a pair of green, square-toed shoes, jammed a peacock-feathered fascinator on my head and took out a boxy, straw handbag that looked like a mini picnic hamper.

'Why Cinderella, you SHALL go to the ball!' Bridget had tears of mirth in her eyes. 'May I join you?' She tugged a silver sequinned jacket with shoulder pads over her nightshirt and tucked it into a pair of black leather trousers that clung to her backside. 'How do you do?' she said, slipping a pair of Dad's Buddy Holly style reading glasses on. 'Do you come here often?'

Weak with laughter, we paraded about, talking to imaginary wedding guests. 'This little number?' I nudged my fascinator. 'I bought it from the nineteen eighties dahling, for a footballer's stag do. Isn't it *soooper*?'

'Does my bum look big in this?' Bridget flapped her eyelashes and stuck out her bottom, which looked like a beach ball in a bin bag.

My ribs ached from laughing as she pretended to take a Kim Kardashian style selfie, then got angry when she couldn't get the trousers off. 'How the hell did Mum ever squeeze into these?'

'Why, is surely more to the point.' I buckled with fresh laughter as Bridget wriggled and writhed on her back on the bed. 'Here, let me help.'

By the time we'd wrestled the trousers off, Romy had materalised, rubbing her eyes and smiling uncertainly.

'We're helping Auntie Tilly look for something nice to wear,' said Bridget, apparently forgetting she was supposed to feed Romy something nutritious the second she opened her eyes. 'Do you want to help?'

Romy nodded, threw down Teddy and went straight to the wardrobe. 'I fink THIS!' She tugged a piece of fabric that turned out to be a fairly harmless tunic dress in black, with a block of embroidered swirls around the hem.

'Actually, I think that will do,' said Bridget, holding it up. 'It's straight up and down, which is more you than something clingy and blingy.'

I checked she wasn't being facetious, but she looked like she was picturing me in the dress and liking what she saw.

'It'll show off your amazing legs,' she added, her impression of Rufus prompting more laughter, which produced a twang of guilt. I thanked her and Romy for their help, and went to my room to try the dress on, deciding I liked New Bridget a lot.

'Wow,' she said, when I eventually sidled into the kitchen, squirmy with embarrassment. 'Romy is obviously going to be a stylist when she grows up, because that dress really suits you.'

Romy pursed her rosebud lips as she looked me up and down. 'Yes!' she pronounced, which made me think of *Say Yes to the Dress*, and the night that Bridget had arrived with Romy – a stranger in her own home. It felt like a lifetime ago.

'I don't really know what to wear with it.' I smoothed my hair, which I'd straightened after my shower so it was swingy and shiny around my cheeks – like shampoo-advert hair.

'Those tights look fine.'

'Obviously, they're Mum's,' I said. 'I never wear tights.' They were too tight, like sausage casings, and I hoped to never wear a pair again.

'And you could wear the blazer I wore the other night,' Bridget suggested. 'The sleeves will be a three-quarter on you, which is fine.'

'Footwear?'

She glanced at my feet. 'Don't you have any nice shoes?'

'The closest I've got are some black suede ankle boots.'

'They'll do,' she said. 'You need a pinker lipstick.' She reached for her bag and pulled one out. 'I hardly ever wear it these days.'

'Thanks.' I went to the mirror in the hall and smoothed some on, trying to work out how I felt, and wishing I didn't keep thinking about Jack, and the fun we could have had. It was probably because I'd never been to a wedding before, never mind with a... my head wanted to say *boyfriend*, but my heart wouldn't quite let me.

When Rufus turned up, five minutes early, my stomach was twanging with nerves, which had nothing to do with meeting a bunch of people I'd never clapped eyes on, and everything to do with sharing a confined space with Rufus for two hours – more if we ran into traffic on the way there and back. We'd never even spent a full night together. And this was his brother's *wedding*. There'd be alcohol at the reception, and I had a feeling Rufus wouldn't be holding back. Combined with his complicated relationship with his brother – who was marrying a woman Rufus had been secretly in love with for goodness knew how long – would it be a recipe for disaster? Or, at least, a punch-up. I really hoped not, and reminded myself that Rufus was besotted with me, and probably wasn't in the mood for a fight at a wedding.

'You look stunning,' he said, holding the car door open, and leaning in to softly kiss my cheek. He'd scrubbed up well in a grey, double-breasted suit that flattered his colouring, and went well with his crisp white shirt and bottle-green matt silk tie. He smelt nice too (why hadn't I thought to wear perfume?) and as I folded myself into the car, my nerves steadied. It *would* be nice to have a day out. Even the sun was trying to appear, peeking between rushing clouds – although it was eye-wateringly cold, and I hoped we wouldn't be standing around too long after the ceremony, waiting for photographs.

'It's made of fine corduroy,' Rufus said from the driver's seat, fingering the hem of his jacket when I told him he looked nice. 'It's flexible, so good for throwing some shapes on the dance floor.' He demonstrated a few moves with his shoulders and fists, eyebrows jigging up and down. He hadn't shaved his head, as he'd said he was planning to do (Jason Statham needn't worry) but had arranged his hair so it looked like he had quite a bit more than he did.

'We're not staying too late, are we?' I hadn't meant to sound edgy, but Rufus's smile didn't budge.

'Let's see how the day plays out.'

'I have to get back,' I said. 'I've work to do.' The words increased the jitteriness in my stomach. Cassie had messaged to say Danny didn't know anyone available at short notice to lay a floor, but despite offering his services – *he's willing to give it a bash!* – I'd assured her it was fine. In fact, I'd lied, and said I'd found someone, anyway.

'It's the weekend, Tilly.' Rufus over-pronounced my name, as if proving he was saying it right, and gave an indulgent chuckle. 'And since when did you care about work?' His confidence seemed to have grown now he finally had me trussed up in his car (not in a kidnap-victim way, though I experienced a pinch of panic as I turned to wave at Bridget and Romy, watching from the doorstep) and he pulled away from the kerb like a man who very much knew what he wanted.

Far from finding this attractive, I felt suddenly trapped. 'I care when I've made a promise.' *Even if it was only to myself.* I adjusted my seat belt as he approached the main road at speed. 'I have to be back by six. Seven at the latest,' I said, unsure why it was so important he understood.

He threw me a smile that revealed his strong, white teeth. 'Like I said, let's see how things go.' He reached over and squeezed my knee. 'My family are going to love you,' he said. 'My sister says you probably don't deserve me, but she's wrong.'

I had a feeling I wasn't going to get on with his sister. 'Seriously, I need to be back this evening.' I stared at his smooth, pale hand and held my breath until he moved it back to the steering wheel.

'OK, whatever.' He shook his head indulgently, as if to say *what are you like?* and it hit me on some instinctive level that he'd already booked a hotel room as a 'surprise'. My heart gave a jolt. The car felt too hot, but I didn't fancy taking my jacket off, and tugged my dress over my knees. He kept darting looks at them, as though they were cream cakes he fancied biting into. 'Do you mind if I turn the heating down?'

'Actually, I do, I'm really cold.' He grinned. 'Joking,' he said, and flipped the switch.

We drove along the A38 and through Buckfastleigh without speaking. Rufus switched the radio on, and cocked his head to show he was listening to the presenter, who was talking about schools in northern Nigeria sending students out to beg.

'Maybe some music?' I leaned forward to twiddle with the knob, hoping some Christmas tunes might lighten the mood – my mood at least – but Rufus lightly slapped my fingers away.

'I was listening to that.' He flashed another smile. 'I like to broaden my mind while driving,' he said. 'It keeps me interesting.'

Really? I suddenly felt like saying. *It's not working.*

Chastised, I sat back, feeling like someone I didn't know in his strongly pine-scented car, clutching a gold-clasped bag that belonged to Mum. I didn't possess a handbag. I used a small rucksack if I was carrying more than I could keep in my pockets and it felt odd, like holding a tray or a brick.

'Any subjects I should avoid talking about at the wedding?' I said, but the presenter had moved on to advances in molecular biology – Rufus's area – and he held up a finger to shush me.

Resisting an urge to snap it off, I turned to look out of the window at the scenery flowing by under a snow-white sky, wishing now that I'd thrown his bouquet away, instead of putting it in a jug in Dad's office, out of the way. The questions I'd planned to ask seemed completely inappropriate – worse, I realised I didn't care what his favourite colour/ animal/food was, or whether he wanted children, and he didn't seem inclined to ask me anything about myself.

How would we survive a whole day together? And how would I get back if he'd been drinking and was determined to stay and 'throw some shapes' before luring me to his seedy hotel room? Obviously I didn't know it would be seedy, it was just the vibe I was getting.

It was as if my true feelings had floated to the surface, perhaps jolted by the potholes in the road, or by Rufus's close proximity; so different to being with Seth, when conversation flowed without any prompting or awkwardness.

'You know, I never really thought that painting my feelings would work,' Rufus said unexpectedly, turning the radio down.

'Sorry?'

'Last time I did it, I almost got arrested.' His eyes were too bright – almost glassy – and I spotted a patch of stubble by his ear he must have missed while shaving. 'Luckily, she didn't press charges, but I still ended up moving back to Ivybridge because of her.'

'Hang on.' I swivelled to face him. 'You've got form?'

'Form?' He pulled his chin back, slowing the car as we approached a set of roadwork traffic lights on red. 'I'm not a hardened criminal.' His glance bordered on cocky as he pulled the handbrake on and turned to shoot me a tight-lipped smile. 'Girls like romantic gestures,' he said. 'You've proved that.' *What?* 'She just wasn't the right girl for me.'

Girl? Ugh. 'It wasn't a romantic gesture, it was damage to public property,' I said, snapping my seat belt off. 'And I'm not the right *girl* for you either, Rufus, I'm sorry. I should never have agreed to come.'

'Wait.' His hand shot out and clamped around my wrist. 'What are you doing?'

'I'm sorry, but I can't go to the wedding with you.'

'But, Tilly, you promised! You said your word is your bond.'

'Rufus, be honest.' I tried to shake him off. 'You want me there as arm candy, to impress your bother, and to prove to his wife that you're over her.' I waited for him to deny it. 'It's not even about me.'

'You know that I think you're gorgeous.' His grip tightened. 'I'm in love with you, *Tilly*,' he said through his teeth, looking anything but loving. 'How many more ways can I say it?'

'None.' I finally wrenched free from his grasp and rubbed my wrist. The lights were still on red. 'I'm sorry if I've misled you, Rufus, I really am, but it's over.' As I reached behind me to open the door I heard a *thunk*. 'Did you just lock me in?'

'I'm sorry, I'm sorry.' Another *thunk* as he released the locks. 'Please, Tilly, just come with me today and I'll never bother you again.'

'I can't.'

'Remember our lovemaking?' His tone became pleading. 'It was something special.'

How had I ever allowed myself to be naked with this... *person*? 'For you, maybe.'

'Look, you're coming with me, whether you like it or not.'

'Go to hell, Rufus.'

His hand fastened around my upper arm. 'Don't talk to me like that.'

I looked into his eyes. His pupils had inflated so his irises looked almost black, and my breath stuck to the back of my throat. Had I really thought he might be my first grown-up relationship? That we might have a future together? No, not really.

'Get. Off. Me,' I said through clenched teeth. 'Right now, or I'll break your balls.'

He automatically clamped his thighs together. 'Is it to do with that man?' he said.

'Man?'

'The one you hugged on the beach, after you saved his son's life?' His voice dripped with resentment.

'I still can't believe you watched all that and did nothing.' As if a blindfold had been removed, I saw that was the moment I should have known we didn't belong together. 'Now, move your hand.'

'I only asked you out to please our dads,' he muttered, releasing his grip and dropping back in his seat. 'You haven't even got a proper job. And I only pretended to like Alanis Morissette. I prefer Meat Loaf.'

'Well, I don't like Stinking Bishop,' I shot back. 'I prefer cheesey triangles.' Before he could respond, I shakily fumbled the door open and clambered out onto the road. The lights were amber, and drivers were revving their engines. I leaned down to look at him. 'If you contact me again, in any way, I *will* go to the police.' I was glad my voice sounded steady. 'Tell your brother I'm sorry.'

I slammed the door as the traffic began to move, and hurried onto the pavement, not sure where I was going – only that I needed to be as far away as possible from Rufus Pillock.

❄ ❄ ❄

I found a café in the little town and ordered a coffee, which I drank at a table by the steamy window, feeling the warmth seep through me as I stared through the window at a Christmas market in the square, where a small brass band was playing carols.

I didn't feel like calling anyone, or thinking about what had just happened, and decided I might as well do some shopping since I had some time on my hands. Pushing Rufus to a distant corner of my mind, I spent an hour or so browsing the fairy-lit stalls and buying Christmas gifts – including a squeaky toy for Digby, a wooden board game for Jack, and a deep-blue hand-knitted fisherman-style sweater that I knew would look good on Seth.

Bridget and I hadn't exchanged gifts for years, but there was a bookshop nearby, and after reading a chapter of a funny new parenting book that made me laugh out loud, I bought it for her (but kept the receipt just in case), then spotted a scarf on a stall that matched her eyes and bought that too.

Pleased with my haul, I drew some money from a cashpoint, and bought a bag of roast chestnuts, which I ate in a taxi on the way back to Ivybridge, and shared with the female driver as I couldn't face making small talk.

I couldn't face returning home either, and asked her to drop me in Seashell Cove, but felt stranded and out of place in Mum's dress and jacket, with my hands full of bags. I was wearing *tights,* for god's sake. I hadn't worn tights since school, and the crotch had sunk almost to my knees. Suddenly, I didn't want to go to the café, *or* the bakery, but unless I returned home to get my car, I couldn't go anywhere else.

As I dithered, shivering in my unseasonal outfit, watching a jogger down on the beach, a car horn made me jump.

'Tilly?'

I jerked round. It was Seth, looking at me through the half-lowered window of his car with a puzzled look on his face. 'I thought you were going to a wedding.'

'I was.' I shook my hair out of my watering eyes. 'I changed my mind.'

He leaned over to open the passenger door. 'Get in,' he said, and for the second time that day, I found myself getting into a car with a man.

Only this time, I wanted to be there.

Chapter Twenty-Five

'I thought your mum was coming over,' I said, relaxing in the warmth of the car.

'She's on her way,' said Seth. 'I thought I'd take Jack swimming first.'

'Good idea.' He was in the back, white headphones over his damp hair, holding his iPad. 'Hi, Jack,' I mouthed.

He gave me a wave and I waved back, overcome at the sight of his friendly face. 'I'd really like to go to that pantomime, sometime,' I said impulsively.

'It's on until January, I checked.' Seth's gaze was steady. 'What happened?'

I glanced back at Jack, his feet dancing up and down in their blue and white trainers as he lifted his head to gaze out of the window.

'It's OK, he's listening to music.' Seth gave me a heartfelt smile that I had to look away from. I was teetering on the verge of crying. 'I've introduced him to Bruce Springsteen and he seems to like it.'

I cleared my throat. 'Good choice.'

'You look… nice.' His eyes swept over me.

'I look ridiculous.'

'Tilly!' He scanned my face, as if checking I was being serious. 'You couldn't look ridiculous if you tried.'

'You don't have to keep this up you know.'

'Keep what up?'

'Saying nice things, being complimentary, saying I'm amazing and so forth.' I shoved my handbag in the footwell with the rest of my bags. The clasp wasn't closed and Bridget's lipstick rolled out. 'You're not obliged to be nice to me, Seth.' He glanced at me again in astonishment. 'And you should keep your eyes on the road.'

'I'm only doing twenty miles an hour, and there's no one else around,' he said. 'Tilly, I'm not saying things just to be nice, why would I?'

'You know why.' I tipped my head back at Jack. 'I'm happy to help out, if that's what I'm doing, while your mum's here. You don't have to flatter me all the time.'

'Flatter you?' His lips twitched. 'I didn't realise that's what I was doing,' he said. 'Look, I know we met under unusual circumstances, but even if I'd met you some other way, I'd still like you, Tilly.'

Great. Now he was being kind because I was coming across as insecure and needy – two things no one had ever accused me of being.

'If we'd met any other way, you wouldn't have looked at me twice,' I said, unable to stop myself. 'I'm hardly your type.' *Brilliant.* Now it sounded as if I wanted to be.

'I don't have a type of female I want to be friends with,' he said. 'And I'd like to think that's what we are now.'

Friends. Of course we could be friends. What was wrong with being friends? Especially as he was seeing my sister and might marry her one day. We'd be practically related if he did.

'Sorry,' I said, on a wave of exhaustion. 'I've had a really weird morning.'

'So, tell me about it.'

Checking once more that Jack was absorbed by The Boss, I gave Seth a rundown, surprised to see his hands tighten around the steering wheel when I mentioned Rufus grabbing my arm.

'Christ, Tilly, he sounds like a total creep.'

'He is,' I said, admitting it for the first time. 'I don't understand why my dad thought we'd be good together – or why I did, to be honest.'

'I'm sure he wouldn't have if he'd known what this bloke was really like.' Seth parked outside the cottage and switched the car engine off. 'He definitely wouldn't want you to keep seeing him.'

'I'd had some doubts,' I confessed. 'But Bridget was impressed I was in a "grown-up relationship",' I scraped quote marks, 'and I convinced myself it was normal to not be sure, because I hadn't been seeing him for long enough to really know.' I released a sigh, realising how lame it sounded. 'That's why I agreed to go to his brother's wedding, to get to know Rufus better.' I checked Seth's reaction, and saw him listening intently. 'Not that I'm blaming my sister.' I shook my head. 'I'm an idiot,' I said. 'I convinced myself I just needed to try harder to like him.'

Seth surprised me by saying, 'We've all been there.' He pulled the key out of the ignition and tapped his knee with it. 'I kept telling myself I should marry Gina, because on the surface she was everything a man could want, but my gut kept saying she wasn't the one for me.' He lightly touched my sleeve. 'I know you spoke to her the other night, by the way.'

My head whipped up. 'You saw my note?' I'd completely forgotten to mention it.

He nodded. 'If I'd known she just wanted closure, I'd have called her,' he said, a regretful twist to his lips. 'I'm sorry you had to deal with it.'

'I didn't *have* to,' I said. 'She sounded nice.' I wasn't sure nice was the right word, and judging by the look Seth gave me, he wasn't convinced either. 'How did she know you were out with Bridget?' I said.

'She didn't.'

'A *good mamma* for Jack?'

He shook his head, a smile still hovering. 'She obviously meant you.'

My face began to burn. 'Are you going to make me a cup of tea before your mother arrives?' I flung open the car door and got out, welcoming a shot of cold air to my face.

'My pleasure,' he said.

Jack tugged his headphones off and raced inside to greet an ecstatic Digby, who'd brushed against wet paint judging by the badger-like stripe down one side of his fur.

'You leave your front door unlocked?'

'The team are still here,' said Seth, as I followed him inside. 'I decided to leave them to it for a couple of hours.'

Sure enough there was the sound of a ladder clattering upstairs, followed by a shout of, 'Watch what you're doing, Mick, or you'll have me over the banister.'

Seth bent to remove his boots, pretending to shield his eyes from the swirly-patterned carpet. 'They've got a mate in doing some rewiring, then there's just the hall to do and they'll be out of here by Christmas Eve.'

'What about your lovely bathroom?'

He grinned as he hung up his parka. 'That's a job for next year,' he said. 'Regardless of what my mother thinks.'

I hoped he'd let me design it, but it didn't feel like the right time to ask.

'Dad, can I have something to eat?' Seth flattened himself to the wall as Jack pelted past after Digby, who was carrying a half-shredded ball in his mouth.

'There's some vegetable lasagne leftover from last night.'

Jack nodded as he chased Digby back into the living room.

'Vegetable lasagne,' I said, slipping off Mum's jacket, which was too tight around my armpits. 'I'm impressed.'

'I was surprised he liked it.' As he took in the sight of me, head to toe, I wished my tights would evaporate, or at least transform into something fleecy. Mum's dress had long sleeves, and the cottage was warm, but my body temperature had dipped.

'Here.' Seth unzipped his thick black woollen cardigan and handed it to me. 'Put it on,' he ordered.

I gratefully pushed my arms in the sleeves and zipped it up to my chin. The wool smelt deliciously of him. 'This is getting to be a habit.'

'It suits you.' He nodded his approval. 'You don't want to catch a cold right before Christmas.'

'Not when I've still got work to do at the café,' I said, feeling like myself for the first time all day – including the bit that was worried that work was at a standstill. 'Now, where's that cup of tea?'

In the end, Seth warmed up the vegetable lasagne in the microwave, and the three of us ate at the kitchen table, while Digby chewed his rubber bone on the mat in front of the fireplace. It was an oddly domestic scene, and when Felicity appeared in the doorway, her face registered horrified surprise – as if she'd stumbled across a vicious crime scene.

'Well, isn't this cosy?'

'Hello, Mother.' Seth made an effort to sound welcoming, but looked resigned.

'Hello, Grandma.' Jack wiped his mouth with the back of his hand, which drew a frown as Felicity put down her leather bag, unwound her tartan scarf and unfastened what looked like a shooting jacket.

'Napkin, Jack,' she scolded.

'We haven't got any.' Seth handed Jack a sheet of kitchen roll, which he scrunched up and put on his plate.

'Hello, Felicity,' I said in a friendly manner. 'Would you like something to eat?'

She looked at me as though I'd offered to trim her toenails. 'Is it your place to ask?'

'It's the servant's day off,' I couldn't resist saying, and Seth pressed a hand to his mouth to hide a smile.

'What's a servant?' Jack enquired.

Felicity seemed about to speak when Digby flew at her, growling deep in his throat and we watched, transfixed, as she stared him down until he retreated to the door with a whimper.

'Please can I play with Digby in the living room, Dad?' Jack was already down from the table.

Seth nodded and ruffled his hair. 'Of course you can.'

'You're too soft with him,' said Felicity, when Jack had fled with Digby hot on his heels. Still wearing her coat, she peered into the hall then shut the kitchen door.

'What are you doing?' Seth had half-risen, but sat back down again.

'I need to talk to this young lady in private,' she said, as if I wasn't there, and when she fixed me with a penetrating gaze, I wished I wasn't. 'Why are you wearing my son's cardigan?'

Was that all? 'I was a bit chilly,' I said, fingering the zip. It was cosy in the kitchen, as Seth had got the fire going in the grate, and I'd unfastened the cardigan while we were eating.

'Rather dressed up for a *nanny*,' she said, eyeing my outfit underneath as though I'd rocked up in a cocktail dress. 'Wouldn't you say?' This last bit she directed at Seth.

'Please don't be rude to Tilly.' He was tight-lipped as he gathered our plates and stood up. 'Why does it matter what she's wearing?'

'It matters because this woman is an imposter.'

I wondered whether she'd been reading some Agatha Christie, because surely no one spoke like that in real life.

'Imposter?' Seth's voice was drenched with disbelief. 'This isn't *Murder on the Orient Express*.'

It was as if he'd caught my train of thought, and I threw him a little smile, which Felicity caught.

'Why are you smiling at my son like that?'

'Sorry?'

'Mum,' Seth began, but Felicity was jabbing the air in front of my face.

'I know you're not a nanny.' Her eyes had narrowed to slits. 'I looked you up.'

'Mother, if you keep talking to Tilly like that—'

'Don't you care?' Lifting her chin, she glared at him, her face tight with annoyance. 'This woman has wormed her way into your life under false pretences.'

Seth put the plates down and rubbed the crease between his eyebrows. 'She hasn't,' he said, with weary forbearance.

'What did you find online?' I was genuinely curious. I wasn't active on social media, I didn't have a website, and I hadn't done anything interesting enough to warrant my name coming up in a Google search.

'You don't have a website and you're not on social media, which rang alarm bells for a start,' she said, finally thrusting her coat off and draping it over the back of a chair. 'Although I did come across a photo of you in a so-called design magazine with some *friends*, one of whom was smoking *weed*.' I knew the picture she was referring to. It had been taken the night I was out with the group of designers I'd studied with, one of whom had just won an award. 'It wasn't weed, she was vaping,' I said.

'That's just as bad as smoking.'

'Technically, it isn't.'

Felicity was wearing a crimson turtleneck, and pushed the sleeves up as if preparing for a fight. '*And* you're not registered *anywhere* as a childminder, *or* a nanny.' There was a lot of emphasising going on.

'That's because—'

To stop Seth saying 'she's not' I said, 'Why do you think I'm here, then?'

That seemed to throw her. 'That's not the point,' she blustered, brushing a loose strand of hair off her forehead.

'You said I was here under false pretences.'

She opened and closed her mouth then said, 'You obviously know my son is famous in some circles and have insinuated your way into his life to either take advantage of him, or his son.' We'd moved into bad movie territory now.

'Why on earth would I do that?'

'You might be planning to kidnap Jack and hold him to ransom, or work some magic on my son to get him to marry you.' OK, we'd moved into the realms of very bad television drama.

'That's ridiculous,' I said.

She fingered her pearls and darted a look at Seth, who'd tipped his head to look at the ceiling as if hoping he could shoot right through it. 'Look at him!' The words blasted out like bullets. 'He's a catch for any woman, but he's been badly hurt once before and I don't want that to happen to him again.'

Seth's head came down, and as his eyes grazed mine before meeting hers, I registered his surprise. 'Mum, it's not like that.' He spoke more gently than I felt she deserved. 'Tilly's here for Jack and, no, she's not a trained nanny, and I'm sorry I let you believe that she was, but Jack likes her, and so do I, and that's all that really matters.'

'Of course it isn't,' she snapped, as if ashamed by her show of vulnerability, and I wondered suddenly, what it must have been like for her, knowing Seth was racing around a track somewhere in the world, perhaps waiting for a call to say he'd been hurt – or worse. Perhaps she hadn't been able to bring herself to watch. I wasn't sure I could have, in her position, and felt a small and unexpected swell of sympathy.

'I would never do anything to hurt Jack… or Seth.' I didn't look at him as I said it, and wondered whether it would help to mention Bridget. Explain that Seth's social circle was widening, and might include his future wife and stepdaughter.

Wow. That would be weird. Seth would be Romy's *stepfather.*

But I didn't get round to saying anything else as she picked up her bag and strode to the door. 'Well, now you've finished taking me for a fool, I think it's time I checked on my team,' she said. 'Registered workmen, with business cards and a good reputation,' she added, presumably for my benefit, colour on her cheeks. 'And then I'll go and sit with my grandson, if that's OK with you.'

'Of course it's OK with me,' said Seth, scratching the back of his neck. 'You don't need to be so dramatic, Mum.'

'Don't tell me what I need.' She rounded on him. 'I've given you every opportunity to do the right thing by Jack, and instead you're…' she swept an arm between us '… sitting around, playing happy families with a woman who doesn't even have a job, as far as I can tell.'

Why did people keep saying that?

As she ran upstairs – no doubt to find fault with her *team* – I pushed back my chair and stood up. 'I should go.'

'Please don't.' Seth shoved his hands through his hair, his face crumpled with misery and embarrassment. 'I'm so sorry about that.'

'I don't want to give her any more reasons to think Jack would be better off with her.'

He let his mouth twist into a wry smile. 'She'll find plenty more, if she puts her mind to it,' he said. 'And you can't go home, you don't have any transport.'

'I can walk to the café from here.' Even so, I didn't move. 'I've work to do, anyway.' Why did I keep saying that, when there was nothing I could do?

'Dressed like that?'

'Eighties couture is the new overalls.' It didn't make much sense. 'I'll manage.'

Seth gripped the worktop behind him. 'I'm sorry Mum said that. About you not having a proper job.'

'It's not the first time I've heard it today.' I zipped Seth's cardigan back up. 'It was Rufus's parting shot, too.'

'Mum was just lashing out.'

'They're both right, though. Apart from doing up the café, I don't have a proper job.' I dropped back on the chair and looked at the table. 'It was one of the things that Bridget had a bee in her bonnet about, and that's why she thinks I'm giving your cottage a makeover,' I said. 'It was part of my business plan…' I said *business plan* in a silly, posh voice '… to become a bona fide, full-time interior designer.'

'Is that what you want to do?'

I considered his words. 'It's what I think I *should* do. Don't get me wrong,' I said, looking up as he started to speak. 'I really enjoy it, but I like doing other things too, like walking tours in the summer, and I was thinking I might take that swimming instructor's job you told me about at the pool. I'd rather take design jobs by word of mouth, if they appeal to me, than get all websitey and businessy.'

'What's wrong with that?' Seth sat opposite, and while I knew he was just being polite because... well, because I was Jack's saviour, I found myself saying, 'I feel guilty, I suppose.'

'Guilty?'

'Because I had it easy growing up, compared to Bridget. Dad was working all hours – he hadn't won any awards back then – and money was really tight. The nice holidays didn't happen until after I was born.' I paused as Digby came in and gulped water from his bowl. 'Bridget was always ambitious and driven,' I said, when he'd gone. 'She thinks I'm a lazy, over-privileged brat, which I suppose I am.'

'That wasn't the impression I got.' Seth's smile was one of puzzled amusement. 'I mean, I got the whole "exasperating kid sister" vibe, but she's obviously fond of you.'

'She was in a good mood because she was having dinner with you.'

'I don't think it was just that.' He shook his head. 'If you don't want to work full-time, then don't,' he said. 'If we're in a position to choose what we do with our lives, why shouldn't we, providing we're not hurting anyone else?'

I struggled to find an argument and failed. He made it sound not only possible, but desirable. 'The guilt though...' I let the words trail off.

'Guilt can be a good motivator, but it seems to me you don't need one.' He prodded the table for emphasis. 'You have a gift for doing the right thing at the right time... what?' he said, as I covered my eyes and groaned.

'We're back to me being on the beach at just the right moment,' I said, but when I peered through my fingers he was vigorously shaking his head.

'No, it's not that. You make people happy.'

'Rubbish.' Even so, his words ignited a warm glow in my stomach that I did my best to ignore. I laced my fingers together and studied my nails. I'd forgotten to paint them for the wedding – not that it mattered now. I wondered how Rufus had explained my absence to his brother, and decided I didn't care. 'But thanks for being nice.'

A look of mild frustration crossed Seth's face, but before he could speak there was the sound of drilling upstairs and Felicity stuck her head around the kitchen door.

'There's no need to stay now I'm here,' she said, with chilly restraint. 'You probably have things to do.'

Ignoring Seth's urgent protest, I pushed my chair back. The toxic atmosphere would ease if I left. 'I'll get my bags from the car and be out of your hair,' I said.

Chapter Twenty-Six

It was dark and cold as I approached the café, and no lights were on inside. It closed earlier during the winter months, and Gwen would have locked up in good time to catch her bus to Bigbury-on-Sea where she lived with her cousin.

The security light came on as I walked through the empty car park to the function room, glad of the parka Seth had lent me.

'You'll have no clothes left at this rate,' I'd said, prompting an unexpected image of him bare-chested in a rolled-down wetsuit, which had quickly warmed me up.

I wasn't warm now, having been buffeted by a salty wind racing off the sea, working its way through my layers. I couldn't even feel my knees, which proved how useless 'natural' ten denier tights were, unless you were attending a garden party thrown by the Queen.

I'd rejected Seth's offer of a lift, aware that Felicity was watching from the window as I retrieved my bags from his car, and told him I'd enjoy the walk.

'Don't be a stranger,' he'd said, hands bunched in his jeans pockets, hair tossed by the breeze, and I'd sensed again his reluctance to let me go. No wonder, as I'd been a buffer between him and his mother, I reflected, striding away as if I didn't have a care in the world, in spite of what felt like a gale-force wind in my head, tossing my thoughts about.

I hadn't even said goodbye to Jack.

Reaching the door, I rummaged in my pocket for my keys, before remembering it wasn't my coat and they were in the handbag I'd brought for the wedding. Putting down the bags of Christmas gifts, I unclasped the handbag and felt around inside. Nothing, apart from my phone, my leather wallet, and a pen that must belong to Mum.

The lipstick wasn't there either, and I suddenly remembered it rolling out in Seth's car when I'd dropped the bag. Perhaps the keys had fallen out too.

'Crap,' I muttered, switching on my phone torch and checking all the bags, but I knew the keys had been in the handbag – I remembered putting them there, and I hadn't used them all day.

I leaned my forehead against the cold, glass panel of the door and peered inside, but there was nothing but empty space. It was becoming impossible to imagine it with a proper floor and lights and a Christmas tree, and filled with people holding drinks, singing carols, and generally having a good time. Or, in Jerry's case, trying to escape Gwen's clutches. Remembering my promises, I quickly tried Gwen's mobile on the off-chance she might have missed her bus and could let me in through the café. Guessing she'd want to know how I'd managed to secure an electrician after hours on a Saturday, at this time of year, I mentally rehearsed some answers.

He's the friend of a friend, and desperately needs some the cash to buy Christmas presents for his children. No. She wouldn't want some 'desperado or conman' on the premises, bound to 'make a balls-up'.

The original electrician has said he can do the floor one-handed… too ridiculous.

I felt a blast of relief when she didn't pick up, and remembered her saying the mobile reception at her cousin's house was terrible. She must be there already.

I just about had time to walk back to the cottage but couldn't face Felicity again, and really didn't want to call Seth and ask him to check his car. Then again, I didn't have much choice if I wanted to get into the function room. I rang his number.

'Hello?'

I almost dropped the phone. 'Bridget?

'Tilly!'

'Why are you answering Seth's phone?'

'Why are you calling him?' She lowered her voice before I could respond. 'My god, his mother's a nightmare,' she whispered. 'Talk about suspicious. She's already accused me of using my daughter to try and trap Seth – did you know his actual name is Ainsley? – and warned me I won't win. I've only been here ten minutes.'

'What are you doing there?'

'Romy kept saying Jack's name and, to be honest, I was bored, so I thought I'd give him a ring and suggest we take the kids bowling in Kingsbridge.'

'Isn't Romy a bit young for bowling?' I'd gone Mary Poppins again. 'And what about her bedtime routine?'

'She had a long nap this afternoon,' said Bridget. 'She's bouncing off the walls right now. I needed to get out.'

Not the most romantic of reasons, but a good excuse to see Seth again.

'Where is Seth?'

'He had to nip upstairs and investigate some rewiring that's being done,' she said. 'I suppose your team need some supervision while you're not here, though I imagine his mother will enjoy wielding the whip while we're out.'

I imagined them packed in Seth's car, driving to the leisure centre in Kingsbridge, where I'd bumped into Seth and Jack at the swimming pool. 'Does she mind you all going out?'

'I don't think she's got much choice,' said Bridget. 'Seth looked pretty hacked off when I got here. I got the sense they'd had words.'

I had a feeling my name might have come up. 'Will he mind you answering his phone?'

'He asked me to, on his way upstairs,' she said. 'How was the wedding?'

It took a moment to make the mental shift. 'Oh,' I said. 'I didn't go.'

'WHAT?' Digby gave two loud barks, as if startled by her shout. 'What do you mean you didn't go?' she said. 'Where have you been all day?'

'It's a long story.' I was suddenly desperate to get off the phone. My teeth were chattering and my feet had gone numb. My boots definitely weren't made for walking, and hadn't been designed for warmth. 'I'm fine,' I said, trying to sound jolly. 'Have a nice evening, and I'll see you later.'

'But you haven't got your car.' If I didn't know better, I'd have said my sister was worried about me.

'When I'm done here, I'm off to meet Cassie and Meg at the Smugglers Inn,' I said, making a snap decision. If necessary, I'd ask every person there if they knew how to lay a floor, and offer to buy them drinks for life if they'd do the job for me. 'I'll get a taxi home.'

I hadn't looked at my phone since leaving that morning, and saw that Cassie and Meg had messaged to ask how the wedding was going.

So, is he the One? That was Meg.

Cassie's had asked *Have you found your 'forever man'?*

I replied in our WhatsApp group. *Rufus IS the One – most likely to bury a body under his patio one day. Not so much forever man, as 'never man'.*

There was another message I'd missed, from a number I didn't recognise. It was the electrician, and as I read it, my heart dropped like a stone. *Sorry, can't do the job tonight after all, wife sick, got to take my kids to a Christmas party in Truro.*

I closed my eyes; thought about screaming, or having a quiet sob, but instead went back to the WhatsApp group. *Either of you free for an emergency drink at the Smugglers? XX*

'I knew there was something off about Rufus, when you told us he didn't like dogs,' said Cassie, flipping a peanut in the air and catching it in her mouth.

'I wish you wouldn't do that, you might choke,' said Meg.

'I mean, who doesn't like dogs?'

'People who like cats,' I said miserably. 'Although, he doesn't like cats either.'

'I can't believe he tried to lock you in his car.' Cassie pushed the bag of peanuts across the table. 'And you reckon he's gone all stalkery before?'

'From what he said.' I paused as a group of revellers entered the pub, almost toppling the heavily decorated Christmas tree by the door. Decor wasn't the landlord's forte – the whole pub was a throwback to the eighties – and Bill hadn't matched the size of the pot to the tree, which was topped by a glowing Yoda wearing a Santa cape, and holding a lightsabre, which made me think of Jack. 'I feel like an idiot for not trusting my judgement in the first place,' I said. 'But he's out of my life for good now.'

Meg raised her voice over a blast of, 'We Wish You a Merry Christmas' from the bar area. 'Maybe you should report him to the college.'

I shook my head. 'I don't want him to lose his job,' I said. 'I just want to forget I ever met him.'

'You should have called us,' said Cassie. She was wearing a paint-patterned shirt and I guessed she'd come straight from her easel, while Meg had a dusting of flour near her hairline that suggested she'd been baking more mince pies. Our motto *sisters before misters* still held true – but I wondered for how much longer. In less than nine months, Cassie's priorities would shift, and Meg would be splitting her time between the bakery, and trips abroad with Nathan. Bridget would be returning to her house in Notting Hill in March, and I'd still be at home with Mum and Dad.

'What is it?' Meg stretched a hand across the scarred wooden table and gripped my fingers, and the sight of her clean, short fingernails made me feel a bit teary. 'Are you still shaken up?'

'Honestly, I could kill him,' said Cassie, pushing her glass of untouched white wine aside and taking my other hand. 'Tell us what you'd like us to do.'

'Cyanide poisoning might be the way to go.' Meg's blue eyes sparkled with intent. 'I could slip some into a cake and have it delivered.'

'Um, I'm not sure where to get hold of cyanide.' I blinked, already feeling better.

'Public humiliation might be easier.' Cassie gave a wicked grin. 'I could do a cartoon sketch, highlighting his less flattering characteristics,' she made the recognised symbol for a tiny willy with her little finger, 'and stick copies to lampposts all over Devon, with his name attached.'

'I like that idea.' I took a gulp of cold beer. 'But maybe it's best if I ignore him altogether from now on.'

'Spoilsport.' Meg smiled and let go of my hand. 'Let us know if you change your mind.'

'I still can't get over the sight of you in a dress.' Cassie leaned down the side of the table to take in the full spectacle, while I discreetly scoped the pub for possible electricians and floor fitters. 'I don't remember ever seeing you in tights.'

'Do you mean my itchy leg shackles?' I said. 'I noticed when I came in, they're completely laddered.'

'I prefer thick black ones. Like the ones we wore at school,' said Meg. 'I think I've still got a pair, somewhere.'

'Shame on you.' My phone gave a melodic tinkle. 'Uh-oh, talk of the devil,' I said, seeing a text had arrived. 'It's Rufus.'

'Oh my god, what a nerve.' Cassie craned her neck to look at the screen. 'He'd better be doing some sorries.'

Meg came round, enveloping me in her sweet, rose-garden scent. 'What's he got to say for himself?'

'There's a photo.'

'You got a dick-pic?' said a barrel-shaped woman on her way to the ladies, peering over my shoulder with a raucous cackle. 'Get a lot of them on Tindall.'

'I think she means Tinder,' said Cassie and we exchanged horrified giggles.

'I really hope it's not a dick-pic.' I opened the attachment, which – to my relief – revealed a scarlet-faced, grinning Rufus with his shirtsleeves rolled up, and his arm draped around the shoulders of a sweet-faced red-head gazing at him adoringly. 'Christ, I think he's pulled.'

'Maybe he's got a gun pressed to her side,' said Cassie.

'She actually seems really happy,' Meg observed. 'Or drunk.'

'Listen to this.' I read his text aloud. 'I'm sorry you couldn't make it today, Tilly, and wanted to let you know that I've met someone at Grant's wedding. She's called Sophie, she's a teacher like me, and we've really hit it off. I'm sorry, but I don't think we can see each other again.'

'What the actual…?' Cassie's jaw dropped. 'He's actually *breaking up* with you?'

'Even though you've already broken up with him?' Meg squeezed my shoulder. 'What a bloody cheek.'

'Oh, here comes another photo.' This time, Rufus and Sophie were standing beneath some mistletoe, doing an open-mouthed kiss.

'Ew,' said Cassie. 'It's like watching cats licking each other's faces.'

'Who's even taking those photos?' Meg looked queasy.

'They're selfies,' I said. 'You can see from the angle of his arm.'

'Talk about making a point.' Cassie made a retching sound. 'It's revolting.'

'I suppose if it makes him feel better to think he's the one doing the breaking up, I'm not going to complain.' I swiftly typed *She looks lovely. All the best x*

'Shouldn't you be warning her off?' said Meg. 'What if he turns dodgy?'

'She looks into him.' I risked looking at the photo again. 'It might be different this time.'

'See, there's a bit of romance in you after all.' Meg nudged my hand. 'Now, delete his number and those awful pictures, and finish your drink.'

'Good plan.' I felt lighter once they'd gone, and had a feeling I wouldn't be hearing from Rufus again.

'So, are you back on track for the party?' said Cassie.

My heart tripped. 'Definitely!' There was no way I could go around asking for help, when she and Meg thought everything was under control.

'You're sure?' Meg flashed me a significant look. 'You know you can say if you're not, right?'

'I've told you, the room will be ready on the night.' My gaze slid to my glass, which was almost empty. 'Stop hassling me, bitches.'

'There's only one full day left before our parents get back,' Cassie pointed out, as if the date wasn't emblazoned in neon across my frontal lobe. 'And it's a Sunday.'

I lowered my head to the table and let it rest there a moment.

'Tilly, what's wrong?' Meg touched my hair.

'Tilly?' Cassie picked up my hand and let it drop. 'Are you ill?'

'I'm not ill.' I raised my head and looked at them. I was *so* tired. I hadn't even realised how tired I was until that moment, and the crowd at the bar, now doing shots and singing the first verse of every Christmas song ever made, was making my scalp throb. 'I don't think I cope well under pressure.'

'Oh, Tilly, you should have said.' Cassie sounded stricken. 'I wouldn't have…' She slid a look at Meg.

'What?' Meg blinked slowly, like a doll.

'Nothing.' Cassie ate a handful of crisps, while I tried to accept that the room might not be finished, and their Christmas Eve would be ruined.

'Well, *I've* put pressure on her too,' said Meg. 'No wonder she's in a state.'

'What sort of pressure have you put on Tilly?'

'I just… I…' Meg picked up her phone and fiddled with the case. 'I kept saying how much I was looking forward to the party on Christmas Eve, that's all.'

'Me too,' said Cassie, then blurted, 'I'm pregnant.'

'Oh my god, I KNEW it!' Meg's voice was a strangled squeal. 'When you didn't eat your mince pie or drink your coffee yesterday,

I had a feeling there was something you weren't telling us. And you haven't drunk your wine.'

'I wanted to announce it at the party,' she said, returning Meg's bear hug, and grinning at me over her shoulder. 'You know I'm no good at keeping secrets, but I only told Tilly because I wanted to check the party was going to happen.'

'Well, I'm arranging a wedding for Mum and Dad.'

'Shut UP!' Meg fell silent and Cassie giggled. 'It's a saying,' she said. 'Like, you *cannot* be serious!'

'I know.' Meg grinned. 'And I *am* serious, but honestly, Tilly,' she leaned over again and lifted my limp hands off the table, 'we could always shift the party to my house. I mean, it'll be a bit tight because it's not very big, and they'll be loads of people coming, but we'll manage. Just say the word.'

I looked at their beautiful faces, and the urge to cry was overwhelming.

'You guys.' I gave them my best Canadian accent. 'That party's gonna happen where it's supposed to, you'd better believe it.' They raised their glasses, and I lifted my beer bottle, marvelling at the scale of my delusion. 'But it's the last time I'm doing a project with such a tight deadline, because it's turned me into a psycho.'

'We'll drink to that,' said Meg, shaking her head when Cassie and I fell about laughing. 'Obviously you're *not* a psycho,' she said.

'Well, I'm glad we've cleared that up.'

'Hey, you two can be godmothers, how about that?' said Cassie.

As we lifted our glasses again, it struck me that nothing could ever be really bad as long as I could talk to my best friends about it – only, I still couldn't bear to spoil their Christmas Eve plans. 'Cassie, do you have a spare key to the café that I could borrow?'

'There's one at Mum and Dad's,' she said. 'If you like, we can go and get it, why?'

'Do you trust me?'

'With my life.'

'Good,' I said. Because I was going to get the floorboards down and sort out the wiring if it was the last thing I ever did.

Chapter Twenty-Seven

I was never going to get the floorboards down *or* sort out the wiring. I'd even watched a YouTube tutorial enticingly titled 'How to Lay Wood Flooring over Concrete' but was crucially missing some polyethylene sheeting to 'minimise moisture migration' and a few other vital tools, and I already knew in my heart I'd need more than a screwdriver to get the electricity working. I'd somehow convinced myself on the way over that I'd be able to improvise, forgetting I didn't have my car with my toolbox in the boot.

It didn't help that the room was almost dark as the café lights barely filtered through, and I was nervy about having them on in case they attracted attention. I'd found a torch in the office, but the beam wasn't very strong, and the one on my phone drained the battery too quickly. I was down to one bar after watching the stupid tutorial.

I sank to the cold floor and wondered whether it was worth putting a plea on social media for some emergency tradesmen. Then I remembered, I didn't have any followers so there wasn't any point. If I'd admitted I was stuck, I could have asked Cassie and Meg to try, but it was too late for that.

Groaning, I threw my phone across the floor, then scrambled to get it back. There was literally nothing I could do but admit defeat, and the last bus from Seashell Cove arrived in around five minutes; I should make it if I left now. Once home, I'd phone my friends – and Gwen – and break the news that the function room wouldn't be ready for the party. Knowing I'd let everyone down made me want to howl, but I couldn't keep hoping for a miracle, and alternative arrangements had to be made.

It felt spooky being at the café on my own at night, especially once I'd switched off the lights in the café. A half-moon shone in, casting a silvery glow and glimmering off the Christmas tree decorations. I half-expected Dickens to sidle through, but Gwen would have carted him home on the bus in his fancy carrier. He'd be curled on her lap by now, no doubt being fed caviar from a silver spoon.

My stomach gave a treacherous growl. Cassie would be tucking into a gourmet dinner cooked by Danny, and Meg had said she was meeting Nathan at his brother and sister-in-law's for a meal. Not that I deserved a nice dinner. Eyes prickling with tears, I let myself out and locked up, and started when my phone buzzed in my hand.

Can you believe his mother insisted on coming? Bridget had attached a picture, shot from below, of a coat-and-boot-clad Felicity watching, stony-faced, as a blurry Jack hurled a bowling ball down the alley with both hands. I actually could believe it. I headed up the path to the bus stop, blinking as a car drove past, headlights cutting through the darkness, trying to picture the scene. So much for their cosy, festive outing. I couldn't imagine a bigger downer than having Felicity tag along. She'd probably called her friendly judge to update him on the terrible way her grandson was being treated – doing something as common as bowling with his loving dad, accompanied by an accomplished, attractive, single mum and her daughter, and probably eating pizza!

I still couldn't imagine a judge – even one who was a friend of Felicity's – opting to remove Jack from his father's care, and felt hopeful that her plan would come to nothing. I even found myself feeling a bit sorry for her. She was sure to lose Seth *and* Jack if she kept doggedly pursuing custody. It was only a matter of time before Seth cut her off completely.

Deep in thought, I barely registered the sound of footsteps behind me, and let out a choking gasp when a hand landed on my shoulder and someone spoke my name. I dropped my bags and spun round, ready to kick out at whoever it was – if my tights would let me. It was a man. A tall, broad-shouldered man, wearing a thick coat and a hat with earflaps.

'Seth!'

'Sorry, I'm sorry.' He backed away with his hands up as though I'd whipped out a sword. 'I didn't mean to scare you.'

'What… why are you here?' I felt for my phone, which I'd dropped in the pocket of my coat. *Seth's coat.* 'You're bowling,' I said. 'I got a text.'

'From me?' He sounded confused.

'Surely you'd know if you'd sent me a text.' I was breathless with fright – and something else I wasn't willing to name. 'From Bridget.'

'Oh, right.' He lowered his hands. 'She must have sent it earlier.' He stepped forward. 'We just got back and I spotted your keys in the car,' he said, holding them out so they jangled. 'I thought you might need them.'

'You could have given them to Bridget and asked her to come and get me.'

'Romy was a bit overexcited.' He dropped the keys in my palm, and I slid them into my (his) pocket. 'Bridget wanted to get her home, so I offered to come.'

'What about Jack?'

'My mother's a very efficient babysitter, in case you hadn't noticed.'

'Oh, right,' I said. 'Sorry. I don't mean to keep implying you've left him at home alone.' My brain struggled to keep up – to accept he was even there, though mostly in silhouette, shadowed by darkness.

'Bridget said you were meeting your friends at the pub once you'd finished working, but when you weren't there, I guessed you might have come back here.'

'I did.' I remembered the headlights I'd seen. 'That was your car,' I said.

'I didn't realise it was you at first, you were practically running.'

'I was trying to catch a bus.' I looked up the road, but could only see an endless stretch of velvet-black sky, carpeted with stars. 'It's the last one and I've probably missed it.' I sounded as close to tears as I felt.

'I'm sorry.' Seth's breath hung in the cold air between us. 'So, you haven't finished whatever you had to do?'

I dropped my bags at my feet and blew on my hands. 'No,' I said, incapable of dressing it up. 'I'm no good at the hands-on stuff, apart from painting and sticking up the occasional roll of wallpaper. I'm good at seeing what needs to be done and organising people to do it, and I love the finishing touches. That's my forte. It was all going according to plan until that bloody leak, and the floor took ages to dry, and then the floorboards were wrong and had to go back, and then Ted couldn't fit the work in, and the electrician broke his arm and I couldn't find another – electrician, not arm – and now there isn't time to get the room ready before the Maitlands come back.'

A couple of tears spilled over. 'Sorry,' I said, flicking them away. 'It's just that it sucks, because all sorts of things were supposed to happen at the party on Christmas Eve.'

'What sort of things?'

'Well, for a start, my friend Cassie's boyfriend is planning to propose, then she's going to announce that they're having a baby...' I stopped.

He'd stepped closer, wrapping a hand around mine as gently as if he was picking up a newborn kitten. 'Gwen, the manager, is planning to make a move on the guy who works behind the counter because she fancies him – not that he knows it,' I continued in a shaky voice, 'and Meg has arranged a surprise wedding for her mum and dad, and it's really important because she thought her dad was dead until earlier this year, and her mum doesn't like going out so it's meant to be informal and the setting's perfect, or would be if I'd got my act together and got the place ready in time, like I promised.'

'Whoa,' said Seth. He produced a tissue from his coat pocket and pressed it into my free hand. 'This is all meant to be happening at the party?'

I nodded, scrubbing the tissue across my eyes. 'It's top secret, so I shouldn't even be telling you.' I let out a sob – the first time I'd cried in I couldn't remember how long. 'I've promised them all the function room will be ready and now I'm going to have to let them down, which I hate, because I *always* keep my word.'

'Well, sometimes that's just not possible.' Seth's voice was gentle. 'You've tried your very best, haven't you?'

'Well… yes, but no one's available to work now this close to Christmas Eve, which, as everyone keeps reminding me, is *the day after tomorrow*.'

'But that's not your fault.' He gently pressed my fingers. 'You weren't to know there'd be a leak, or the floorboards would be wrong, or that the electrician would break his arm.'

'I should have been able to work around it.'

'You've tried your best, by the sound of things.'

'Bridget would say it's typical of me.' I gave an unladylike sniff, and tipped my head to stop more tears falling. 'That I dilly about too much.'

'Dilly about?' His tone was teasing. 'You need to remember your sister was probably holding onto some jealousy about you. She talked about it a bit, while Mum wasn't listening,' he added, when I made a sound of surprise. 'She thinks coming home, and your parents being away, has helped her see things differently. That *you've* helped her see things differently.'

'She said that?'

'I told you.' The pressure on my hand increased. 'You have a way of bringing out the best in people, of saying the right things.'

'It hasn't worked on your mother.' I said it more to deflect his words, which had sent a spread of heat through my whole body. 'I'm starting to wonder whether she even has a best side.'

'I've wondered that myself,' admitted Seth. We'd been officially holding hands for more than a minute and I was no closer to letting go. 'Her saving grace is she thinks the world of Jack and, although she's going about it the wrong way, I know she thinks she has his best interests at heart.'

'She's got a funny way of showing it.' But it was nice to hear him defending his mother, in spite of everything. 'Anyway, thanks for coming to find me, and I'm sorry about… you know.' I held up the soggy, crumpled tissue.

'You don't need to apologise.'

As I met his eyes, the whites gleaming brightly, a flurry of snow began to dance around us.

'Oh wow.' Seth looked up, and held out his free hand as if to pocket the flakes. 'I hope it settles this time,' he said, a smile breaking out. 'Jack's desperate for it to snow.'

'It's a shame we can't order it specially,' I said, smiling too. 'You should get back to him.'

'Not until I've driven you home.'

'Don't be silly, I can easily call a taxi.'

'It's the least I can do.'

'Not this again.' It came out as a wail. 'Please, Seth, stop proposing favours.'

'You haven't heard what I'm going to say next.' Now he was holding my other hand and despite the cold, I felt as if I was melting. 'I think you're going to like it,' he said.

My heart started racing. 'Go on.'

'You should have said sooner you were struggling to get the room finished,' he said, still smiling. 'But then we wouldn't be standing here, and I think this might be the best night out I've had in ages.'

He must really like bowling, and freezing his toes off with grizzling females. 'Will you just say it?' I blinked snowflakes off my eyelashes, my heart bumping harder.

'You can have the team for the day tomorrow.'

'The team?' I was momentarily confused; pictured footballers prancing on a snowy pitch.

'You might have noticed there are workmen at my cottage,' he said, with exaggerated patience. 'Including an electrician. Although, I expect they've downed tools for the night and gone back to their hotel to drink, and bitch about my mother.'

'Oh my god.' Remembering I'd briefly thought before about asking if I could borrow them, I felt a frisson of excitement. 'Are you saying…?'

He nodded. 'All yours.'

'But… there's quite a lot to do.'

'So?' He gave my hands a gentle shake. 'I'll pay them double, triple, whatever they want and they're fast,' he said. 'It'll be a challenge, like that sixty-minute makeover programme I was hooked on for a while.'

Hope rose, warm and bright, inside me. 'But, your mum,' I said, not daring to believe it. 'She'll be furious.'

'She'll have to live with it.' He squeezed my hands, and I squeezed back, as it fully sank in that, if the team really was coming over, the function room could still be ready for the party. I wouldn't have to let anyone down. 'And this is your final payback?' I said. 'You'll stop going on about owing me anything afterwards?'

'Promise,' he said, teeth flashing.

On impulse, I leaned in and kissed his cheek, which wasn't as cold as I'd have expected. The words *hot-blooded* shot through my mind. He smelt of warm skin with a hint of garlic from the vegetable lasagne we'd eaten earlier, and as I pulled away, he turned his head so our lips were barely millimetres apart.

'Thank you,' I murmured. Our eyes locked. A snowflake landed on the tip of his nose and I wanted to lick it off.

I sprang back, releasing his hands. 'It's going to be a long day tomorrow.' I bent to pick up my bags, which were already dusted with snow. 'I should get an early night.'

When I looked up, he was watching me with a look I couldn't describe – mostly because it was dark, and my vision was obscured by falling flakes. 'Come on,' I said. 'I'll race you back to your car.'

Chapter Twenty-Eight

'Did you get everything done last night?' Bridget asked, as I headed for the door the following morning eating a Marmite sandwich. She was coming downstairs with Romy clamped to her back like a koala.

'Tilly!' Romy squealed, looking cute in a snowman-patterned onesie.

'Romy!' I blew her a kiss, which made her giggle. 'Not quite,' I said to Bridget. 'Actually, not at all.' I decided I wasn't going to lie to her any more. 'Seth's lending me the team from the cottage to help me finish in time.'

True to his word, he'd called them and explained what needed doing, and asked them to be at the café by 8 a.m. 'I offered to pay them extra, but they said they'd be glad of a change of scenery, which I took to mean a break from my mother breathing down their necks,' he'd reported over the phone, half an hour after dropping me off, and when I thanked him again he said, 'Believe me, Tilly, this gives me so much pleasure, I should be thanking you, but I think I'll be doing that forever, anyway,' which had made me go hot again. I'd already been struggling not to keep replaying the way my heart had kicked when our lips had almost touched, or how good it had felt being beside him in the car on the journey home, the charged atmosphere becoming more relaxed as I steered the conversation to his glory days as a Formula One champion.

'It wasn't always as glamorous as people assume,' he'd said, driving carefully through a blizzard of snowflakes. 'Unless you're Lewis Hamilton and have a reputation to play up to.'

It had involved a lot of travelling, he'd said, to races all over the world: Dubai, Kuala Lumpur, New Zealand. 'I tried to visit the main attractions there, but a lot of my teammates weren't interested. They wanted to get laid, or go drinking, and I fell into it too for a while, but it wasn't really me, in spite of what the press reported.' There'd been memorable times – 'Obviously winning a few Grand Prixs and Le Mans, and meeting some elephants in the middle of the highway in Bangkok on the way to the track' – and sad times too – 'Losing a teammate was horrifying, and made me question whether it was worth carrying on. Especially after Jack was born.' His face had darkened. 'But I was in too deep, worth too much to the sponsors, and they'd always persuade me to compete just one more time.' Seeing his jaw tighten, I'd wanted to say something reassuring, but he'd added that it had been his choice; no one had made him compete. 'But maybe if Charlotte hadn't made things so difficult when I was at home...' His words had trailed off. 'She enjoyed the lifestyle,' he'd said. 'Anyway, although I had a couple of near misses, broke my collarbone, my ankle, I was lucky I was never seriously injured. But I was completely ready to give it up at least a year before I retired.'

He'd asked how I got into interior design, and I told him I'd always enjoyed rearranging the rooms at home, and that I'd redesigned Cassie's bedroom. Seeing it since coming home, I'd been surprised to find it looked exactly the same. 'But not half as nice as I remembered,' I told him. 'It was way too green – like Kermit-green.'

He'd laughed and said something about us all having to start somewhere, and then I was home, and the snow had stopped as though it had been switched off. I climbed out of the car with my bags and said goodbye and thank you, still embarrassed I'd kissed him – albeit it a chaste one on the cheek.

'*Lending* you?' Bridget set Romy down on the floor, and I watched as my niece raced into the living room with the early morning enthusiasm of the very young. 'I thought they were *your* team?'

I took a breath and nearly choked on my mouthful of sandwich. 'I'm not working at the cottage,' I said, once my throat was clear. 'I was planning to, but Felicity kind of took over.'

'That figures.' Bridget folded her arms. 'I thought *I* was a control freak, but she makes me look like… like…'

'Homer Simpson?'

She nearly smiled. 'That'll do.'

'You should probably wash Mum's dressing gown before she gets back,' I said, noticing a coffee stain on the pocket.

Bridget ignored my weak attempt at distraction. 'Why did you lie about the makeover?' I gave her a long look and she coloured. 'OK, I get it, I've been a judgemental bitch about your career. Or lack of one. I'm sorry.'

'It's fine, I should have been honest,' I said. 'As pathetic as it sounds, I wanted you to be pleased I was working hard.'

'Oh.' She pressed her fingers to her lips. 'That makes me feel even worse.'

'Hey,' I said, taking pity on her. 'Maybe we've both got issues.'

'Your only issue is *me*.'

Sensing tears were imminent, I went over and gave her a hug, holding on even when she tensed up. 'We're moving past all that now.' I kissed her temple. 'Honestly, Bee, we'll be like twins this time next year, communicating telepathically and everything.'

She gave a snorty laugh and relaxed against me for a second. 'Wait.' She pulled back and dashed a hand across her cheeks. 'Why have you been hanging about at Seth's if you're not working there?'

The back of my neck grew hot. 'I've been sort of pretending to be Jack's nanny,' I said.

'Oh my god! *Tilly*!' It was clear she was torn between laughing and telling me off and settled for saying, 'You're actually great with kids.'

'*What*?'

'He'd be lucky to have you as his nanny.'

'Wow!' I pretend-staggered backwards. 'Something amazing must have happened to put you in this charitable mood.'

'You're in a good mood too.'

'That's because I've got a team to help me at the café today.' I felt the same lurch of pleasure that had kept me flipping about in bed for most the night, pitching in and out of sleep. Remembering the text that Bridget had been so enigmatic about, I said, 'Aren't you going to let me in on your secret?' Maybe Seth was going to whisk her and Romy on holiday, after Christmas.

'All will be revealed at the Christmas Eve party.' Dry-eyed now, she gave a stagey wink.

'Oh god, not you too.'

'What do you mean?'

'Nothing.' Perhaps they were going to publicly announce they were a couple. Not wanting to examine the thought too closely, I grabbed my keys. 'And Felicity's rumbled I'm not a nanny, so I won't be hanging around at the cottage any more.'

'Oh.' Her brows rose. 'But I thought you and Seth had become friends.'

'Well... I...' *Did she mind?* 'I suppose, yes, we are, but—'

'Banana!' Romy ran out. 'Can't undo.' She held it up to Bridget, and I took the opportunity to slip out.

❄ ❄ ❄

''Cor, this looks a bit of all right.' Gwen – sporting 'festive' green and red stripes where her eyebrows had been, drawn on with felt-tip pens – was gazing at the sweep of floorboards gleaming warmly under the overhead lights. 'I'll just double check the electric is definitely workin' 'cos you can't be too sure, an' I don't want 'em going orf the minute people start arrivin' tomorrow evenin'.' She made her way back to the panel of switches that controlled the café's lighting, and clicked the newest one on and off several times, while I gave Mr Berryman an apologetic smile.

'Sorry about that,' I whispered. 'She likes to be thorough.'

'No worries,' he said, with a grin. He and the team had worked flat out, without a word of complaint, just lots of friendly banter. 'She's a duchess compared to Mrs Donovan.'

''e's only sayin' that cos I've kept 'em supplied wiv cake,' Gwen cackled, though how she'd heard from so far away was a mystery.

'Anything else we can do?'

I shook my head. 'You've been amazing,' I said. 'I can't thank you enough.'

'Our pleasure.' He gave me a military style salute I was sure he wouldn't have dared give Felicity, and went to join his workmates, who were sharing a pot of tea and some reindeer-shaped cookies that Meg had brought over as an excuse to check that the flooring was really down.

As the afternoon drew to a close, all that was left to do were the finishing touches. The floor space was needed, so the chairs and tables wouldn't go in until after Christmas. If anyone needed to sit down at the party they could use the café area, which meant all I had to do was put up and decorate the Christmas tree, currently stashed in the storeroom, string fairy lights around the room, pin some mistletoe in the archway, and hang the pictures that Cassie had painted: a series of watercolours of Seashell Cove in winter.

'Oh wow, it looks fantastic,' she said, when she dropped them off, before charging to the toilet to be sick.

'I reckon she's in the family way,' Gwen observed, when Cassie emerged looking pale but happy – not at all in keeping with the bout of food poisoning she'd mumbled about as she fled.

'Don't say anything,' I urged.

Gwen mimed zipping her mouth shut. 'We know all abart secrets, don't we?' She swivelled her eyes in Jerry's direction and winked. He almost dropped the cup he was drying and did a little dive to catch it. 'Look at 'im.' She made a noise that might have been a lovelorn sigh if it hadn't been so wheezy. 'They don't make 'em like that any more,' she said.

'Wasn't your ex in the SAS?'

Averting her gaze, she pulled a spray gun from her cleaning belt. 'Nah,' she said, squirting the nearest windowpane, which I was planning to decorate with removable vinyl snowflakes. 'I should never 'ave said that. I were coverin' up to save face, if I'm bein' 'onest.' She rubbed the window as though she was trying to erase it. 'We ran a pub togevver in the East End, but 'ad a difficult relationship on account of 'im bein' a cheatin' bar steward.' She paused to wipe the back of her hand across her forehead. 'He liked the ladies, did my Jimmy. But 'e 'ad an affair wiv me sister and when I found out I chucked 'im art… no, I didn't chuck 'im art,' she amended, seeming not to notice my mouth was gaping.

'I begged 'im to choose me, but 'e chose 'er, so I left and lived on the streets for a bit, then came to live wiv Maureen and I ain't looked back.'

I looked at her closely. 'Is that a storyline from *EastEnders,* Gwen?'

'Wish it were, duck,' she said, unoffended. She stopped polishing and tucked her cloth away. 'It's all true, you can ask Maureen if you don't believe me.'

'I'm sorry,' I said, tugging my shirtsleeves up. 'I just… it was unexpected, that's all. But it must have been horrible.' I considered giving her a cuddle but she was emitting enough *don't touch me vibes* to repel even the most committed hugger.

'It weren't nice.' She pointed to Jerry. 'Now, *'e* would never let a lady darn, I can tell.'

'How do you know, Gwen?'

'I've got that thing like gaydar these days, only for blokes what are decent.' She smoothed a hand over her bristly hair. 'I'm tellin' you, 'e's desperate for me to make a move.'

As she strolled back to the counter – was she swaying her *hips*? – I remembered what Meg had said about love being transformative, and hoped for Gwen's sake that my suspicions were true, and Jerry would be receptive to her advances.

I tried not to think of Seth as I set about bringing the room to life, with Meg's assistance – Cassie had gone to babysit her nephew – or to wonder what Jack was doing, and whether Felicity would persuade them to go back to hers for Christmas. It seemed unlikely, but Seth might agree to appease her if she played the card about Christmas being for families.

By the time I'd finished, I had a pounding headache, but the room looked like a classy, grown up Santa's grotto – without the Santa – and I could finally imagine it filled with people, holding drinks, and plates of food, and having a brilliant time.

'It's just how I imagined it would look.' Meg slid her arms around my waist from behind, and pressed her face to my back. 'You're a superstar, Tilly. I knew you'd get it done.'

'With a little help.' I'd confessed I'd been struggling and that Seth had lent me his team.

'I like that man more every day.' She gazed around shiny-eyed, hands clasped under her chin, and I knew she was imagining the scene that would unfold on Christmas Eve.

'Everything going according to plan?' I said, snapping a couple of photos on my phone and sending them to Bridget. Now she'd parted the gates of communication, I was determined to keep them open.

'Perfectly.' Meg dived into shot doing jazz hands. 'It's been hard hiding it from Mum, but I don't think she suspects a thing.'

'How are you going to get her into a wedding dress?'

Meg's eyes widened. 'I'm not,' she said. 'Any sniff of an event, and she'd stay in her bedroom all night.'

'I did wonder about that.'

'She'll pick something nice to wear, with a bit of encouragement from me and Dad, and whatever it is, it'll be perfect.'

I felt a bit choked up. 'You're amazing for doing it,' I said. 'Who would have thought that by the end of this year, your parents would be back together and getting married for the first time?'

'Not me.' She swung her hair, which was as shiny as her eyes. 'Talking of which, I'd better go and finish decorating the wedding cake, and then I'm going to have an early night.'

After a final check around the room, and a slight adjustment of the lights on the Christmas tree, I finally removed the plastic sheeting from the archway dividing the rooms, and heard a slow handclap from the counter.

''Bout bleedin' time,' said Gwen.

Chapter Twenty-Nine

Arriving home at seven-thirty, tired but elated, I pricked my finger on a giant holly-and-acorn wreath adorning the front door, and noticed the porch was illuminated by flashing colours. Bridget had clearly gone overboard with Christmas decorations. In the hallway, a garland, threaded with fairy lights, was twined around the banister; tinsel had been draped around picture frames, and Christmas cards dangled from a thread of ribbon on the wall.

'Wow,' I said, impressed. I'd campaigned to carry on decorating throughout the house, but Bridget had thought it would look 'over the top' so I'd let it drop. 'Have you been in the attic?'

'Obviously,' she said. 'I remember some of this stuff from when I was a kid, and Romy helped me put up our old stockings – though she's filled them with her Enchantimals toys.'

'I'm surprised they're in a fit state to hold anything,' I said, 'never mind those creepy crossbreed dolls.'

Bridget had also spent the day cleaning, judging by the shiny floor, and was leaning on a mop, looking tired but elated – which was odd. I knew she liked cleaning, but not that much.

'Where is my niece?'

'Worn out and fast asleep,' she said. 'She's over-excited about Mum and Dad coming home.'

'Do we have an estimated time of arrival?'

'Around half ten.'

I threw my jacket off and looked around, the scent of cloves, cinnamon and nutmeg carrying me back to childhood. 'You found Mum's Christmas candle?' She'd bought the same one for years, lighting it for an hour or two every day in the lead up to Christmas, so the house always smelt delicious.

'It's on the kitchen windowsill, out of harm's way,' said Bridget. 'Now, hang your coat up.' She smiled. 'Just kidding.'

I dropped it on the floor.

'No really, hang it up,' she said.

In the kitchen, she put the mop away, then took some clean washing out of the dryer and began to fold it. 'All done at the café?' Her eyes were sparkling. She'd washed her hair and wound some old-style rollers at the front (Mum's, obviously) and – in one of Dad's shirts and a pair of tracksuit bottoms – resembled an eccentric, yet very attractive cleaning lady. 'It looked great in the photos. Very festive.'

'All done, thank god.' I dropped at the table, reliving the utter relief that had washed over me as I left the café and texted Seth *THANK YOU!!* Whatever happened now, I'd kept my promise, and the room was ready for business. 'Let me do that.' I stood up, and plucked Mum's freshly washed dressing gown from her hands. 'You've done enough today, by the look of things.'

'Thanks.' She tuned the radio to a carol concert at the Royal Albert Hall, and the sound of a choirboy piping 'Oh Come all Ye Faithful' filled the air.

'You're looking forward to tomorrow then?' I said, as Bridget sank onto a chair, and picked up a half-empty mug of coffee, a smile playing over her face.

'Hmmm?' She looked up, her eyes all dreamy. 'Oh, definitely,' she said. 'I might be a bit late to the party though.'

I folded the dressing gown and picked up a little pinafore dress of Romy's. 'And you're definitely not going to let me in on your secret?' I gave her a winning smile. 'I'm good at keeping them,' I said. 'You'd be amazed to know what else is going to be happening.'

'Oh?' Her gaze sharpened. 'Do tell.'

'Only if you do.' I added Romy's dress to the growing pile and picked up Seth's jumper, which I'd finally got around to putting in the wash, resisting an urge to press it to my face. It wouldn't smell of him anyway, now, and Bridget would think I'd lost my mind. 'Come on, Bee, I'm dying to know what's got you smiling at least forty-five per cent of the time.'

She plucked a grape from the fruit bowl and lobbed it at me. 'OK, I'll tell you,' she said, as if she hadn't needed much prodding after all.

'Go on.' My curiosity levels shot skyways as I sat down, still clutching Seth's jumper. 'It had better be good.'

'It is.' She plucked another grape and popped it in her mouth.

'Bee!'

'I'm working up to it,' she said with a chuckle. 'OK, here goes.' She dusted her hands and rested them on the table between us. 'Chad's coming back.'

'Chad?' I stared. 'Romy's dad?'

Her eyes danced. 'I don't know any other Chads, do you?'

'But…'

'He did it, Tilly.'

'Did what?' My imagination ran riot. *He's killed someone. Bridget's going to hide him. He's a fugitive. Romy's going to grow up on the run.*

'His invention,' she said. 'You remember the plastic handle for cans?'

Switching scenarios, I blinked and nodded. 'The one Dad refused him investment for?'

Bridget nodded. 'Not that I blamed him,' she said. 'I thought it was a completely ridiculous idea, but…' Her eyes widened. 'He's found a big investor in Chicago.'

'What?'

'It's going to be placed with some major retailers over there, and there's interest from other countries.' Her face was growing pinker. 'He's going to make a fortune, Tilly, and, even better, they're interested in some of his other ideas.'

'Well, he was never short of those.' Her excitement was catching. 'That's amazing, Bee.'

She nodded so hard one of her curlers fell out and rolled across the table. 'Isn't it?'

'None of us had faith in him.'

'I know.' She fingered her hair. 'I feel bad about that.'

'You shouldn't,' I said. 'He didn't have the best track record, and anyway it doesn't matter now.' I rolled the curler back to her. 'He said he'd come home when he could make you proud, and he has.'

Her smile flew back. 'I've never stopped loving him,' she said, with feeling. 'And Romy will be *so* excited. I just can't wait to see her little face—'

'Hang on.' I stood up and turned the radio down mid-chorus. 'Where does this leave Seth?'

'Seth?' For a moment, it was as if she'd forgotten who he was.

'Er, Seth Donovan… the "date of your dreams",' I reminded her.

'Oh, Seth!' She made a swoony face. 'Seth's lovely, I like him a lot, but there wasn't any chemistry,' she said. *How could there be no chemistry with Seth Donovan? He was a walking chemistry lab.* 'To be honest, seeing him made me realise that Chad's the only one for me and, even if he hadn't made it, I was going to ask him to come home and give us another chance.'

'Right.' Did Seth know any of this? 'Have you told him about Chad?'

She shook her head, her freed curl bouncing on her forehead. 'I got a bit drunk when we went out to dinner…'

'I can't say I noticed.'

'… and was all fan-girly about his career,' she continued, with a rueful smile. 'And we had a great time, and have texted each other, but then I got the message from Chad and I've been on cloud fifty-nine ever since.'

'Ah.' I sat back, slightly deflated. 'That's why you've been unusually nice to me.'

She paused in the act of removing the rest of her curlers. 'What?'

'You were on a "Chad-high",' I said. 'Love is transformative and all that.' I supposed I should have known it was less about her seeing me differently, and more about the love of her life coming home.

'Actually, it had nothing to do with it.' She shook out her hair, which was truly enormous, and bounced around her head. 'Come with me.'

'Where?'

She stood up and held out her hand. 'Come.'

I let her lead me upstairs and into her room where she pulled my old DVD player from under her bed. 'I got it out of your drawer, like you said.' She sat on the bed and patted the duvet beside her. 'You told me to watch it so I did.' She opened the player and switched it on, and I sat gingerly beside her, hardly daring to believe it.

'You saw it all?'

'I did.'

I looked at the screen, and saw Dad swinging me in the air, like I'd seen him do with Romy. I must have been her age, my hair as dark as Romy's was fair. Then the scene cut to Mum in her shed with her pottery wheel, re-enacting the scene from *Ghost* with a giggling Bridget. 'I'd forgotten that,' murmured Bridget, her fingers closing over mine. Next up, was Bridget in her first bikini – green-and-white polka dots – showing me how to dive in the water at the lake house where we'd been staying on holiday. I'd been about four – too young to remember much about the trip, apart from the joy of the bracing water, and the way Bridget's hands had caught mine and pulled me to the side, while Mum cheered her on from the jetty. 'I taught you to swim.'

Tears threatened. 'Yes, you did.'

Bridget's laugh was shaky. 'Look at Mum.' The outline of her legs was visible in her cheesecloth skirt, which the sun had turned see through. 'Look at the cuddles she gives us when we come out, even though we're dripping wet.'

'You were never keen,' I said, smiling as Bridget pulled away from Mum, her long red hair dripping down her back.

'I was a right moody cow.'

'You were a teenager, with an annoying kid sister.'

'We had some nice times, though,' she said. 'I'd just forgotten.'

'Perception's a bitch.' I pulled her hand into my lap. 'Sometimes the bad bits stick.'

'They weren't even that bad.' Her shoulders drooped. 'I blew things way out of proportion,' she said, watching the pair of us cartwheel across the screen, in the garden at our old house, Bridget in her faded denim jeans, me showing my daisy-sprigged knickers. 'So, I had a much younger, cuter sister. It's not like our parents were druggies and I was forced to take you begging on the streets.'

'Maybe you could let them know that.' I gave her a nudge. Her cheeks were shiny with tears. 'Hey, don't cry.'

'Do you think they'll ever forgive me?'

'Bee, you're their daughter.' I brought her hand to my lips and kissed it. 'As far as they're concerned, there's nothing to forgive.'

'I suppose if they forgave you for that...' The scene switched to Meg, Cassie and me belting out an All Saints song in Cassie's back garden, her brother playing the keyboard, assembled family and neighbours clapping along. 'What was it you called yourselves?'

'Legal Mystics,' I said, grinning at our carefree, fifteen-year-old selves, thinking we were on the cusp of greatness. 'It's an anagram of Cass, Meg and Tilly.'

'That's right, I remember Mum mentioning it,' said Bridget. 'Quite inspired.'

'That was Cassie.'

'Obviously.' Bridget gave me a good-natured shove and we carried on watching, laughing softly when the camera wonkily zoomed in on Mum and Dad smooching in the kitchen to 'Santa Baby'.

'I shot that on Christmas Day,' I said, realising how much I'd missed them. The lens wavered towards seventeen-year-old Bridget, curled in the armchair reading Nelson Mandela's *Long Walk to Freedom*. She tutted as she watched her younger self glance up from the pages and stick her tongue out at me.

'I left home the year after.'

'Well, you're here for Christmas this year.' I pressed the off button. 'And we couldn't be happier.'

We jumped as Romy charged in and threw herself on the bed between us. 'Father Christmas been?'

'Not yet, cherub.' I moved to tickle her, as Bridget leaned over to switch on a lamp, her hair bouncing around her face.

'Come on, pickle, let's go downstairs and play a game while we wait for Gran and Gramps,' she said, scooping up her daughter, her eyes soft as they met mine. 'We've a lot to tell them.'

I smiled, feeling sentimental, and more relaxed than I had in ages – even as part of my brain was wondering how Seth would take the news that my sister and her ex were getting back together – and was deciding whether to take a shower, or look for something to eat, when my phone began to ring.

'Seth?' It was as if I'd conjured him up.

'Tilly!' He sounded frantic, or as though he'd been running. 'You haven't seen Jack today, have you?'

'Jack?'

'Jack!' shouted Romy from the doorway, and Bridget's head snapped up.

'No I haven't.' A cold hand gripped my heart. 'Why?'

Seth voice fractured as he spoke. 'He's missing.'

Chapter Thirty

'What happened?'

Seth's expression had been stripped back to panic, his face a shade of pale that made everything else about him look darker. 'After dinner, he asked my mother why she didn't like you and she said it was because you were only pretending to look after him, and he told her she should be happy because you saved him from drowning and he could have been dead.'

Tears started racing down my face. *Dear, sweet Jack.*

'Mum lost the plot, said she couldn't believe I'd allowed him to go near the sea on his own, that I wasn't a fit father and it proved she was right to take Jack away from here.' The pain in his eyes was almost too much to bear. 'Jack overheard, said he didn't want to go. She said he didn't have a choice and told him to go to his room.'

I managed to choke out, 'But he didn't?'

Seth nodded. 'He did. I went straight up to talk to him, but he wouldn't respond, so I sent Digby up to keep him company and came back to talk to my mother. We just ended up rowing as usual, and when I went back up he wasn't there.'

'Where's Digby?' I looked around, half expecting to see the dog on the rug in front of the blazing fireplace.

'He's gone too.'

I swiped my hand across my nose. 'That's good,' I said. 'That he's gone with Jack.'

'How, exactly?' I spun round to see Felicity standing by the window, looking older than the last time I'd seen her. Her eyes were cavernous and her hair had dropped, as though it didn't have the heart to stay up. 'This isn't an episode of *Lassie*,' she said. 'The dog's not going to run in and bark a few times, and lead us to my grandson.'

'OK, well, have you double-checked every room?' I looked back at Seth. 'It sounds silly, but my friend and her boyfriend once lost his little sister, but she'd been hiding in her bed all along and had fallen asleep.'

'For heaven's sake.' Felicity's expression stretched with disbelief. 'We're not imbeciles.'

'Mum, stop it.' Seth was pacing the kitchen in his coat, his hair pushed into peaks, a powerful looking torch dangling in one hand. 'We've double-checked inside and out.' I spotted a rim of sandy mud circling the toes of his and Felicity's boots. 'He's taken his coat and wellingtons, his rucksack, and Digby's lead.'

I met his eye, and knew he was thinking the same thing. If Digby was on his lead, there was less chance of him running into the sea.

'I thought he might have found his way to your house, there's a bus service, I checked, because he couldn't walk that far…'

'Would he have any money on him?'

Seth pushed a hand through his hair again. 'I don't think so, he has a savings account, but no cash.'

'It's gone nine o'clock,' I said. 'It's time to call the police.'

'Oh god, do we have to?' Felicity's voice rose with fright, and I sensed it was because the arrival of uniformed officers would make Jack's disappearance real.

'Yes, we do.' A strange calmness settled over me. 'It's dark and it's late. We need all the help we can get.'

Seth motioned to the handset on the worktop. 'I was about to, but hoped you might have spotted him on the way over.'

'Oh my god, he could be lying dead in a ditch,' Felicity wailed.

'Not helpful.' I fixed my eyes on Seth's. 'You've searched the beach?'

'First place I looked, after…' He eyed his mother who was reeling around with her hands clamped to her mouth. 'After last time.' He looked as if he might be sick at the realisation that, once again, his son had left the cottage without his knowledge. 'There were no footsteps or paw prints that I could see, but I'm going to look again.' He was already heading to the door. 'Call the police, the lifeguard… everyone,' he ordered his mother.

She pressed a shaking hand to her throat as he left. 'You saved my grandson's life,' she said, as if that part had just sunk in. 'Please help find him, Tilly.' She held out a wavering hand. 'I can't bear that this has happened because of what I said.'

I snatched up the handset and thrust it at her. 'Call for help, *now*,' I instructed. 'Stay here, in case Jack comes back.'

Outside, the wind cut through my denim jacket – the first thing I'd picked up after telling Seth I was on my way, leaving Bridget with instructions to call me if Jack should, by some miracle, turn up at the house.

The moon was high in the sky, lighting a path to the beach as I ran after Seth. 'I don't even know where to look,' he said as I caught up. He spun back and forth, swinging the torch to and fro. The tide was creeping in, the surface rippled by the wind, waves frothing at the sand. 'There's no one around, so we can't even ask if anyone saw him.'

'I think he'd stick close to the headland, after what happened before,' I said. 'Let's try over there, and see if we can pick up a trail.'

I could hear the sound of our breathing and the echo of my heartbeat in my ears.

'Tilly, look!' I ran over to where Seth was shining the torch. 'Do these look like paw prints to you?'

I peered to where the beam was pointing. 'Definitely.' As I looked around, Jack's voice zoomed into my head. *Dad, can we go to the smugglers' cave on the beach?*

'I think I know where he might have gone,' I said.

Seth shone the torch at my face. 'Where?'

Shielding my eyes, I said, 'The smugglers' caves I told you about, when he asked if you could take him there.'

'You think?' The hope in his voice was hard to hear.

'He said he had a map on his iPad,' I said. 'Do you know if he took it with him?'

He smacked a fist to his forehead. 'I didn't think to look.' He groaned. 'Mum's right. I'm the worst bloody dad ever.'

'No you're not.' I punched his arm. 'Come on. I know where they are.' I didn't add that we needed to hurry as the incoming tide would flood the caves within half an hour, but Seth was already charging ahead, torchlight bouncing. I also didn't add that he didn't need it, the moon was bright enough, because I knew he needed to feel he was doing something useful.

'I should have just taken him that day,' he said as I caught up. 'I know I can't keep him wrapped in cotton wool, but then he does something like this and I want to keep him locked inside forever.'

'It's a balancing act,' I panted, as though I'd had experience. 'Hardly anyone gets it right all the time.'

'Are we far away?'

'Another few minutes.' I picked up speed so I was almost running, wishing I'd pushed my feet into my boots instead of the sheepskin slippers nearest to the front door. It was a measure of how serious the situation was that no one – least of all me – had noticed until now.

'It'll be freezing in those caves.' Seth was keeping pace, his coat flapping around his knees. It was his purple-lined pea coat, and I thought how incongruous we would look to anyone watching.

'At least he dressed sensibly.' Even so, I knew the temperature would be arctic. Those caves were chilly even in summer. I'd explored them once with Dad, ages before I met Cassie and Meg. I'd thought it would be exciting, like in the Enid Blyton books I'd read, but had found them claustrophobic and scary.

'I'm not going to let Mum take him.' Seth's voice had hardened. 'The set-up we've got isn't perfect, but it'll get better.'

'Of course it will.'

'If anything's happened to him…'

I caught the sheen of tears in his eyes. 'Don't think like that.' I reached over and touched his hand and he caught my fingers.

'Thanks for coming.'

'Let's just get there.' A sudden choke of fear rushed up my throat. 'We can't be far away now.'

'Jack!' Seth called, his voice snatched by the wind.

'Digby!' I was rewarded by a distant bark. 'Did you hear that?'

Seth was already stumbling ahead and, rounding a curve, I realised we were there. The mouths of the caves gaped like missing teeth and behind us the sea lapped closer. I shivered as Seth passed me the torch and cupped his mouth with his hands.

'*Digby!*'

A volley of barks echoed back, followed by a wavering cry of, 'Dad?'

'Jack!'

'In there.' I pointed to the nearest cave.

Seth plunged in and I followed, shooting a hand out to the damp-slicked wall, blinking in the salty darkness. Now we needed the torch, the beam had faded.

'Jack!' I yelled. The sea shushed behind us. I estimated we had around fifteen minutes to get out and pressed forward, almost crashing into Seth. One of my slippers came off. I felt cold, compacted sand underfoot, but knew there were stones and rocks further inside the cave.

'*Jack!*' Seth's shout bounced around us.

'Dad!' Jack's voice broke on a sob. 'I've hurt my ankle.'

'Hang on, son, we're nearly there.' Seth sounded grimly determined now, pushing further into the tomb-like interior.

More barking, closer this time, and a pair of glowing eyes appeared in the weakening cone of torchlight. 'It's Digby.'

He lolloped over, pranced in a circle twice, then headed back the way he'd come.

'He's doing a Lassie.' Hysterical laughter rose. 'He's leading us to Jack.'

'I bloody hope so.' Seth spoke through gritted teeth as he tripped over a protruding rock. 'Jack!' he called again.

A ghostly white light appeared. 'What's that?' Seth paused in a half crouch and held up a hand, like a modern-day Indiana Jones.

'It's his iPad,' I said. 'He must have brought it with him.'

'*Dad!*'

Seth clattered forward. 'I'm here, Jack.'

I lurched behind, stifling a yelp when my foot caught the craggy edge of a rock, and as Seth dropped to hold Jack in an awkward hug, murmuring endearments, I saw that Jack's ankle was trapped inside a narrow crevice.

'I was climbing over, so I could get to the dry bit where it's safe from the sea,' he said, his eyes like big dark puddles in the bright light of his screen. 'Digby and me were going to stay here until Grandma goes home, but I fell and my foot got stuck.'

'Oh, Jack,' said Seth, stroking his son's hair. 'You know I'm not letting you go back to live with her, don't you?'

'She might make you.'

'No chance,' said Seth. 'I'm your dad and I love you, and you're staying here with me.'

'And he doesn't mean in this cave,' I said, relief making me silly.

'I left a note to say where I was.' Jack had started crying in little gulps. 'I didn't want you to be worried.'

'I didn't see it.' Seth sounded as if he was trying not to weep too.

'I said not to look for me until tomorrow,' Jack said, burying his head against Seth's shoulder. 'I want to go to the party like Romy.'

Seth kissed his head. 'And you will,' he said fervently. 'I promise you that.'

The sea had reached the mouth of the cave, sloshing gently.

'We have to go, if we don't want to be stuck here until the tide goes out,' I said to Seth.

Picking up on my tone, he looked to where Jack's foot was stuck fast, his leg twisted awkwardly. He shifted round. 'OK, buddy, just a couple of minutes and we can go home and have something to eat.'

'It hurts a bit.' Jack had stopped crying, his voice wobbly but brave.

'It's because you've fallen over.' I bent to take a closer look. 'He's at an angle,' I told Seth. 'If you can lift him up a few inches so his leg straightens, we should be able to get his foot out of his wellie.'

'Let's do it.'

Digby darted back and forth, barking at the water. He was skittish; sensing danger – or picking up on our tones.

'Try and wiggle your toes,' I said to Jack, to distract him as Seth slipped his hands under Jack's armpits and carefully raised him off the ground, so his leg was level with the rock.

'Ow, ow, ow,' cried Jack, and Digby rushed to lick his face.

'Nearly there,' I said. I nodded at Seth who gave a gentle tug as I held onto the toe of Jack's boot. 'Once more.' The icy water was lapping around my feet now. Seth gave another yank, and this time I felt Jack's foot move. 'Again.'

It was heart-wrenching hearing Jack sob, and I sensed Seth's hesitation. 'Now,' I said. He pulled again and Jack screamed as his foot was wrenched from his boot. Digby whined and growled.

'It's OK,' I said. 'We're done.' I grabbed Jack's rucksack and iPad and the torch, which had finally died, while Seth waded through ankle deep water to the mouth of the cave with Jack in his arms. The moon had dipped, but there was just enough light to make out the steps carved into the hillside, which I remembered climbing years ago, and Digby led the way to the top where we carried on walking, and didn't stop until we were back at the cottage.

Chapter Thirty-One

'I don't know how to thank you for what you've done.'

Felicity faced me across the kitchen table, all airs peeled away. Her eyes were red-rimmed and she kept passing a crumpled tissue across her nose. 'If you hadn't remembered those caves…'

'If Seth hadn't found him, the police would have.' I sat down to roll on the clean, dry socks she'd found in the airing cupboard while Jack was in the bath. 'They would have known where to look, and Digby kept running out of the cave and barking, trying to alert someone.'

'I take back everything I said about that dog.'

Digby wandered in, as though sensing he was being talked about. He wagged his tail, then picked up his rubber bone and trotted upstairs to where Jack was being tucked into bed by Seth. His ankle was badly bruised but not broken, and thankfully there were no signs of hypothermia.

By the time we'd staggered inside, the cottage had been filled with paramedics and the police, about to call out a search and rescue team, but once Jack had been examined, and the police had determined there was no need for further action, they'd left with hearty wishes for a Merry Christmas, leaving us dazed and slightly euphoric, like train wreck survivors.

'You know, he'd pushed a note under his father's bedroom door so Ainsley… Seth would see it when he went to bed.' Felicity's voice was barely a whisper. 'As if he'd have gone to bed, knowing his son wasn't here.'

'Children see things differently,' I said, and finished the mug of hot sugared tea that Felicity had made – the first domestic task I'd seen her undertake. 'It probably didn't occur to him the police would be involved. He just wanted to escape for a while.'

'Because of me.' Her mouth wobbled around the rim of her mug and she put it back down. 'What can I do?'

Before I could speak, Seth popped his head round the door, with the look of a man who'd been given a new lease of life. 'He wants you to say goodnight,' he said, and when Felicity rose, added coolly, 'I was talking to Tilly.'

As he retreated her face fell and I felt a rush of pity. Leaning forward, I took hold of her bony hand. It was icy, despite the warmth of the kitchen. 'I'll tell you what you can do,' I said. 'Have some faith in Seth and drop this custody battle, or you'll lose them both.'

I left her stroking her pearls, staring wide-eyed into her mug, and headed upstairs. Jack was propped against his pillows, his iPad recharging on his desk. 'Will it snow tonight?' He looked hopefully at the window.

'It might.' I rested my arms on the side of the bed, careful not to jolt his foot. 'According to the weather forecast, it's going to be a white Christmas.'

'Cool,' he said, snuggling down, wincing slightly. 'Thank you for coming to get me out of the cave with Dad.'

I kissed his cheek, breathing in the clean, sandy scent that made my brain go fuzzy. 'You're welcome.'

He gave a pleased little smile. 'Can we come to your house when it's Christmas?' he said. 'I've got a present for Romy.'

'I'm sure that can be arranged.' I remembered that Chad would be back, and that soon, Bridget and Romy would return to their London home. 'She'll be pleased to see you,' I said, a lump rising in my throat. 'We all will.'

'Can Digby come?'

'Of course he can.'

'Time to let Tilly go.' Seth was leaning against the door frame, bathed in light from Jack's rocket lamp, the curl of a smile on his face. 'It's getting late.'

I stroked his hair and stood up. 'See you at the party tomorrow night, if your ankle's OK.'

'Yay!' He was on the verge of sleep, worn out by his adventure. 'Can Digby come too?'

'We'll find out about that tomorrow,' said Seth, mouthing *no* to me as I joined him in the doorway. 'Get some sleep now, buddy.'

We stood for a moment, until Jack said, 'Go away,' which made us laugh and we crept downstairs where Seth helped me into my jacket. 'Sure you won't stay and have something to eat?' He sounded hopeful, and I knew he was facing a difficult evening with his mother.

'I can't,' I said. 'My parents are back, and they'll be dying to tell us all about their trip.' I'd called Bridget while the paramedics were checking Jack, to let her know he was safe, and she'd been expressing her relief, when I'd heard Dad boom, 'Anyone home?' and Romy shriek 'Grampdad!' and Bridget had said, 'My god, they're so tanned you're going to laugh,' before hanging up. 'Maybe you and your mum can have a civilised chat.'

'I'll try,' he said, looking at my feet. 'You can't leave in socks.'

'I came out in slippers.'

'Wear Mum's shoes.' He indicated a pair of fawn brogues that almost blended into the carpet. 'You're about the same size.'

'Won't she mind?'

'You can probably get away with murder now you've saved Jack again.'

'Not hers, I hope.'

He laughed, a warm rich sound that made my heart feel full. 'Your work here is done, Poppins.'

'Shame you can't say something similar to your workmen.' I looked around the dingy hall, which I'd grown to rather like. 'They could have done this today if they hadn't been working for me.'

'It can wait until the New Year.' He touched the battered skirting board with his foot. 'I'm sick of the smell of paint, anyway.'

'You don't know what you're missing,' I said, which made him laugh again. Our eyes snagged, and it was hard to look away. 'I'll see you at the party tomorrow, all being well.'

'Oh, you will.' He held me in his gaze a moment longer.

'Right then.' Confused, I opened the front door, and he followed me out to my car, which in my haste, I'd parked at a peculiar angle and hadn't bothered to lock.

'It's been an eventful day,' I said, patting my pockets for my keys, aware I was being too jolly. 'I'm surprised I'm not more tired.' In fact, I'd felt more alive in the past week than I had for ages, and I recalled the exhilaration I'd felt, plunging into the sea after Jack. It was as if I'd been woken up, and ever since had let myself be drawn deeper into their lives, despite all its complications.

I'd changed. Or, maybe, I'd become me.

Unsure of where my thoughts were heading, I tugged out my keys. 'It's supposed to snow tomorrow,' I said, and gave an exaggerated shiver even though I wasn't cold.

'So they keep saying.' We looked up at the sky, and it occurred to me that I'd seen a lot of sky over the past twenty-four hours.

'I should go,' I said, dropping my eyes from his.

'Not until I've done this.' Before I knew what was happening, Seth had leaned in and kissed me on the mouth. It lasted a mere second, but I felt as if I'd been attached to a defibrillator. 'I've wanted to do that since you came out of the sea, like Ursula Andress, in your bra and jeans.'

My lungs felt a size too small. 'To say thank you for saving Jack.'

He pulled back, his eyes tracing mine. 'You really need to stop this,' he said softly. 'Yes, I'll never be able to thank you enough for what you did that day. It's imprinted on my heart forever, but that isn't why I wanted to kiss you.'

'Why, then?' I jerked away, unexpected tears flooding my eyes. 'I thought you had feelings for Bridget.' I wondered when she was planning to tell him about Chad. 'You can't switch them on and off.'

He reached for my hand and tried to tug me towards him. 'I like your sister, but there's nothing going on.' He stroked a tendril of hair behind my ear.

'But you kissed her, and sent her a text the night after your dinner,' I said. 'What was that all about?'

'Actually, she kissed me.' A smile hovered around his mouth. 'If you hadn't ducked away from the window, you'd have seen me untangling myself.' Blood whooshed to my face. 'And I wanted to let her know that although I'd had a nice time and hoped we could be friends, I didn't want a relationship.' He gave a one-shouldered shrug. 'She replied that she felt the same, and was still in love with her baby-daddy.'

'She'd never say baby-daddy.'

'She did.'

My heart was behaving in a way I'd never experienced – all fluttery and fast – and I was overcome with an urge to laugh and cry at the same time. But mostly laugh. And then cry.

Seth took my other hand and pressed my palms to his chest. 'I was never in danger of falling for your sister, Tilly.' His eyes moved to my lips, and he cupped my jaw with one hand and rested the other on my waist. 'I'm already in love with you.'

Even as my head began to spin, his words opened up an acknowledgement deep inside me; that I'd fallen for him that day on the beach, when he'd wrapped me in his sweater like a gift. 'Me too,' I whispered, curling my arm around his neck. 'I mean, with you.' And in the second before his lips met mine, I knew.

This was going to be the most significant kiss of my life.

Chapter Thirty-Two

The Christmas Eve party went *almost* according to plan.

The guests were wowed with the function room, the oak floor in particular drawing oodles of compliments, and by the end of the evening there were several bookings for birthday parties, and Bill Feathers had asked if I'd consider giving the Smugglers Inn a long overdue makeover.

'It's time to get rid of the sticky carpet,' he said, drunk on mulled wine, and I decided to wait and see if he asked me again when he was sober before committing.

The music went down a storm – mostly requests for Christmas songs because... well, it was Christmas, and Danny managed to discreetly propose to Cassie by the tree in the café that we'd decorated together. Obviously, she said yes, and agreed they could choose a ring together, but she decided not to announce her pregnancy, as nearly everyone had guessed already, due to her not drinking alcohol, and rushing off to be sick every half hour.

'It gets better after four months,' her Mum reassured her, glowing with happiness and excitement, and an almost radioactive tan.

Dad had a word with a man in the planning office and got the OK for the wedding to go ahead, so Meg's Mum and Dad were married by Nathan's brother's friend, who looked a lot like Donald Trump which added a touch of hilarity. There wasn't a dry eye in the room as they exchanged their vows. Meg's three-tier wedding cake, decorated with cascading holly and berries, drew a roomful of gasps, and ensured a rush of orders for the bakery.

'I think this might just be the best day of my life,' she said. 'Not every child gets to be at their parents' wedding.'

Bridget arrived as the ceremony ended, with a triumphant and handsome Chad, which caused a stir for no one apart from our teak-tanned parents, who were thrilled to see their oldest daughter so happy and relaxed, for once, and their granddaughter joyfully reunited with her father.

'I don't know exactly what's happened, but I'm so glad my lovely girls are here for Christmas,' Mum cried, hugging us both at once, her tinsel necklace scratching our cheeks.

Gwen engineered her kiss with Jerry under the mistletoe. I noticed he didn't put up a fight and had actually been hovering near it for most of the evening, in his Santa jumper – though her technique left onlookers open-mouthed.

'Ain't you lot never seen a proper movie kiss?' she demanded, after dipping him over her knee in a way that can't have been good for his back. Not that he was complaining. I caught them looking at the sky together on the terrace, Dickens tucked under Jerry's arm. 'If 'e's good wiv me pussy, he's a keeper,' she said, winking at me over her shoulder.

Seth arrived with Jack, who made a beeline for Romy to show her a *Star Wars* sticker book his grandma had bought him for Christmas but decided to let him open early, and Seth told me he'd ordered a lightsaber, which had arrived that afternoon.

Digby stayed at home, probably enjoying having the place to himself for a few hours. Felicity had gone home, but had invited Seth and Jack to Oaklands during Jack's first school half-term in February. 'As long as you'll come too,' Seth said, nuzzling my neck as we swayed together to 'Last Christmas'. Felicity had agreed to stop fighting for custody and was hopeful relations would improve, and Seth was giving her the benefit of the doubt. 'Jack deserves a relationship with his grandparents,' he said. 'And maybe she'll come to see I'm not such a bad dad.'

'You're not,' I said, pulling him towards the mistletoe. 'And you're not a bad kisser either.'

'You two are adorable.' Meg hugged me as I joined her and Cassie by the buffet laid out in the café, mostly comprised of turkey sandwiches, and made me pull a Christmas cracker with her. 'Can you believe we're all ending the year coupled up?' she said, trying on a gold paper crown.

'What a horrible term.' But I couldn't stop smiling – especially watching Seth dance Romy and Jack around the room, his head stuffed into a Christmas elf hat complete with pointy ears.

'I *knew* there was something that day he came into the café.' Cassie handed me another Christmas cracker. 'It was written all over you both.'

❄ ❄ ❄

The only thing that didn't go to plan was the weather. Despite predictions, it didn't snow until the end of January when it barely stopped for a fortnight. It was the heaviest snowfall south Devon had ever seen, and I took plenty of photos to prove it.

One in particular has joined the little gallery beside Jack's bed, next to the one of him with his mum – a photo of Jack and Seth, their faces bright with laughter, building a sand snowman on the beach at Seashell Cove.

A Letter from Karen

I want to say a huge thank you for choosing to read *The Christmas Café at Seashell Cove*. If you did enjoy it, and want to keep up-to-date with all my latest releases, just sign up at the following link. Your email address will never be shared and you can unsubscribe at any time.

www.bookouture.com/karen-clarke

It was wonderful to return to Seashell Cove at Christmas to tell Tilly's story and catch up with some familiar characters. I particularly enjoyed revisiting the café, which gave me the opportunity to pop in lots of references to favourite festive cakes!

At the heart of the story was Tilly's difficult relationship with her older sister. I'm happy to say, I had no such issues with mine growing up. We had lots of laughs back then, and it's lovely to have a sister who's also a friend, but I wanted to explore the effect a ten year age gap would have, and how different perceptions of their upbringing impacts their lives.

My biggest challenge was writing about Tilly's love of swimming – despite growing up by the seaside, I cannot swim, and am terrified of being in water. Maybe, one day, I'll pluck up the courage to book some lessons.

I loved writing about Seth and Jack, and now know far more about motor racing than I ever thought possible – enough to be thankful that neither of my sons plan to take it up!

I hope you loved *The Christmas Café at Seashell Cove* and if you did I would be very grateful if you could write a review. I'd love to hear what you think, and it makes such a difference helping new readers to discover one of my books for the first time.

I love hearing from my readers – you can get in touch on my Facebook page, through Twitter, Goodreads or my website.

Thanks,
Karen

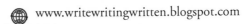 www.writewritingwritten.blogspot.com

 karen.clarke.5682

 @karenclarke123

Acknowledgements

A lot of people are involved in making a book, and I would like to thank Oliver Rhodes and the brilliant team at Bookouture for making it happen. Particular thanks to my wonderful editor, Abi, for her insightful guidance, to Jane for copy-editing, Claire for proofreading, Emma and Nikki for my gorgeous covers, Alex for marketing, and Kim and Noelle for spreading the word.

As ever, I owe my lovely readers a massive thank you, as well as the blogging community, whose reviews are a labour of love, and Amanda Brittany for her tireless feedback and friendship despite a difficult year.

And last, but never least, thank you to all my family and friends for their constant encouragement, my children, Amy, Martin and Liam for their unwavering support, and my husband Tim for endless cups of tea, and for everything else – I couldn't do it without you.